PRAISE FOR THE NOVELS OF
#1 NEW YORK TIMES BESTSELLING AUTHOR
BARBARA FREETHY

"In the tradition of LaVyrle Spencer, gifted author Barbara Freethy creates an irresistible tale of family secrets, riveting adventure and heart- touching romance."

*-- NYT Bestselling Author **Susan Wiggs***
on Summer Secrets

"This book has it all: heart, community, and characters who will remain with you long after the book has ended. A wonderful story."

*-- NYT Bestselling Author **Debbie Macomber***
on Suddenly One Summer

"Freethy has a gift for creating complex characters."

*-- **Library Journal***

"Barbara Freethy is a master storyteller with a gift for spinning tales about ordinary people in extraordinary situations and drawing readers into their lives."

*-- **Romance Reviews Today***

"Freethy's skillful plotting and gift for creating sympathetic characters will ensure that few dry eyes will be left at the end of the story."

*-- **Publishers Weekly** on The Way Back Home*

"Freethy skillfully keeps the reader on the hook, and her tantalizing and believable tale has it all– romance, adventure, and mystery."

*-- **Booklist** on Summer Secrets*

"Freethy's story-telling ability is top-notch."

*-- **Romantic Times** on Don't Say A Word*

Also By Barbara Freethy

To Anne, Sara, Christie, and Grace,
the wonderful writers who helped me brainstorm this romantic adventure
on a writing retreat in Lake Tahoe,
I couldn't have done it without you! And the coloring books were fun, too!

LIGHTNING LINGERS

Lightning Strikes Trilogy #2

BARBARA FREETHY

HYDE
STREET
—PRESS—

HYDE STREET PRESS
Published by Hyde Street Press
1325 Howard Avenue, #321, Burlingame, California 94010

Printed in the United States of America

Cover design by Damonza.com

ISBN: 978-0-9961154-6-9

One

She didn't like storms, especially not on Halloween. But the shiver that ran down Katherine Barrett's spine as she stepped onto the roof of Houston's St. John's Hospital at eleven o'clock at night had as much to do with painful memories of the past as it did with the storm clouds gathering overhead.

There was nothing to be afraid of tonight, and her sense of foreboding was misplaced, she told herself forcefully. Even the ER had been quiet; only a sprained ankle, a broken arm, and a stomachache from too much candy. No one had gotten hurt.

No one had died.

Her stomach twisted painfully at the memory of another Halloween a very long time ago. In her head, she could still feel herself tripping over the long skirt of her costume as she ran through the streets with her friends. They'd gone farther than they were supposed to that night. She'd known it then, but she hadn't stopped. She'd never imagined anything bad could happen.

Shaking her head, she told herself to stop going back in time, focus on the present and not the past.

Today was a celebration, an end of one very long chapter in her life and the beginning of a new one. Eleven years of medical training had come to a finish with her last shift as a medical resident. She was twenty-nine years old and more than ready to start her career as a doctor. She'd thought medical school was difficult, but the past three years as a resident had been brutal. She'd worked eighty-hour weeks, and sometimes she'd been so tired she couldn't remember what day it was. Through it all, she was supposed to be at the top of her game, and for the most part she had been at the top, because she'd given up everything else in her life—friends, family, hobbies—in pursuit of her goal. She'd climbed a mountain, she'd made it, but the hollow in her heart reminded her that she was alone.

Had it been worth it?

Frowning, she couldn't believe she was even contemplating the fact that all the time and dedication *hadn't* been worth it. She was just exhausted. Tomorrow, she'd feel the exhilaration that she couldn't quite seem to find at this moment. Tomorrow, Halloween would be over, and she'd be done with that painful memory, too.

She reached for the locket she'd put on for her last shift. She didn't usually wear it on duty, but tonight it had felt appropriate. She unclasped the necklace and opened the locket to look at the smiling face of Hailey Peters, a beautiful, freckled redhead with a big smile—her face forever captured at twelve years old.

"I did it, Hailey," she murmured. "I'm a doctor."

For a moment, she thought she could hear Hailey's voice saying *I knew you could.* She smiled at the foolish thought, but silently offered up a *thank you,* knowing that Hailey's voice had gotten her through a lot of tough moments in her life.

However, it was another voice that drew her head around. Josie Holt, a fellow resident, walked over to join her. Josie was a gregarious brunette who seemed able to maintain her happy nature no matter the circumstances. She'd also just finished her last day of residency.

Katherine slipped the locket into her pocket as Josie

handed her a beer.

"This should be champagne, but we're not making real doctor money yet, so I settled for beer," Josie said with a grin.

"It's perfect."

Josie raised her bottle. "Here's to us, to a new beginning."

"To us," Katherine echoed, as they clinked their bottles together.

"Can you believe we actually made it?" Josie added, taking a swig of beer. "No more eighteen-hour shifts, no more working every holiday and every weekend, no more taking orders from Dr. Horrible."

Katherine smiled. Dr. Horrible was a nickname for Dr. Mark Hutchinson, the brilliant but rigid physician who had terrorized them for the past year. "Would it sound traitorous if I said I think he might have made us better doctors?"

Josie made a face at her. "He might have taught us a few things, but he didn't have to be such an asshole about it. He hated all of us. Actually, he tolerated you, because you're so damn good. In fact, you're the most single-minded, determined person I've ever met. If you don't know something, you make it your mission in life to figure it out. I've learned a lot from you, Katherine."

"We've learned a lot from each other," she said, not completely comfortable with the compliment. Her single-minded focus might have been good for her career, but it had distanced her from everything and everyone else in her life. She'd left a lot of people behind on her way to this moment.

"So, have you decided which job offer to take?" Josie asked. "Are you going to stay here in Houston, go back to Corpus Christi, or will New York or Los Angeles be lucky enough to get you?"

"I haven't decided yet. What about you?"

"I'm going home to Connecticut to join my uncle's practice. He has a well-established and mostly insured patient base. With all my debt, how can I say no?"

Katherine shrugged. "Do you want to say no?"

"It's not as exciting as hospital work, but it will be nice to get to know my patients, not just meet someone in the middle of a health crisis, not just think of them as whatever part of them is broken or diseased."

Katherine nodded, but she didn't feel the same way Josie did. For her, it was easier to think of the problem than the patient. Emotions only got in the way.

"I'm going to miss this view." Josie waved her hand toward the downtown Houston skyline. "Texas has gotten into my heart."

The city was beautiful at night; the collection of lit-up architecturally magnificent skyscrapers had always been a nice distraction from the chaos of the ER. Katherine had come to this roof many a night when she needed a minute to breathe—not that she ever got much more than a minute—but the view had always calmed and inspired her.

But for her, the real Texas was wide-open spaces, empty highways that went on for miles, spectacular storms, and home in Corpus Christi.

"One thing I won't miss is rain and hail the size of baseballs," Josie added, putting out her hand as drops of rain began to fall. "Looks like another storm is on the way. Thank goodness it cleared up for the trick-or-treating. Fewer sopping wet children on Halloween means fewer kids coming in next week with colds and the flu. Not that we'll be here to deal with it."

"It's weird to think that we won't be." She wrapped her arms around her waist as the wind made her shiver again. "Maybe it's the storm making me feel so edgy." The words slipped past her lips before she could stop them. She didn't normally share her emotions or her mood with coworkers simply because it didn't matter how she felt, only how she performed at her job.

"Is that how you feel—edgy?" Josie tilted her head to the side, giving her a thoughtful look. "What's going on, Katherine? You should be happy. Today is the day of victory.

We climbed Mount Everest, or at least our version of it, but you don't look very excited or relieved."

"I *am* happy. I'm just too tired to celebrate, and I can't quite believe it's over. It hasn't really sunk in yet. I can't imagine what I'm going to do tomorrow when I wake up."

"Well, sleep in for one. Then come join me for a much-needed massage at the Serenity Spa."

"That is tempting."

"Then let yourself be tempted for once in your life. You don't always have to be responsible. We can talk about it over better drinks. David is meeting us at Harry's Bar in a half hour. You should come. He's going to buy us champagne."

"I don't want to be the third wheel on your date. Plus, it's Halloween. It will be crazy busy."

"So what? As you just said, you don't have anything to do tomorrow. David has a bunch of guy friends coming. You'll have fun, I promise."

Out of habit, she hesitated and then thought, why not? She'd turned down hundreds of invitations over the years. "All right. I'll meet you there. I'm just going to finish my beer and enjoy one last night on the roof."

"Really? You're going to get wet."

"It's barely drizzling." She'd spent so many hours of her life inside the hospital that she'd almost forgotten what it was like to be outside, to feel cold, to be out in the world.

"Well, don't take too long."

"I won't."

After Josie left, Katherine took a sip of her beer and then pulled her phone out of her pocket as it started to vibrate.

She frowned as she looked at her screen. The area code wasn't one she recognized, and it was late for a telemarketer. Hopefully, it wasn't one of her mom's caregivers on the phone. "Hello?"

"Katherine?"

"TJ?" Her brother's voice was muffled and scratchy. "What's wrong? Is it Mom?"

"No, it's me. I'm in trouble, Katherine."

"What's happened?"

"They're all dead. I didn't understand how they were all connected, but now I think I do."

"Who's dead?" she asked in alarm.

"Everyone. Jerry. Professor Bryer. Connie. They're all dead," he said forcefully. "And I'm going to be next. They already tried to get me once. I can't wait for them to try again."

"You're not making sense, TJ." The only name she'd recognized was Professor Bryer, the man TJ had worked under at the university, but he'd been murdered a year earlier, and she didn't think that had had anything to do with TJ. "What on earth is going on?"

"I don't have time to explain. There's so much you don't know. It's too late to bring you into it. You can't help me, but you can help Mom. It's on you now, Katherine. She can't stay alone anymore. She's gotten much worse the past few weeks. I've set up round-the-clock caregivers to take care of her for the next two weeks, then it's your job to figure something out."

"Wait," she said, suddenly panicked that he was about to hang up. "Let me help you, TJ. Whatever is wrong, we can go to the police. If you're in danger, they can protect you."

"No one can protect me. They're too powerful, Katherine. And there's no one I can trust. Hell, I don't even know if I can trust you."

Another shiver ran down her spine and the sense of foreboding she'd felt earlier returned. "Of course you can trust me; I'm your sister. Tell me where you are. I'll come to you."

"I won't be here after I throw this phone away. And you can't come after me. They'll be watching you. If you book a flight to Mexico, they'll know I spoke to you. You'll be in danger."

"Mexico?" she echoed in surprise. "What the hell are you doing in Mexico?"

"I was asking myself that question until a few minutes ago. The less you know the better. I'll call you again—if I can. But if you don't hear from me, take care of Mom—"

"Stop," she said, cutting him off. "Tell me where you're headed now."

"I'm not entirely sure."

"You must have some idea."

"I need to disappear. The cities are too dangerous. I'm going to see if I can find the village where the world is stuck in time, where people linger in a civilization that died hundreds of years ago."

His words ignited an old memory in her mind. "Are you talking about where Jake's great-grandmother lives?"

"Maybe if I can turn back time, I can find my way back to who I'm supposed to be."

She'd always thought her brother was a little on the dramatic side, but she could hear the fear in his voice. "TJ, please, tell me where you are right now. I'll meet you. I can fix this."

. "Not even you can fix this, Katherine. Just take care of Mom and if she's lucid, tell her I love her. Good-bye, Katherine."

Her stomach churned. "This isn't good-bye, TJ. We're going to see each other again."

"I hope so. Don't tell anyone I called, Katherine. Promise me."

"TJ—"

"Just promise."

"I promise." She'd barely gotten the words out when the dial tone buzzed in her ear.

Her hand shook as she stared down at the phone. She hit redial, but the call didn't go through.

What should she do?

She wanted to start making calls, but he'd just told her not to tell anyone. Was she really going to do the one thing he'd made her promise not to do?

But she couldn't do nothing.

Her father was dead. Her mother was suffering from dementia. TJ was all she had left of her once vibrant family, and she was the only one who could help him.

But how?

No immediate answer came to mind, but one thing was clear; she couldn't solve the problem from Houston. She needed to go home, see her mom, and then figure out how to find her brother.

—➤◄—

After stopping at home to pack an overnight bag and fill a thermos with coffee, Katherine made the four-hour drive from Houston to Corpus Christi. She'd been wondering what she would do with her first day off in years, and it definitely hadn't been this. She had planned to go home, of course, but in a few days—when she'd had time to sleep and consider her job opportunities.

Guilt ran through her at the selfishness of that thought. She'd let TJ carry the burden of her mom's illness since her father had died a year ago. She'd told herself she'd make it up to him and to her mom when she was done with her residency, when she had more time and more money to help make their lives easier. They'd both told her they understood, but that didn't necessarily make it right.

Well, she couldn't change the past, but she could start being a better daughter and sister today.

It was seven a.m. when she arrived in the modest neighborhood of single-family homes, where she'd lived from age thirteen to eighteen. They'd moved to Corpus Christi when her father, Ron Barrett, had become an English professor at Texas A&M. It had been a good move for him and for her, Katherine thought. After Hailey's death, it had been horribly painful to walk by her best friend's house every day on her way to school.

She pulled into the driveway and turned off the car. As she looked at the house, she felt a mix of emotions. This house had once been the centerpiece of her happy family. Her dad had been a gregarious man who'd always welcomed his colleagues and grad students into his home. Her mother, Debbie, had been a stay-at-home mom, and she'd been involved in everything her children did from soccer to horseback riding and science fairs. Katherine had taken it all for granted. She'd always expected her parents to be here in this house when she came home.

Unfortunately, her father had suffered a fatal heart attack a year ago and without warning he was gone. Shortly thereafter, her mother had had a mini-stroke, the beginning of what had been a mental slide into dementia. Her father was too young to be deceased, and her mother was too young to be losing her mind, but as Katherine had learned the past few years, illness and injury could strike anyone at any time.

Grabbing her overnight bag, she got out of the car and walked across the lawn. When she stepped onto the porch, she was assailed with more memories from the past. The porch swing with its now-faded cushions and rusty iron chains had been her favorite place to read, and she'd always been a big reader. How could she not be with a father who was an English teacher?

Her gaze moved to the boxed planters that had always held a colorful array of flowers but were now nothing more than boxes of dirt. The house needed a new coat of paint and the porch light was holding on by one thin wire. Looking up at that light, she remembered its brightness. Her dad had made sure the porch was well lit, especially when his daughter was coming home with her boyfriend.

Jake had complained that he felt like he was kissing her under a spotlight. Not that that had slowed him down. She sucked in a breath, not surprised that Jake would find his way into her memories. He was one of the reasons she didn't come home as often as she probably should.

She inserted her key into the lock and opened the front door, knowing there would be more memories inside, but not as many of Jake.

When she walked into the living room, the clutter shocked her. TJ had told her that their mother lost track of every project she began, leaving chaos behind her every step.

Katherine had thought he'd exaggerated, but clearly he hadn't. What had once been a neat and tidy living room was now a disorganized mess of books, magazines, knitting projects, and half-drunk coffee mugs and water bottles. The coffee table was overflowing with sales catalogs, and the couch and chairs held numerous articles of clothing from jackets to sweaters to shirts and jeans.

"Mom?" she called.

There was no answer despite the fact that every light in the living room was on, but she did hear the sound of the television coming from the combination kitchen/family room, so she headed down the hall.

Her mother, Debbie Barrett, was snoozing on the couch in her nightgown and robe. She was half-sitting, half-lying against the cushions while the television blared an infomercial on some new miracle skin care cream.

As Katherine moved closer, she could see how thin her mother had gotten. She must have shed at least fifteen pounds in the past year. Her once thick and beautiful blonde hair had grayed, and her skin had a sallow tone to it. As she dozed in front of the television, small snores escaped from her slightly droopy open mouth.

This woman barely resembled her once vibrant mother. Debbie was only sixty-five years old, but she appeared closer to eighty now.

Had TJ told her things were this bad, or had her mother gone suddenly downhill? She certainly hadn't looked this bad when Katherine had last been home, but that was three months ago. She really should have come back sooner.

Glancing around the room, her gaze caught on the

window. A middle-aged woman wearing gray slacks and a white blouse stood on the back deck. She was on the telephone and seemed completely oblivious of Katherine's presence. That must be the caregiver.

Turning back to her mother, Katherine sat down on the couch next to her. "Mom," she said quietly.

Debbie Barrett jerked at the word, her eyes flying open. She looked dazed and scared as she blinked rapidly and then sat up straight. "What?"

"It's me, Katherine," she said soothingly.

"Katherine?" her mom echoed, her gaze still bemused, but the fear slowly leaving her eyes. "Katherine," she repeated, more fully cognizant now as her eyes found their focus. "What are you doing here?"

"I came to visit you," she said, relieved that her mother recognized her. "How are you feeling?"

"I'm so tired I can barely keep my eyes open. I don't know where all my energy has gone."

"It's early in the morning. I shouldn't have woken you."

"What time is it?"

"About seven."

Debbie pulled her robe more tightly around her body. "When did you get here?"

"A few minutes ago."

"I don't understand. Did you tell me you were coming? Did I forget?" Her mother's brows knit together in puzzlement.

"No, it was a spur-of-the-moment decision." She debated what else she wanted to say. She didn't want to worry her mom, but it was possible her mother knew something about TJ's situation. According to her brother, there were times when Debbie was lucid, when she and TJ had coherent conversations. Whether she could remember any of those discussions was another matter. "I got a call from TJ last night," she continued. "He seemed upset. Do you know where he is?"

Debbie's gaze narrowed, and she frowned. "I think he told me. I can't remember."

"That's okay, don't stress out," she said, seeing the frustration in her mother's eyes.

"The hats—they wear the hats." Her mom grabbed her arm. "And they take a nap in the middle of the day. What is that called?"

"A siesta?" she guessed.

"Yes," she said, clarity coming into her eyes. "Mexico. He went to Mexico for work."

That corresponded to what TJ had told her, not that she understood what her brother would be doing down there. "What kind of work would TJ do in Mexico?" she asked.

"I don't know—maybe a conference? TJ is a genius, but I don't understand what he actually does every day."

Her brother was an engineer for Mission Defense Technology, otherwise known as MDT, a huge corporate defense contractor in Corpus Christi, but Katherine didn't really know what he did on a day-to-day basis, either.

"Your hair is getting so long," Debbie murmured, tucking a stray strand of Katherine's hair behind her ear. "It reminds me of when you were a teenager."

And her mother's gentle touch, the love in her eyes, reminded Katherine of those days, too. She savored the moment, wondering how many more like this they would have.

But as much as she wanted to just spend time with her mother, TJ's desperate voice rang through her head.

"When did you last speak to TJ, Mom?"

"Last night or maybe the day before. He's always so busy. You and TJ are changing the world. I never did anything more important than change the sheets and keep the house clean. How did I get such brilliant children?"

"You did more than that, Mom. Don't sell yourself short."

"Something is wrong," her mother said abruptly. "You

don't come home unless something is wrong. What is it? Is it TJ? Is that why you're asking about him?"

Considering her promise to her brother, she didn't know how to answer that question. She settled for a half-truth. "TJ told me that he's going to be out of town for a while. I came home to make sure you have enough help here. Do you like the women who are staying with you?"

"Who do you mean?" her mom asked in confusion.

Katherine tipped her head toward the window. "That woman in the yard is one of your caregivers, right?"

Debbie blinked a few times. "She looks familiar. Oh, yes, that's Margot. She's always trying to feed me." As her mother finished speaking, the woman they'd been talking about entered the room, giving Katherine a surprised look when she saw her.

"Who are you?" Margot asked abruptly.

"I'm Katherine Barrett, Debbie's daughter."

"Oh, of course, you're the doctor," the woman said, relief filling her eyes. "Sorry, you gave me a start. It's so early in the morning, and I didn't know you were coming."

"I didn't know myself until a few hours ago." She paused. "What's your name?"

"Margot Waxman. I was just about to make your mother breakfast. Would you like some?"

"That would be great," she said, her stomach rumbling at the mention of food. "But don't go to any trouble."

"It's part of the job. Are scrambled eggs all right?"

"That would be perfect. Will you be here all day, Margot?"

"No, I cover the nights. Lillian gets here at nine. We both work for the Living Angels Agency."

Katherine got up from the couch and followed Margot into the kitchen while her mother drifted off to sleep again. "Is she always so out of it?" she asked as Margot started taking ingredients out of the refrigerator.

"She's mostly asleep when I'm with her, or dozing off

and on. You should ask Lillian. She's here during the day when Debbie is more alert." Margot set a carton of eggs on the counter. "I'm only here for another two weeks. Your brother said you might want to keep us on."

"I'll have to let you know after I speak to my brother."

"I hope you'll do that soon. Our schedules book up quickly, and I do like taking care of your mother," Margot said, as she put a frying pan on the stove.

"Are you a nurse, Margot?"

"No, I'm just here to help her get dressed, eat, and not burn the house down."

"Well, we appreciate your help very much."

Margot gave her a smile. "Your mother is well taken care of. Now, how do you like your eggs? Runny or well done?"

"Well done. I'm going to wash up."

"Take your time. I'll cut up some fruit before I put the eggs on."

On her way to the stairs, Katherine was surprised to hear the doorbell ring. "I'll get it," she said to Margot and then made her way to the door.

A slender, pretty, dark-eyed brunette stood on the porch. She looked surprised when Katherine opened the door.

"Oh," she said. "I'm looking for Debbie Barrett."

"That's my mother. I'm Katherine. She's sleeping right now. It's very early."

"I know. I'm sorry. I'm on my way to work. I saw the lights on, and I know Debbie doesn't sleep that well at night anymore. I thought I might catch her awake," the woman said. "I'm Jasmine Portillo." She glanced over her shoulder. "Could I speak to you for a moment?"

"Of course. Come in."

"TJ told me you live in Houston," Jasmine said, as she stepped into the house.

"I do. I came home for a visit. How do you know my brother?"

"I work with him at MDT." She drew in a breath and let

it out. "Actually, we have a personal relationship, too. I don't know if he told you..."

"We haven't spoken recently."

"Well, it's kind of new. He was supposed to get back on Thursday from a trip to Mexico, and I haven't heard from him. One of his coworkers told me that they thought he missed the plane. He's not answering his cell phone. I'm worried about him. I thought your mom might have heard from him."

"She told me he was in Mexico," Katherine said carefully. "Should I be concerned?"

"I'm sure he just stayed a day longer or took a sightseeing trip. He was pretty excited about going to Cancun. He said he'd never been to Mexico but had always wanted to go."

"I think it was on his wish list," she admitted.

"TJ is usually really good about calling me back, and we were supposed to get together last night, so I thought it was strange that I didn't hear from him. I probably shouldn't have come over here. Now I've worried you, too."

"It's fine. I'm glad someone is looking out for him." She wished she could tell Jasmine that TJ was all right, but she'd promised her brother not to speak to anyone about his situation, especially not someone who worked at his company. Jasmine seemed genuinely worried, and maybe she was right to be worried, because Katherine hadn't heard from her brother in almost twelve hours. Who knew where he was now or what condition he was in.

"There have been some weird things going on at the company," Jasmine added. "I guess we're all still a little on edge when something out of the ordinary happens."

She thought back to what TJ said about the people in his department who had died the past year. "He mentioned to me there had been some problems."

"The problems are supposedly over, but you never know." She paused and put on a brighter smile. "Anyway, I hope the bell didn't wake up Mrs. Barrett."

"I doubt it bothered her at all."

"How's your mother?" Jasmine asked.

"She's doing well this morning."

"That's good to hear. TJ told me her condition has been getting worse. I went through Alzheimer's with my grandmother so I know a bit about how bad it is."

"It is difficult," she said.

"I won't keep you. If you hear from TJ, could you tell him to call me?"

"I will. It was nice to meet you."

"You, too. TJ talks a lot about you, Katherine. He's really proud of you, just in case you didn't know that. I know how brothers can be."

"I'm proud of him, too," she said, relieved that Jasmine had only heard good things about her from her brother.

After Jasmine left, Katherine went upstairs to use the bathroom, then went into her mother's bedroom to see what condition it was in. Sadly, it was as messy as the rest of the house. There were dozens of clothes on the bed, as if her mom had tried on several different outfits the night before.

There was a pill bottle on the nightstand that disturbed her. Her mother definitely should not have access to medication, since she might get confused about what she'd taken and when she'd taken it.

The prescription was for a medication she wasn't familiar with, but what bothered her more was that the prescribing doctor was not her mother's physician. That was odd. Maybe Dr. Benner had gone out of town and his associate had filled the prescription. She'd have to ask TJ when he got back, or maybe one of the caregivers would know.

Slipping the bottle into the pocket of her jacket, she moved down the hall to TJ's room. He'd always been a nerd, and despite the fact that he was now twenty-seven years old, his bedroom still looked like a teenager lived here. He had Star Wars posters on the wall, and his desk was filled with textbooks.

How had he gone from this geeky innocence to dangerous trouble in Mexico, of all places?

She walked across the room and spun the standing globe by his bed. As the world went around, she thought about her brother's words. He was going to a place where people lived in a lost civilization. Her nerves tingled and her body tensed as her fingers trailed across southern Mexico.

Her high school boyfriend Jake Monroe had wanted to take her to the Yucatan one day. He'd wanted to introduce her to his great-grandmother, who lived in a small village untouched by technology.

Jake had told her and TJ stories about the Mayan legends of his ancestors, the underground caves, hidden sacred pools, and massive ruins left by one of the most advanced civilizations of all time.

TJ had loved listening to Jake's tales. Was it possible he'd decided to hide somewhere in the Yucatan? It made sense if he had to stay in Mexico that he'd go somewhere he'd at least heard about. But what she didn't understand was why he wasn't making his way back to Texas.

Unfortunately, she had no way of reaching him, so until he contacted her, she was going to have to guess where he might be going. And then she would have to find him.

She blew out a sigh. He'd told her to stay away, to not get on a commercial flight, to not tell anyone she'd spoken to him. Was his paranoia warranted?

Until she knew what he was involved in, she couldn't say it wasn't.

So she had to be careful. She had to get to Mexico without anyone knowing. That meant private transportation—a small plane—and she knew just the pilot who could probably help her….Jake Monroe.

Anxiety swept through her at the thought of reaching out to Jake. It had been years since they'd spoken, and she was fairly certain he hated her. She was also fairly certain that she deserved his hate. But her brother's life could be on the line, and Jake was in a position to help her. She had no choice. She had to ask. She was just really afraid to hear his answer.

Two

—⟶≫≪⟵—

Jake walked into his mother's house Saturday morning and paused in the kitchen doorway, feeling unexpected emotion at the scene. His mother Joanna was at the stove frying up bacon. His two younger sisters Danielle and Alicia sat at the kitchen table. All three women were in pajamas and robes.

The scene reminded him of his childhood when he'd bickered with his sisters over breakfast bacon and pancakes. That seemed like a million years ago now.

They'd certainly grown up since those innocent days. He was the oldest at thirty with Danielle at twenty-eight and Alicia at twenty-six. He and Danielle took after their mother, inheriting her green eyes and fairer skin, while Alicia had their father's dark hair, dark brown eyes and olive skin.

Looking around the room, he could see the remnants of Danielle's going away party the night before in the overflowing bag of trash and the wine glasses waiting to be washed. It had been a good sendoff for Danielle. He was going to miss her, but she was moving on to bigger and better things. Alicia had left years ago. Now it would just be him and his mom in Texas. Not that he saw his mother much, either. She had her life, and he had his.

Even though his family had drifted apart, he felt an overwhelming rush of emotion toward the three women in the room. They each brought a strong personality to the table. His mom could be extremely critical and judgmental. She loved to be right and could barely stand it if she was wrong. Danielle was the typical middle child; competitive and ambitious, always trying to make a name for herself and to be seen. And then there was Alicia—the passionate, emotional, imaginative dreamer who chased lightning with her camera and always saw the shades of gray in every black-and-white situation.

He'd thought of himself as the one sane person in the family, but his mother probably wouldn't appreciate hearing that. She'd always prided herself on being the strong, logical parent, while his father had been more like Alicia, a man who always had his head in the clouds even when he wasn't flying an airplane.

Thinking about his dad put an ache in his heart. His father had died ten years ago when his plane had gone down in an electrical storm over the Gulf of Mexico. His death had shattered their family.

He had been twenty at the time, Danielle an eighteen-year-old college freshman and Alicia had been sixteen and finishing up her junior year in high school. Alicia had had it the worst. She was the youngest and the only one still living at home at the time. She'd been the one in the house with his mom, the one to feel the loss, the emptiness every single day.

He hadn't appreciated how difficult it had been for her at the time; he'd been too consumed with his own emotions. The tragedy should have brought them closer together, but it had done the opposite. Their grief had turned to anger, and they'd turned that anger on each other—and to some people outside the family as well.

His gut tightened as he thought about Katherine. She'd definitely been collateral damage, but she'd done her own damage to him.

He shook those thoughts out of his head. The past wasn't important anymore, and while he couldn't predict what would happen tomorrow, he was happy about what was happening today. His family was back together for a brief moment in time, before Danielle moved to Washington DC to work for the US senator from Texas, and Alicia returned to her job as a photographic journalist and storm chaser in Miami, and to her fiancé Michael Cordero. But this morning, it felt good to have everyone in one place—the way they used to be.

He walked into the kitchen as his mom set a platter of bacon on the table.

"Jake, honey," she said with a happy smile. "I'm so glad you came for breakfast. I've got pancakes and eggs warming in the oven."

"You went all out." He sat down in what had always been his chair, noting that Alicia and Danielle had done the same. Old habits died hard. His mom would take her chair, and his dad's chair would stay empty, unless...

He turned to Alicia. "Where's Michael?"

"He went for a run. Unlike me, who reaches for coffee to get the day started, Michael likes the endorphin rush of exercise. I also think he wanted to give me some time alone with the family. There was quite a crowd here last night. It was hard for us to talk to each other."

"Yeah, I was surprised so many people turned up to say good-bye to you, Dani," he teased his sister. "I didn't think you had that many friends."

She made a face at him. "I'm very popular. I always have been."

Since Danielle had always made popularity a priority in her life, he wasn't surprised to hear her defend her status now. In high school, she'd been a cheerleader and part of the *in* crowd, and now she was going to be part of the inner circle of a very powerful man. Only one thing bothered him about that. She always seemed to be the one who was following someone else.

"You know," he began. "You don't have to orbit the moon. You can *be* the moon."

Danielle shot him a wary look. "What the hell does that mean?"

"Yes, what does that mean?" Alicia added.

"It means you should think about running for office yourself, Dani, instead of putting someone else into power," he replied.

"That's down the road. I'm paying my dues and I'm making political connections for when I do decide to put myself into power."

"Maybe you'll be the first female president," Alicia said.

Dani shrugged. "I have a feeling someone may get there before me, but I don't expect we'll have only one female president in our lifetimes." She turned her gaze back on him, a questioning look in her eyes. "Since when do you care what I'm doing, Jake?"

"Since always."

"Yeah, right," she scoffed.

"It's true. I care about both of you, and I try to look out for you. Someone obviously needs to. Alicia almost got herself killed last month."

"But I survived, and I helped solve a triple homicide," Alicia said with pride in her voice. "So you don't need to worry about me, Jake."

"Or me," Dani put in. "I can take care of myself."

"Let's talk about something happier," his mother said, joining them at the table. "Alicia, when are you and Michael getting married?"

Jake laughed at the sudden look of discomfort on Alicia's face. His youngest sister and his mom rarely saw eye-to-eye on anything, and while Danielle would probably love to plan a big wedding bash with his mom's help, Alicia would no doubt walk to her own beat, the way she always did.

"We haven't set a date yet," Alicia said carefully. "It's all really new, but you'll be the first to know when we start making plans."

"I want you to have a real wedding." Joanna shook a

warning finger in Alicia's direction. "No running off somewhere and doing it on your own. Your father isn't here to walk you down the aisle, but Jake will do it, and I want to see Danielle stand up next to you. I want it to be a family affair."

"Don't worry, Mom. There's time to figure it all out," Alicia said.

"Well, I know how stubborn and independent you can be," Joanna said pointedly. "And while I do like Michael very much, I feel a little jealous that you'll be living near his family and so far from your own."

"I'm planning to come home more often," Alicia said. "I miss you guys."

His mother dabbed at her eyes with her napkin. "You never ever say that."

"Well, I'm sorry that I haven't said it more often, because I've thought it a lot. Maybe I just needed some distance to appreciate home."

"You could always move back," Jake suggested. "We have plenty of lightning storms here."

"I won't rule it out," Alicia said. "But at the moment, it's better for both Michael and me to be on the East Coast."

"Just promise to keep me involved in the wedding plans and to come home more often," Joanna said.

"I promise."

As Alicia made her vow, Jake found himself wondering if some of his sister's newfound motivation to come home more often was because of what she'd discovered about one of his father's best friends and what she believed to be a mystery surrounding his father's death. But he didn't want to bring that up now. His father's death was always a painful and disconnecting topic.

"I've been meaning to ask you, Mom," Alicia said. "How is Mrs. Barrett doing? When Jake and I went over there last month, she was not doing well."

"She has round-the-clock caregivers now," Joanna said. "TJ does his best, but he works long hours, and he doesn't want to leave her alone. We still have a neighborhood group that's helping to fill in by making sure she has healthy meals."

"How does TJ afford so much help?" Danielle asked. "That has to be expensive."

"I'm not sure," his mother replied. "He said he's been working extra projects to bring in more money. I'm sure Katherine is helping."

Jake wondered about that. "Are you sure?" he asked. "When was she last home?"

"I don't know," his mother said, giving him a speculative look. "She's not on vacation, Jake; she's completing her residency."

"And that's more important than her mother?" He didn't know why he'd asked the question because he knew firsthand that nothing was more important to Katherine than her medical career.

"I don't think it's *more* important, but she has put a lot of time in; I'm sure she wants to finish," his mom replied.

He shrugged. "All right. Whatever." He was sorry he'd brought up Katherine. "So, what's happening today?"

"Michael and I will hang out with Mom and Danielle today, then fly back to Miami tomorrow," Alicia said.

"And I have to pack so I can leave for Washington tonight," Danielle added.

Joanna's sigh enveloped the room. "I'm going to miss you both so much."

"Hey, I'm still here," he reminded her.

"I know, Jake, and I love that one of my children wants to live by me, but I miss mornings like these, having all my kids in one room, knowing you're all safe." Her gaze drifted to the empty chair.

He thought for a moment she might say something about missing his dad, but she didn't.

His phone buzzed, and he glanced down at the text. It was the dispatch center at the airfield. Someone wanted to talk to him about a charter flight that needed to happen today.

"I'm going to have to run," he said. "Work calls."

"Where are you flying this time?" Danielle asked. "Is it for medical intervention?"

"I don't know. I don't think so, but I'll see when I get to the airport." The charter service he worked for had been flying medical evacuation flights in addition to corporate charters the last year, but he flew wherever he was told to fly.

"I'll walk you out," Alicia said, surprising him with the offer.

"Okay." He paused on his way out of the room to give Dani a hug. "If I don't see you before you go, knock 'em dead in DC."

"I plan to."

"Mom, I'll catch you later."

"Be safe, Jake," his mom said.

Alicia led the way to the front door and then paused. "Before you go, we still need to talk about what Jerry told me about Dad's death not being an accident."

"He didn't say that exactly, did he?"

"Well, he said we didn't know everything about it, and I want to find out what we don't know."

He let out a sigh. Last month, Alicia had gotten involved in a terrible situation involving murder and treason, and his father's former friend, Jerry Caldwell, had tried to kill her. Jerry hadn't been able to accomplish that, but he had managed to leave a tormenting thought in Alicia's head before taking his last breath.

Alicia had tried to talk to him about it before, but he'd always brushed her off. Now that she was here in person, he could see that wasn't an option.

"What do you want to do?" he asked.

"I've spoken to a private investigator, Colin Kenner, and he has agreed to help me look into the crash and also Jerry's relationship with Dad around the time of the accident. I talked to Dani about it last night. She said she'd pitch in on the cost, but she can't get any more involved, not with all she has going on. Plus, she doesn't want to be associated with any kind of criminal investigation. You know how she is about keeping her reputation squeaky clean."

"It will be hard for her to do that in politics," he said dryly. "What about Mom? Did you speak to her?"

"I tried to tell her, but she shut me down. She said it doesn't matter anymore what happened. We can't bring him back."

"She's right about that, Alicia."

"I'm not trying to bring him back. I'm trying to find out what happened, and if justice needs to be served, then someone needs to make sure that happens, and if that's me, then it's me."

He frowned at the intensity of her words. "Alicia, you just got out of a bad situation—are you sure you want to jump into another one?"

"I don't have a choice. I know what I heard. I can't forget it. And unlike just about everyone else, I don't believe Jerry's death was the end of anything. I think it was just the tip of an iceberg. But I can't force the FBI or Homeland Security or MDT to work with me on that, so I'm going to concentrate on the piece of the puzzle that means the most to me."

"Look, I get it, but Jerry could have been trying to torture you. You'd gotten the best of him, and he wanted to pay you back. Why are you so sure he told you the truth before he died? He lied about so many other things. It's clear we had no idea who he really was."

"True. But I've thought there was a mystery surrounding Dad's death long before Jerry brought it up. It's not just that I want your money, Jake; I want you to think it's the right thing to do," she said, meeting his gaze. "I know you don't share my belief that the lightning I chase is trying to tell us something, but we have more than weather to go on now."

He looked into her earnest dark-brown eyes that reminded him so much of his father and knew that he couldn't say no. "I can't imagine what you'll be able to find out, but

I'm in."

Relief filled her gaze. "Good. I'll keep you posted."

The front door opened, and Alicia's fiancé Michael Cordero walked into the house. He wore track pants and a T-shirt, and there was a gleam of sweat on his face.

"Hey," Michael said, shaking Jake's hand. "Are you leaving?"

"On my way to work. There's still plenty of pancakes and bacon."

"Good. Will we see you later?"

"I'm not sure. But if I can get back before you leave, I will. Congratulations again on your engagement. It's going to be nice to add another male to the family. I've been outnumbered for far too long."

"As if Mom doesn't treat you like the king," Alicia teased. "Your life is not that hard, Jake."

He laughed. "Well, I am the oldest, so that does make me the most important."

Alicia rolled her eyes. "In your mind, maybe."

"You two take care. See if you can keep her out of trouble," he added to Michael.

Michael gave a shrug. "I'm not sure I can, but I will try. Your sister can be very stubborn."

"It's a family trait," Alicia said, giving him a pointed look. "Which is why we work better when we're on the same team."

"We are," Jake said. "I'll see you around."

As he left the house, he wondered if he was making a mistake supporting Alicia's desire to search for answers to a decade-old-tragedy.

Were they going to stir up more trouble?

On the other hand, as Alicia had said, if someone had deliberately sent his father's plane crashing into the Gulf of Mexico, that person needed to pay.

⇒▷◁⇐

Twenty minutes later, Jake parked his car in the lot at the Culverson Field Airport, the home base of Culverson Air Charters. As he walked toward the two-story building that housed airport operations, the business offices, a lounge for waiting passengers and a smaller break room for pilots, his thoughts were on his father.

His dad had worked for Culverson after leaving the Navy, and Jake had followed in his footsteps. He didn't want to believe that there was anything mysterious about his dad's death, mostly because he didn't want to relive all that pain again. But he couldn't think of himself; he had to consider Alicia and Dani and his mom, and most of all, his father. If there was a truth to be found, he needed to help Alicia find it.

His dad would have been impressed with how the charter service had grown in the past ten years, he thought, eying the mixed fleet of sleek jets including Citations, Mustangs, and Hawkeyes on the tarmac.

Business had been good in the private aviation industry the last few years, especially in Corpus Christi. The city was the second biggest in south Texas and home to the US Navy as well as several important corporations including MDT, one of the largest defense technology companies in the world. Flying corporate executives and political operatives out of Culverson had given him some solid job security doing work that he loved. Because, like his dad, he'd never wanted to do anything but fly.

He'd grown up at this airfield. His dad had taught him to fly before he'd learned how to drive. They'd made a lot of amazing memories over the years, and he treasured the time they'd had together. He just wished it had been longer.

Stepping into an empty lobby, he made his way to the business office, prepared to find his boss, Rusty Sampson, grumbling about the fact that he'd taken his sweet time to get there, but there was no sign of the burly six-foot-three manager, who had run Culverson Air Charters since Jake had been a teenager. There was, however, another person in the room—a woman wearing dark jeans and a brown leather jacket over a cream-colored sweater, a floral scarf around her neck. Her golden blonde hair swung halfway down her back in thick waves and her steel-blue eyes touched a deep, painful nerve.

His heart came to a crashing halt.

Katherine!

It had been years since he'd seen her in person, but she'd haunted his memories for a decade.

As she stared back at him, it occurred to him that she didn't look as surprised to see him as he was to see her.

"What are you doing here?" he bit out.

"Looking for you."

For years he'd imagined those words coming from her lips. Now, they seemed impossible to believe. "You're the one who wants to charter a plane? Why?"

She drew in a breath as if it hurt to say whatever was coming next. "I need a favor, Jake."

Of course she needed something from him. There was no way she would have come here just to see him. "You think I want to do you a favor?" He was somewhat amazed by that thought. "Have we spoken in the last ten years? Did I miss some texts, some emails, an Instagram?"

"You're not going to make this easy, are you?"

"Why should I? You walked out on me. You told me you didn't love me, and you never wanted to see me again."

"I was twenty years old, Jake. I was angry and confused, and so were you."

He wanted to deny that, but he couldn't.

"Look, I wouldn't be here if I had another choice," she added with determination in her eyes. "I need to go to Mexico to find my brother."

He didn't know what he'd been expecting her to say, but it hadn't been that. "TJ is in Mexico?"

She nodded. "Yes, and he's in trouble."

"What kind of trouble?"

"I'm not exactly sure."

"So take a commercial flight."

"I can't do that, for a couple of reasons."

"What reasons?"

She hesitated, as if not sure how much she wanted to tell him. "TJ called me last night. He's in danger and on the run in Mexico. I don't know the circumstances, except that several people he worked with at his company, MDT, were killed recently. I don't know what those people have to do with him, but he said something about thinking he might be next, and that he wasn't going to let that happen."

His body tightened at her words, at the idea that Alicia was right—that Jerry's death was just the tip of an iceberg. "Go on."

"TJ told me that he's going to disappear to a place where time stands still and people can get lost forever. Does that sound familiar, Jake? All those stories you told TJ about your great-grandmother and your Mayan ancestors apparently stuck in his head."

"That's crazy. Why doesn't he just go to the police?"

"In Mexico?" she challenged.

She had a point. "If not there, then back here."

"He said he doesn't know who he can trust. I wish I knew more, but I have no idea what he's talking about."

"I probably have a better idea than you do," he muttered.

"What does that mean?" she asked sharply.

"My sister Alicia helped unravel the mystery surrounding the murders TJ told you about. She spoke to TJ about the professor he worked for last month. I was with her when she went to see him and your mom."

Surprise widened her eyes. "You went to my house?"

"Yes. I saw your mom. TJ wasn't there, but Alicia spoke to him later." He paused. "Your mother is in bad shape, Katherine. Where the hell have you been? Why aren't you taking care of her?"

"I'm very aware of my mother's illness," she snapped. "I'm doing the best I can."

"Your best doesn't impress me."

"Well, I'm not trying to impress you," she said, anger in her eyes. "This was a mistake."

"Hell, yes, it was a mistake."

She bit down on her bottom lip, and the action took him back to when she was a teenager struggling to contain her emotion. For some reason, she'd always seen tears as a sign of weakness, and Katherine Barrett hated to be weak.

"Okay, look, this isn't about us," she said, taking a breath. "This is about my brother. I'll pay you whatever you want to fly me to Mexico."

"So you're rich now?"

"I'll find the money somewhere. This isn't just for me. My mom needs TJ to be okay. He's her rock. Just think of me as the messenger."

"The messenger is the one who usually gets killed," he said darkly.

She didn't waver under his angry gaze. "I'll take that chance. I need to fix this, so will you help me or not? Because if the answer is no, then I need to move on."

"You're really good at moving on, aren't you?"

"And you're really good at helping people who are in trouble, or at least you used to be."

"You don't know me anymore, Katherine."

"And you don't know me."

"You can get another pilot."

"The man I spoke to earlier said you're the only one available, and the truth is I want it to be you, because you can tell me where to look for TJ. You know the area. So, what's your answer, Jake?"

He hesitated for one long minute, if for no other reason than to make her squirm, but deep down he'd known he was going to say yes from the second she asked him for the favor. "All right. I'll do it," he said slowly.

"You will?"

"Don't make me say it again."

"How soon can we go?"

"I need to talk to my boss, fill out the necessary paperwork, see what plane we have available." He glanced at the big clock on the wall. It was a little after nine. "If there aren't any snags, we should be able to take off by noon."

"Thank you, Jake."

As he looked into her eyes, he felt like the years between them suddenly fell away. They were young. They were in love.

And then they weren't...

He straightened and broke the connection. "Before we go, I think we should talk to Alicia. She's at my mom's house." He pulled out his phone. "I'll tell her we're on the way."

"I'm not supposed to talk to anyone about this, Jake. I shouldn't have even told you."

"Alicia knows more than you do about TJ's situation. She talked to him about the murders at MDT, and she's been in touch with the police and the FBI and God knows what other agencies. You need to get up to speed on the situation your brother may be involved in, and so do I. If I'm taking you into danger, I'd like to know what we're getting into."

Indecision played through her eyes. Katherine wanted to say no, but she was a smart girl, and she had always, always done her research. "I suppose that makes sense."

"Why don't you wait for me outside? I'll get the paperwork started for our flight, so we'll be ready to go when we get back."

"How long will that take?"

"Not long."

"Is there any way you cannot put my name down as the charter or the passenger? TJ was concerned that someone might be checking the airline database for any attempt I make to go to Mexico. I didn't even know that was possible."

"I'd have to check with my boss."

"It's important."

"Like I said, I'll look into it."

"All right." As she turned to leave, his boss walked through the door. Rusty was in his late sixties and had a square face, intelligent brown eyes and a full head of copper-colored hair that had given him his nickname when he was a small boy.

Rusty gave Katherine a nod. "I see you've met Jake, Ms. Barrett."

"Yes," she said shortly. "He's agreed to fly my charter."

"I'll fill Rusty in," Jake said, cutting her off.

"Okay." She paused, her hand on the door. "Just don't change your mind, Jake."

He really didn't know if he could promise that, but thankfully she left without waiting for an answer—probably because she didn't want to hear his answer.

Rusty walked around the counter and set down the coffee cup in his hand. "So you're taking her to Mexico?"

"Apparently, you told her I was the only one available."

"Well, she asked for you first," he said, a twinkle in his eyes. "And since she's a beautiful blonde, I figured you'd be interested. If I were thirty years younger, I'd take her wherever she wanted to go."

"That's because you don't know her."

"And you do?" Rusty shot back.

He frowned, wishing he'd kept his mouth shut. "I used to. We were together a long time ago—in high school and part of college."

"I didn't know that. What happened?"

"It doesn't matter. It ended. That's that."

"Or that was that until now…"

He ignored that comment. "Can you get started on the paperwork? And I'll need you to dummy up the passenger information."

Rusty raised an eyebrow. "So she's not only trouble, she's

in trouble?"

"Not her; her brother. She needs to get down to Mexico without anyone noticing. Is that going to be a problem?"

"As long as I can make a copy of her passport, and you vouch for her, I'm good with it."

"Thanks. I'd like to get in the air by one at the latest, but I have to run out for about an hour."

"You still like her, don't you?" Rusty gave him a knowing look.

"Not even a little," he lied.

Three

Katherine got into her car and pulled out her phone. Since she had a little time, and she really didn't want to spend it thinking about Jake and how shaken she felt after seeing him again, she decided to call one of the few friends she had left in Corpus Christi.

She'd met Rebecca Saunders sophomore year in high school, and they'd clicked right away with their passion for medicine. They'd started out at different colleges until Katherine had transferred junior year. Then they'd gone through medical school together.

Unfortunately, they'd lost touch a few years ago when Rebecca had decided to do her residency in Corpus Christi at the Halliwell Medical Center. But despite the time that had passed between now and their last conversation, Katherine felt fairly sure Rebecca would be able to help her with her mother's situation. Besides being a friend, Rebecca was also a neurologist who specialized in diseases of the brain. In fact, she really should have gotten Rebecca involved before, but her mom had been insistent on working with her long-term physician.

She punched in the number she had for her and was happy to hear Rebecca's voice come over the phone.

"It's Katherine," she said. "How are you?"

"I'm great. What a crazy coincidence. I was thinking about you yesterday. You finished your residency, right?"

"Last night at eleven. What about you?"

"Two weeks ago. Congratulations. Are you coming back to Corpus Christi?"

"I'm not sure yet."

"I bet you have a lot of options, but the medical center here is really good. They've updated all the equipment, the labs. It's first-rate."

"I'm keeping it in mind. I actually called because I need a favor. I think I told you my mom had a stroke several months ago."

"I did hear that, not from you, from my mom."

"Of course. The neighborhood grapevine has always been strong."

"How's she doing?" Rebecca asked.

"Not good. I called Dr. Benner this morning, and I was informed that she's no longer a patient of his, which doesn't make sense because she's been seeing him for thirty years. I looked at one of her pill bottles, and the prescribing physician was no one I'd ever heard of. His name was Malcolm Watkins."

"I've never heard of him. Did you try his office?"

"Yes, but I didn't even get an answering service. It just rang and rang, then disconnected. I don't know what's going on. My mother told me she switched doctors, because some nice woman told her to. I don't know who that was. And her caregiver said that she doesn't deal with the doctors; she's just there to make sure my mom has her daily needs met."

"Well, what about TJ?"

"He's out of the country, and I can't reach him. I have to go away for a few days, and I really need someone to check in on my mom, and I'm hoping you might make a house call. I know it's a big favor to ask. I'm just in a bind, and I don't want my mom taking the wrong medication."

"I'd be happy to look in on her, Katherine, as long as

she's okay with it."

"She won't know if she's okay with it or not. But I think if you remind her that we went to school together, that you used to love her peanut butter cookies, she'll be happy to let you take a look at her."

"Sure. I'm off tomorrow, so I can go by then. Do you want me to call you afterwards?"

"That would be great. My cell service might be spotty, but I will call you when I can."

"Where are you going?"

"I'll tell you when I get back."

"That sounds mysterious. Is there a mystery man involved—someone tall, dark and handsome?"

Jake's image flashed through her mind. "There is a man," she conceded. "But he's not the man for me."

"Maybe you should give him a chance."

"Believe me, he doesn't want one. I'll talk to you soon. Thanks again."

She ended the call, feeling better about leaving her mom now that she knew Rebecca would check on her. Now, she just had to figure out how she was going to deal with Jake.

As she saw him walking across the parking lot, her heart squeezed tight with that long-ago familiar sensation of need and desire. That should have passed by now. Why hadn't it?

And it wasn't fair that Jake was even more attractive now than he'd been ten years ago. Old boyfriends should never look better with age. Why couldn't he have lost his hair or turned gray or gotten fat? Why did his body have to be broader, stronger, and more masculine?

And those eyes of his—a light piercing green that always seemed to see more than she wanted him to see—were still as unsettling as ever. She wanted to find something wrong with him, but his scruffy beard, faded jeans, navy T-shirt, and black leather jacket only added to his attractiveness.

Maybe it was a good thing he still hated her—because she was having a hard time remembering why she'd ever walked away from him.

You know why, she told herself forcefully.

She wouldn't be where she was now if she'd continued her relationship with Jake. Just because he could still make her palms sweat and her pulse race didn't mean a damn thing. She wasn't a hormone-driven teenage girl anymore, and Jake wasn't the boy she'd fallen in love with.

Besides, he probably had someone in his life now—a girlfriend, maybe even a wife. That thought should have made her feel better, but for some reason it didn't.

"Ready?" he asked, as he opened the passenger's door.

"Yes." She was happy to be in the driver's seat. She liked to be in control. Jake wasn't going to go anywhere she didn't want to take him, at least not right this second.

As Jake settled in next to her, a wave of nostalgia put a knot in her throat. Jake had taught her how to drive. Her dad had always been too busy, and her mother had been too nervous, so she and Jake had gone out together on the weekends. After the driving lessons, they'd usually climbed into the back seat and fooled around. She'd lost her virginity to Jake in the back seat of her dad's Ford Explorer. It had seemed wildly passionate and amazing at the time.

Actually, if she were honest, it still was one of her most vivid memories. There had been a lot of things that had gone wrong between them, but being together like that had never been one of them. They'd been as combustible as a match to gasoline—the good girl and the bad boy. And it had never ever been like that with anyone else.

Which was a good thing, she reminded herself. She'd lost her mind with Jake and almost given up on her dreams. Thankfully, she'd found the reins and pulled back just in time. She knew Jake didn't see it that way. But they'd both been on the wrong road, and now they weren't—at least she wasn't. She didn't know about him.

She started the car and pulled out of the lot, keeping her gaze on the road as she drove back to the neighborhood she'd just left. Jake's mom's house was only a few blocks from her mother's house, another reminder of just how closely intertwined their lives had once been.

She was a little surprised that Jake didn't say anything on the ride. No snarky comments. No insults. Nothing. The silence was highly unusual, because Jake almost always had too much to say.

Finding the quiet a little too intense, she broke through with a question. "Why is Alicia here in Texas? I thought she moved to Florida."

"She did. She came back for Dani's going away party last night."

"Where is Dani going?"

"Washington DC. She got a job with Senator Dillon. She's headed for Capitol Hill."

"That sounds interesting."

"She's excited about it. She loves politics."

"I remember the campaign she ran when she wanted to be sophomore class president. She made posters, videos, and had her own street team of lobbyists," she said.

"She turned our house into campaign headquarters that year. She was obsessed. But she won, so I guess it was worth it."

"What's Alicia doing now?"

"She's a photographer at a newspaper in Miami. In her spare time, she chases storms and photographs lightning strikes."

She shot him a quick look, hearing a dark note in his voice. "She's still crazy about lightning?"

"As much, if not more, than she ever was. She's convinced there's an answer to my dad's plane crash in every flash of lightning."

She'd known that Alicia had taken her dad's death very hard, but she hadn't realized just how much of a long-lasting impact it had had. "What answer could there possibly be?"

"A few weeks ago, I would have said none, but now..."

As his voice drifted away, she glanced over again. "What's changed?"

"Alicia got some information that suggests my dad's crash might not have been an accident."

"What?" She was shocked by his words.

He shrugged. "A former friend of my father's claims there are things we don't know."

"What things?"

"He didn't specify. It could all be bullshit. In fact, I'm fairly certain that he was just yanking Alicia's chain, but she's not going to rest until she knows for sure that there's nothing to find."

She couldn't imagine what anyone could find now. "Wasn't there an exhaustive search for your dad's plane?"

"Yeah," he said shortly, turning his head to meet her gaze. "But it's possible there was a rush to judgment to call it an accident. At least, that's what Alicia thinks."

"What do you think?"

"I haven't made any decisions. I've agreed to help finance an investigator to look into the accident. We'll see what he comes up with."

"Do you really want to go back there, Jake?" The question slipped past her lips before she could stop it.

"No, I don't want to go back there," he snapped. "It was the worst time of my life."

"Then why do this?"

"Because my sister is convinced there's more to find out, and if there's some small chance that she's right and someone had a hand in my dad's death, then I couldn't live with myself if I didn't help her get to the truth."

Jake had always been an intensely loyal person and very protective, especially when it came to his family. "What does your mother think about all this?"

"She doesn't want to talk about my father—not his life, not his death. For the time being, we're going to leave her out of the loop until we figure out if there is something for her to know."

"Has she ever remarried?"

"No. She still works at the university. She has a lot of friends and seems happy enough. She's sad to see Dani leave and wishes Alicia would move back, but she seems to have accepted the fact that the girls are going to go their own way."

"She still has you."

"Yeah, but I don't go shopping with her," he said dryly.

"Well, I'm glad she's doing well." Jake's mom had been very nice to her when they'd been together, but after the breakup, she'd delivered a few choice words to Katherine—words she probably deserved. But with all that was going on in her life, she didn't know if she could handle dealing with Jake's mother, too. "Is your mom home now? Will we see her?"

"I have no idea. She was there earlier, but who knows? Why?" He gave her a thoughtful look. "Do you have a problem with my mom?"

"I think she might have a problem with me."

"Not that I've seen," he muttered. "She loves to tell me how great you're doing."

"Really? After we broke up, she wasn't too happy with me."

"How do you know that?"

"We ran into each other at the store one day. She said a few things."

"What kind of things?"

"I don't remember exactly. It doesn't matter."

For a moment, she thought he might argue the point, but then he said, "You're right, it doesn't matter."

And they went back to a tense silence.

Ten minutes later, she parked in front of his mom's house and then followed him inside.

Alicia was waiting in the living room. She looked as exotically pretty as ever with her dark hair cascading in waves down her back, her deep-brown eyes and warm smile.

"Katherine, it's been so long," she said with a smile, giving her a hug. "How are you?"

"I'm all right." She wasn't sure what Jake had told Alicia on the phone, and she was actually a little surprised at Alicia's warmth. She didn't think his sisters had been any happier with her than his mother had been after she'd walked away from their relationship. But apparently Alicia hadn't held a grudge.

"I want you to meet my fiancé," Alicia said, grabbing the hand of a darkly handsome man. "This is Michael Cordero. He's a brilliant architect and real-estate developer, and he's also going to be my husband once we set a date. Michael, this is Katherine Barrett—Jake's high school girlfriend—and a brilliant doctor."

Michael smiled and shook her hand. "From one brilliant person to another—it's nice to meet you."

She smiled back. "Alicia exaggerates."

"I know it," he said. "But as long as it's in my favor, I don't care."

Alicia playfully punched Michael's arm. "I spoke only the truth—about both of you." Then she turned to Katherine. "So what's going on? Jake didn't say anything except that he was bringing you by and that you wanted to talk to me about TJ. I have to admit I'm surprised that you and Jake are talking about anything together."

"Why don't we sit down?" Jake suggested, waving Katherine toward an armchair.

She took the chair while Michael and Alicia sat down on the sofa together and Jake perched on the arm of another chair. As everyone settled in, she debated what she wanted to say. She'd made a promise to TJ to keep quiet. On the other hand, as Jake had said, going to Mexico without as much information as she could get wasn't smart, and she'd always prided herself on making intelligent decisions.

"You can trust Alicia," Jake told her. "And we don't have all day, so…"

"So," she continued, very aware of the ticking clock. "TJ

called me last night. He mentioned several people he worked with at MDT had been killed. He said he was afraid he might be next—that he knew too much about whatever they were involved in. He was calling me from Mexico. He said someone was after him, and he didn't think he could get on a plane so he was going to hide. I'm on my way to find him. Jake agreed to fly me down there, but he wanted me to talk to you first. He said you know something about the recent problems at MDT."

"I do," Alicia murmured, exchanging a pointed look with her fiancé, before adding, "I wish I could say I'm surprised that TJ is now in danger, but I had a feeling this wasn't over."

"What is *this*?" Katherine asked.

"It's a long story," Alicia said.

"Can you give me the highlights?"

"Let's see. Your brother worked for Professor Bryer before getting a job at MDT."

"I know that part," she said.

"When Professor Bryer was moonlighting as an engineering consultant at MDT, he discovered that one of the employees, Connie Randolph, was selling classified weapons information to a former MDT employee by the name of Jerry Caldwell. Jerry was also a friend of my father's. They flew together in the Navy. I thought he was a good guy. He wasn't. When Connie realized she'd been made, she turned to Jerry for help. He assured her he'd take care of the professor, but what he did was kill both Connie and Professor Bryer, framing Bryer's wife for the murders. He almost got away with it, but the wife appealed her conviction, and in unraveling that case, we discovered that Jerry was the guilty party. He went after me to shut me up, but fortunately I escaped. Unfortunately, a lot of innocent people died before Jerry did."

Katherine's stomach turned over with Alicia's words. "That's awful. And TJ knew this Jerry?"

"And Connie, and, of course, Professor Bryer," Alicia

replied. "After Jerry's crimes were revealed, the police and several federal agencies worked with MDT to make sure that there were no other employees involved in Jerry's scheme to leak classified information. At that point, I was cut out of the investigation but told everything was being done that needed to be done. The fact that your brother is in hiding suggests they missed something."

"And TJ might have found whatever they missed," she murmured, feeling overwhelmed by the magnitude of the problem.

"If he calls you again, you need to ask him what he knows," Alicia said.

"You should probably go to the authorities," Michael suggested.

"I do have the name of an FBI agent who wasn't as dismissive as the others," Alicia added.

"I can't do that. TJ made me promise not to tell or trust anyone," she said. "I'm already breaking my promise by talking to you."

"You can trust us," Alicia said. "But you're probably smart not to trust anyone else." She paused. "If I were you, I'd look for TJ on my own. MDT is a huge corporation, whose board members are closely tied to the government. It's possible that the reason no one found out anything after Jerry died was to save MDT's reputation or government contracts. If TJ thought he could trust someone at MDT, he would have already called them."

She nodded. "That's what I think, too. I need to find TJ so I can help him figure out how to get out of the mess he's in. Since he's going into hiding in Mexico, I believe he's going to try to get to your great-grandmother's village. He was always enthralled by the stories Jake told him about that part of the world."

"You're going to Nic Té Há, Jake?" Alicia asked in surprise, referencing the town where their great-grandmother lived.

"I'm just flying Katherine down there. Then she's on her own."

"But if you're that close, you should go see Mamich. You should tell her what's going on."

Jake shook his head. "She's an old woman now, and she was heartbroken after Dad's death. I don't think we need to hurt her again by telling her it wasn't an accident."

"I already wrote to her after Jerry tried to kill me. I told her what he said."

"Why the hell would you do that?" Jake asked in annoyance.

"Because she's the only one who believes the way I believe. The lightning showed me what I needed to see. It led me to Jerry and to this clue about Dad. I don't believe that's a coincidence."

"Well, what did she say?"

"She hasn't answered my letter yet. It usually takes a few weeks to hear from her. She doesn't have a computer, and I think the mail only goes out once a week. Plus, she said her arthritis has gotten worse, and sometimes she has to wait for one of the women from the village to help her write down her thoughts. You need to go see her, Jake. She might be able to help you find TJ. She knows everyone in that part of the country."

"Alicia is right," Katherine broke in. "Your great-grandmother could be a valuable resource. And it's been years since you saw her."

Jake held up a hand. "Don't push it, Katherine. I said I'd fly you to the nearest airport. That's it."

She wanted to argue, but decided to save it for later. She didn't want Jake to back out of flying her to Mexico. Once they were on their way, she'd try to convince him to go a little farther.

"Don't be such an ass, Jake," Alicia said. "You can help Katherine out."

"I am helping her out, and you can stay out of it, Alicia.

You and your lightning obsession are not part of this."

"Of course I'm part of this. That's why you brought Katherine here to talk to me."

"Well, I'm already regretting that." He got to his feet. "If we're going, we need to go."

"All right," Katherine said, standing up. "Thanks, Alicia."

"Keep us posted. And stay safe," Alicia said. "I'm not going to stop worrying about you until you come home."

Alicia's words sent a chill through Katherine's body, but they were going to come home safe, and they would bring TJ back with them. Failure wasn't an option.

Four

―――≫≫⫸⫷≪―

They drove back to the airport in silence. When they pulled into the parking lot, Jake told her it would probably be another thirty minutes to get the plane ready to go. She could either leave and come back or wait in the lounge. Since she already had her bag in the car, she decided to stay at the airport so that they could take off as soon as possible. She was actually happy to have a little time on her own to catch her breath and regroup. Alicia's story had given her a lot to think about. She still didn't know exactly what TJ was caught up in, but she was more convinced than ever that he was in danger.

As she entered the airport waiting room, she saw a stand filled with maps, and she was thrilled to see one of Mexico.

She took the map over to a table and opened it up. Jake's great-grandmother, who he fondly referred to as Mamich, the Mayan nickname for great-grandmother, lived in Nic Té Há which loosely translated from Mayan dialect to Flower Lake, a small village in the Mexican state of Chiapas located in southern Mexico near the Guatemalan border. She couldn't find the village on the map, but she was able to locate the closest airport in Tuxtla Gutiérrez.

Chiapas had diverse geography with several mountain ranges as well as one of Mexico's largest areas of rainforest.

There were also hundreds of cenotes, which the Mayans called sacred wells, and a multitude of ruins that paid homage to a lost civilization. Reading about the area reminded her that she and Jake had talked about going to Mexico together, exploring the ruins, boating the rivers, listening to the howler monkeys in the rain forest. But their romantic adventure had never materialized. They'd broken up and Jake had gone to Mexico on his own.

She hoped she could convince him to go with her now. Looking at the map, she couldn't imagine how TJ would find his way to a remote, unmarked village, or how she would find Nic Té Há on her own. She would have to hire a car or a guide or both, but that meant bringing some other individual into the situation, which she didn't really want to do. Maybe Jake would change his mind once they were on their way to Mexico. He would have the opportunity to see his great-grandmother again. That had to be worth something to him.

Setting aside the map, she pulled her laptop out of her bag and got on the Internet to do some research. She wasn't used to going anywhere without a plan. She didn't like to be unprepared, and she preferred to know as much as possible about whatever she was doing before she did it, which meant she needed to do some quick cramming on not just Mexico but also her brother's company.

She typed in Mission Defense Technology. There were hundreds of items that came up on the search. She skimmed through the first several articles, noting that MDT employed over 30,000 people around the world, that the company was run by the Packer brothers, Reid and Alan Packer, who had inherited MDT from their father, who still held a seat on the board of directors.

In addition to weapons defense technology, the company had numerous other divisions that worked on everything from telecommunication to artificial intelligence and aviation systems. They were one of the top companies in the world and were always first in line for large government contracts.

No wonder all the governmental agencies had gotten involved when two employees had been murdered by a former employee who had admitted to selling secrets. MDT was hugely important to national security. What she couldn't understand was how her twenty-seven-year-old brother had gotten himself into so much trouble. He was a small cog in a very big wheel.

The only thing that made sense was that he had had a tie to Professor Bryer, and he was working in the same area where Bryer had been consulting, so it was possible there was someone else in the company doing some double-dealing. Maybe TJ had found out about it. But why couldn't TJ take his concerns up the chain or to one of those governmental agencies investigating the company?

He obviously didn't know who to trust, but hiding away in Mexico wasn't going to be easy. He could run into a lot of other problems that were even worse than those he was running away from, like drug cartels and corrupt police officials.

She shuddered at the thought. She needed to find TJ...and fast.

Jake came through the door, and she jumped to her feet. "Are we ready?"

"We are."

"Good." Now that the actual moment had arrived, she felt a sudden and deep sense of foreboding, as if her next move was going to be a defining one in her life. Unfortunately, it was too late to turn back, so she put the map and computer into her bag and followed Jake outside and across the tarmac.

As he put her rolling suitcase on board, she eyed the small plane with some misgiving. It looked a lot older and smaller than the sleek jets she'd seen on the other side of the airfield. "This is what we're taking?"

"Only plane available on short notice."

"Will it get us there?"

"I'd be more worried about what you're going to do after

we land."

He had a point. "How long is the trip?"

"About five hours."

"That long? I didn't realize."

"Yeah, we'll have lots of time together," he said dryly.

As she got into the plane, she headed toward one of the six seats in the cabin, but Jake waved her toward the cockpit.

"You might as well sit up front with me," he said. "I assume you did some research on MDT while you were waiting. You can fill me in."

She wished she could tell him he was wrong, but of course he wasn't. While she would have rather taken one of the seats in the cabin and not talk to Jake at all, he was calling the shots now.

Jake slid into the captain's seat, his attention focused on his preflight checklist.

She got into the copilot seat and fastened her seat belt. She tried not to look at Jake, but the cockpit was not that big, and this man had always been a huge physical and emotional presence in her life.

Her phone rang, startling her out of her thoughts. She reached for her bag.

"You're going to need to turn that off, Katherine," Jake said.

"I will. One second. It's a local number. It could be related to my mom." She answered the call. "Hello?"

"Katherine Barrett, please," a woman said.

"This is she."

"This is Brenda Hooper, Miss Barrett. I work in human resources for MDT. Your brother missed a company flight from Mexico to Corpus Christi on Thursday and didn't report to work yesterday. His manager is concerned about his well-being. We've tried to reach Mr. Barrett on his phone, but the line appears to be dead. I'm hoping you can tell us how we can reach him."

"No, I'm sorry. I haven't heard from him," she said,

trying not to let any emotion show in her voice. "What was he doing in Mexico?" After asking the question, she saw Jake motioning for her to put the call on speaker. Since he was the only one helping her at the moment, she did as he asked.

"Mr. Barrett was attending a business conference in Cancun. One of his coworkers tried to reach him when he didn't meet them at the plane, but she wasn't able to connect."

Brenda was probably talking about Jasmine. She wished she could tell this woman that her brother thought he was in danger from someone in the company, but this could be a test to see how much she knew. She had to be smart.

"Are you telling me that my brother is missing in Mexico?" she asked, thinking that would be a normal response. "Should I be concerned? Should I be calling the police?" She tried to act the way she would have if she'd gotten this call without hearing from TJ first.

"I wouldn't say he's missing. It's quite possible he had a side trip planned, and he just didn't let us know. I did speak to the manager of the hotel where Mr. Barrett was staying, and the man said that your brother checked out on Thursday morning as he was expected to do. The valet saw him get in a cab."

"But you're saying he didn't go to the airport?"

"I'm saying he didn't get on the plane. I have no idea where he went after he left the hotel. I contacted the police and local hospitals in the area, but there was no report of an accident or anyone in trouble."

"That's a relief. You must have been really worried to do that." It seemed like the company had gone to extraordinary lengths to find someone who'd only been missing for forty-eight hours.

"It was a company trip. MDT takes the safety and security of its employees quite seriously. TJ's supervisor, Thomas Mueller, asked me to make the calls out of concern for your brother. It's certainly possible that there is nothing to worry about, but I did want to check in with you just in case your brother told you he would be traveling somewhere else before returning to Corpus Christi."

"He didn't tell me anything about his trip to Mexico," she said, which was in fact the truth. "How did you get my number?"

"Your brother put you down as his emergency contact."

"Oh, of course."

"Would you mind calling me if you hear from him? And, of course, if you do speak to him, tell him to get in touch with Mr. Mueller as soon as he can. We just want to make sure he's all right."

"Was Mr. Mueller on the trip?"

"No. There were six employees who attended the conference, but he was not one of them."

"Would it be possible for you to give me the names of the other attendees so that I can speak to them about my brother?"

"I'm afraid I can't do that."

"Why not?"

"It's against corporate policy, but I have personally spoken to everyone, and no one saw or heard from Mr. Barrett since early Thursday morning."

She wanted to argue, but the cool steel in Brenda's voice told her that would be pointless. "Well, please call me if you hear anything more. You've got me worried."

"I will definitely be in touch," Brenda said.

Katherine ended the call and looked at Jake. "What do you think?"

"That some people at MDT are concerned enough about your brother's missed flight to get human resources on the phone on a Saturday."

"That's true. Why wouldn't she tell me who was on the trip with him?"

"From what Alicia has told me, MDT rarely answers questions about anything and always claims national security as the reason."

"I don't want to believe TJ's problem is tied to national security."

"Well, I'm sure he'll tell you when you find him."

He made it sound so easy. "I should do some more research into MDT while we're flying down there."

"Good idea, but you'll need to do that after we take off. Are you ready?"

She put her phone into her bag. "Sure."

Jake gave her a speculative look as she clasped her hands tightly together in her lap. "You're not nervous, are you?"

His question took her back to a hot summer day when they were eighteen years old. Jake had just gotten his pilot's license. He'd been flying for years but never alone, never with a passenger, and he'd asked her to be the first.

She'd been terrified of getting into the small plane with him, but she'd been too crazy in love to think of saying no. She'd sweated buckets during takeoff and hung on for dear life as they flew through the clouds. Jake had laughed and told her to trust him, and she'd eventually managed to breathe again, to have faith in Jake and his ability to keep them in the air.

She had to have the same faith in him now. And why shouldn't she? When it came to flying, she doubted there was anyone better than Jake Monroe. He was born to sit in the pilot's seat. Nothing had ever fit him better. And he'd always known that. He'd never had a doubt about what he wanted to do with his life.

It was actually something they'd had in common. They'd both set their career paths at an early age. Unfortunately, those paths had taken them very far apart.

"Katherine?"

"I'm fine," she said, realizing Jake was still waiting for an answer.

"You don't look fine. You always hated giving up control."

"A lot of people do."

"But you more than most."

She couldn't deny she had issues with control, but today she was unwilling to admit that she was feeling anything but determined. "Just go, Jake. The sooner we get to Mexico, the sooner you can be rid of me."

"Those are inspiring words," he said, his voice dry.

"But true, right?"

He didn't answer, but his gaze lingered on her face for a long moment. Then he looked away and started the engine.

Within ten minutes, they were airborne.

As the land fell away behind her, she had the feeling that nothing would ever be the same again.

"You can breathe now," Jake said, feeling Katherine's tension as if it were his own. He'd always wanted her to love flying as much as he did, but in order to do that, she had to come to terms with the fact that her life was in someone else's hands, his hands specifically, and she'd never been able to trust him enough to relax and let him protect her.

A small voice inside his head reminded him that he might not have always been completely worthy of her trust, but he didn't want to listen to that voice now. Katherine had a lot more to apologize for than he did. Not that either one of them was going to waste time saying sorry for a breakup that was ten years old.

He just couldn't quite believe they were actually together again or that they were on their way to Mexico, of all places.

He'd wanted to take her to Nic Té Há many times. He'd wanted her to meet his great-grandmother, but those plans had never gotten beyond the dreaming stage. It was surreal to be going there now.

As the plane stabilized, Katherine let out a breath and released her hands from the death grip she had on the armrests. "We're okay now, right?"

"We've been okay the whole time."

"Taking off never feels natural to me. And it's strange to be sitting up here and not in the back of the plane."

"My dad always told me it's the best view in the world, and he was right."

"I suppose." She gave him a considering look. "Do you really think that your dad's death wasn't an accident?"

"I don't know. I never had doubts the way Alicia did. All these years, I thought she was just trying to find some story that would help her get through her grief. She needed to have a reason, but I didn't. I just accepted that accidents happen."

"But, now you're not as sure?"

"I can't discount the fact that someone who was once very close to my father said there are things we don't know about my dad's death. How we're going to figure out what those things are might be a challenge, though. Jerry is dead and so is my father. I don't know who an investigator talks to or where he goes to look for information. There were several searches for my dad's plane. I guess he'll start there."

"Is there any possible way your father isn't dead?" she ventured. "No one ever found his plane or his body."

His lips tightened as he shook his head in denial. "Alicia probably has some crazy hope that a miracle will happen, and we're going to find my dad alive, but I don't think so. If he were alive, he would have come back to the family. It's been ten years. There's no way he would have hidden away for that long. And there was no reason for him to fake his death."

"At least not that you know of."

He gave her an irritated look. "What does that mean?"

"I just wonder how much any of us really knows about the people in our lives."

"Just because you don't spend enough time with your family to know them doesn't mean that I don't. I knew my dad well. We spent a tremendous amount of time flying together. We talked about everything under the sun. We were as close as a father and son could be. He was a good man, and he wouldn't desert his family for anything."

Katherine didn't say anything, and her silence bothered him.

"You know better than anyone how close I was to him," he reminded her.

"I know the two of you were tight, but that was when you were a kid, Jake. Your dad had another life before you were born. Maybe there's something you don't know about that life, about his past—the past he shared with his friend Jerry."

He wished he could say there was nothing he didn't know, but of course she was right. And his confidence in what he thought he was certain about had taken a hit when Jerry, a man he'd regarded as an uncle, had turned out to be a traitorous murderer.

"Well, if there's something I don't know, maybe Alicia's investigator will figure it out," he said.

"Alicia is beautiful and so grown up. I remember her as a skinny stick of a girl who was always hiding behind a camera."

"You can still usually find her behind a camera, but she's definitely come into her own. She's smart, stubbornly independent and very strong-willed. I just wish she didn't let her imagination overtake her good sense. She's still obsessed with lightning. You heard her back at the house. She believes, as my great-grandmother does, that lightning shows us what we need to see."

"What does that mean exactly?"

"I have no idea. I think Alicia hangs on to the lightning legends, because a love of lightning is something she had in common with my dad. He would tell us crazy stories about lightning sprites dancing through the sky. I bought into the stories when I was a kid, but I can't say I've ever seen what he claimed to see as a pilot. I can't convince Alicia that weather is just weather. She's been chasing storms the last ten years. And the last one she chased got her involved in this MDT mess."

"Well, if lightning can show us what we need to see, I hope it will show us TJ."

"Looks like clear skies ahead. I don't think you're going to get that lucky."

"I know. I'm going to have to do this the hard way, and apparently all by myself, unless you reconsider taking me from the airport to your great-grandmother's village."

He saw the hopeful look in her eyes, and his stomach twisted into a knot. There had been a time in his life when he would have done anything to make her happy, but that wasn't his job anymore. He wasn't her boyfriend. He wasn't even her friend. So why did he feel himself weakening?

"I'm sure you can hire a guide, but getting to her village won't be easy. It's quite remote. The roads get washed out with the rains. You might have to hike in. That's what I had to do the last time I was there."

"When was that?"

"I went right after we broke up. So, I guess it's been about ten years. I needed to get away, and I'd been meaning to take Mamich something of my dad's since she couldn't come to the funeral."

"What did you take her?" she asked curiously.

"A very old pocket watch that belonged to my great-grandfather. When she saw that watch, she started to cry. It had been fifty years since she'd held it in her hands."

"Tell me their story again. How did they meet?"

"Mamich was seventeen years old when she met my great-grandfather, Howard Monroe. He was a twenty-three-year-old engineer, and he'd gone to the Yucatan to build a bridge. They met at a carnival in Cancun. Mamich had gone there for the weekend with her friends. I guess she wasn't always so happy to stay in her remote village. They both said they fell in love immediately. They got married and pregnant really fast, and they had one daughter, my grandmother Elisa."

"But the marriage didn't last, right?"

"No. Within a few years, it became quite clear that the cultural differences between them were too great. Mamich's parents were old. They needed her to come back to the village to take care of them. So they split up. Mamich took Elisa back to the village with her. When Elisa grew up, she also married an American man. They had my father Wyatt. My grandparents' marriage had problems, too. I think they were close to splitting up when my grandmother died unexpectedly. My grandfather and my dad ended up moving back to the states when my dad was about ten years old. Falling for the wrong woman seems to be a Monroe family trait."

"Your parents stayed together."

"Until my dad died. I wonder if they would be together now if he hadn't passed away. They didn't always get along very well."

"I remember," she murmured.

He looked over at her, and as their gazes met, the years in between seemed to drift away. She wasn't a hard-edged, ambitious, driven doctor—she was just Kat, beautiful, smart, and in love with him. She was the girl he told his problems to, the one he let all the way into his heart. His breath caught in his chest, and he forced himself to look away. Because she wasn't Kat anymore, and she certainly wasn't in love with him.

He wasn't in love with her, either, he reminded himself.

"You need to take me to your great-grandmother's village, Jake," Katherine said. "You know the way, and you know your great-grandmother. She might be able to help me, but she's not going to want to talk to me. I'm a stranger. You're not."

"I have a job, Katherine."

"I'll pay you for your time."

"I don't want your money."

"What do you want?"

That was a loaded question. A few really inappropriate

ideas came to mind, but thankfully he had the good sense not to say them aloud.

"Just think about it," Katherine said when he remained silent. "Think about TJ. You always liked him, and he idolized you."

"Fine, I'll think about it." He couldn't take any more of her pleas right now. He was too close to saying yes and turning his entire life upside down to help the woman who'd broken his heart.

"Good. Can I turn on my computer now?"

"Go for it." He turned on the Wi-Fi in the plane, happy not to be talking anymore.

Katherine pulled out her laptop and got on the Internet. She was quiet for a few moments, her fingers flying over the keys. Then she said, "I found Brenda Hooper on social media. She lists her job title as Human Resources Manager at MDT, so that checks out. I also looked up Jasmine Portillo."

"Who's that?"

"She told me she's TJ's girlfriend. She came by my mother's house this morning. She told me she was worried about him because she couldn't get him on the phone, and he'd missed his flight."

"Did you believe she was his girlfriend?"

"She was his age, pretty, and she seemed genuine. She asked me questions about my life and my mother that suggested TJ had told her about us." Her fingers flew across the keyboard as she spoke. "Here she is on social media." She turned the computer so he could look at the photo.

"She is pretty," he agreed.

"It says she works in corporate communications for MDT, which is what she told me. Her profile is private, so I can't see her photos or anything. I'm not getting very far, am I?" She yawned and closed her computer. "I'll look for more information later. Do you mind if I close my eyes for a few minutes? I drove all night. I can't remember the last time I slept."

"Why did you drive all night?"

"My last shift ended at eleven, and TJ called me shortly after that. I hopped in the car and drove home."

"Your last shift—that sounds final."

"It is. I'm done with my residency. It's still a little difficult to believe, not that I've had any time to celebrate." She settled back in her seat. "It's been a long, rough road, so much harder than I ever imagined. There were days I wasn't sure I could make it."

"I can't believe you ever had doubts."

He glanced over at her when she didn't reply and realized she was already asleep. She really had been exhausted.

A knot clenched his stomach as his gaze ran over her face. For the first time since she'd suddenly reappeared in his life, he had the chance to really look at her.

She had a heart-shaped face, creamy skin that turned honey gold in the sun, soft, full lips that she tortured with her teeth when she was nervous or stressed or filled with reckless desire. He could remember in vivid detail watching her bite down on that soft bottom lip the first time he asked her if she wanted to have sex.

They'd been seventeen years old, and she'd wanted him as much as he wanted her, but Katherine always had to answer a million questions in her own head before she could ever say yes. That's when she'd worried her lip, and he'd finally swooped in and stolen a kiss and made love to her the way he wanted to—the way she'd wanted him to—but hadn't had the guts to say.

They'd been good together back then. She'd been the one for him. He couldn't go five minutes without thinking about her, wanting to kiss her, touch her, discover a world of passion with her. Because once Katherine had let go, she'd surprised both of them.

Damn. The memories stabbed him like a knife.

He let out a heavy sigh, wishing he could stop the assault of images running through his head like an endless slide show: watching scary movies with Katherine at her parents' house, laughing when she covered her eyes every other second because it was just too terrifying; sharing the triple decker banana split at Conroy's Ice Cream Parlor; walking barefoot on the beach; studying in the university library and then making out in between the dusty shelves; staying up all night just talking...

His chest tightened even more.

He needed to stop thinking about the good times. He needed to remember the end: the pain of her leaving, the harsh horrible words she'd uttered, the way he'd felt when she was gone. He needed the anger to keep the barriers up, and he also needed to get her to Mexico fast, so he could go back to his life and forget about her again.

But was he going to be able to leave her at the airport?

He wanted to think so, but could he really let her make that trip alone? Would she be able to make it on her own?

On the other hand, if he and Katherine spent that much time together, they might kill each other.

The plane jerked, and he suddenly realized that the weather had changed drastically. The blue sky had disappeared behind angry, mile-high clouds. How long had he been daydreaming about Katherine?

He changed altitudes and checked the weather. A huge storm cell was suddenly in front of him and all around him.

The plane hit a bump, and Katherine woke up with a jerk.

She rubbed her eyes as the plane dropped again. "What's going on?"

"A little storm," he said, downplaying the danger. He didn't know how the storm cell had grown so large or moved so quickly into his path. Radar hadn't shown anything this big.

The plane took another hard bounce, and Katherine put her hand on his arm. "Jake, are we going to be okay?"

"Sure, it's just a little weather."

"Can you go around it?"

"I'm trying to do that. It's a huge cell. It came out of nowhere."

She took her hand off his arm, only to put it back on when the plane took another dive. "Jake," she said, panic in her voice.

"It's going to be okay," he reassured her, but he was beginning to have a few doubts of his own.

A jagged streak of lightning lit up the black clouds they were flying through. It was an eerie reminder of their very recent conversation about lightning, and a chill ran down his spine.

He changed course again, but the plane was bouncing around like a small ball being kicked by the clouds.

Another streak of lightning flashed bright right in front of them. The instrument panel crackled. Alarm bells went off. He reached for the radio to check in, but he couldn't get a signal or a response. Every screen in front of him went black.

A roar of thunder, then three jagged lines of lightning came straight at the plane.

He was blinded by the light. Instinctively, he wanted to close his eyes, but he couldn't, because in the now lit sky he could see another man—a man who looked like his father.

His dad waved to him, as if saying: *follow me.*

And then the plane spiraled out of control.

Jake battled to stay in the air, but the plane fought his every move.

"Jake?" Katherine asked, terror in her eyes.

"Hold on, babe."

"You have to get us down. You have to."

He sure as hell wanted to set them down, but he was caught up in a monster storm in a plane that wasn't responding to anything he was trying. They were losing altitude fast, and he had no idea what was below—water, mountains, rain forest…

He couldn't give up—not until the bitter end. And that wasn't now.

"I'm going to set us down," he said as the clouds parted, and he caught his first glimpse of land.

"Where?" she asked, her blue eyes wide with fear.

"Wherever I can," he said grimly.

Her hand tightened on his arm. "You can do it, Jake. I know you can. I believe in you."

Words he'd wanted to hear for a very long time. But not like this.

The ground got closer way too fast. He clipped the tops of some trees, aiming for what looked like a clearing in a thickly forested area. He was almost there, but a tree branch took off the right wing tip.

He had the terrible and shocking feeling that this might actually be the end after all...

Five

⟶⟶⟫⟪⟪⟵

Katherine woke up with a jolt, disoriented and shaken. Where the hell was she? She wasn't in her apartment in Houston. She wasn't in the lounge at the hospital where she sometimes caught a nap in between shifts.

It was the seat belt cutting into her chest that made her realize she was in a plane—Jake's plane. She hadn't been dreaming. The nightmare was real. The cockpit window was smashed, the branches of a tree coming through the jagged glass. She saw cuts on her arms and hands, and her face stung, but she was breathing, and her heart was still beating in what seemed like a miraculous way.

She turned her head and her joy at being alive vanished as she saw Jake slumped in his seat. He was knocked unconscious, blood dripping down his face.

Her brain immediately jumped into doctor mode. She fought her way out of her seat belt and unhooked Jake's belt. "Jake," she said, putting her hand on his neck. He had a pulse, thank God.

She gently pushed back the hair on his forehead to see a gash. It wasn't too bad. He could probably use a stitch. What she needed to do now was stop the bleeding. She pulled the scarf off her neck and wiped the blood from his face, applying pressure to the wound.

Jake stirred, groaning as he came back to consciousness. He swatted away the scarf, and she paused in her efforts as he opened his eyes. Seeing his amazing green eyes focus on her filled her with relief. "Jake."

"Kat," he murmured.

The shortened version of her name on his lips had always been sexy, seductive and tender—at least before they'd broken up—which was probably why it brought a pang of yearning to her heart now.

"How do you feel?" she asked.

"Like I just hit a tree," he said with a wince.

"Good guess."

"Not really a guess." He tipped his head toward the branches coming through the cockpit windows.

"We're alive. That's the important thing. I can't quite believe it."

"I never had any doubt."

The cocky light in his eyes reassured her. "I'm sure you didn't. Is there a first-aid kit on board? You cut your head."

"It's in the cabin. Are you all right, Katherine?" His gaze swept her face. "You've got some cuts, too."

"Nothing bad. I'm more worried about you. You might have a concussion. Let me ask you a few questions."

"Not necessary. I know who I am. I know who you are and what happened. Does that cover it?"

"Okay." She let out a breath of relief. "Do you also know what we're going to do now?"

"I'm still working on that." He reached for the radio, but it was as dead as the rest of the instrument panel. He pulled out his phone. "No signal."

She scrambled around the seat to grab her bag. Her phone was intact but also showing no signal. "Mine isn't working, either. Do you have any idea where we are, Jake?"

"We're in a heavily wooded area somewhere in Mexico."

"I can look out the window, too."

He shrugged. "Everything went off when the lightning hit

the plane. I have no idea how far we were blown off course. But we're on the ground, and we're alive, so I'm going to count this as a hard landing and not a crash."

"A hard landing? The wing came off."

"Not all the way." He got out of his seat and entered the main cabin. She followed close behind, curious to see the damage.

The cabin was fairly intact. A couple of the windows had blown out, and there was glass and debris from the storage area, but at least they had some shelter while they figured out what to do next. "Do we need to worry about fire?" she asked, taking a sniff.

"I don't smell any smoke, and it's raining pretty good out there, so I think we're all right."

"Okay, good. I want to fix that cut on your head," she said, spying the first-aid kit.

"I'd rather get outside and see where we are before it gets dark."

She caught him by the arm. "First I clean your wound and put a bandage on your head."

"All right, Doc, if you insist."

"I do." She pushed him into the front seat and then opened the first-aid kit, happy to see everything she needed. She cleaned his wound and bandaged it, noting that the skin around his eye was turning purple. "You're going to have a shiner."

"It won't be the first time."

No, it wouldn't, she thought, remembering the black eyes he'd sported during football season. Jake had always been an athlete, and he'd pushed himself to the limit, no matter the activity or the safety factor.

"Done," she said, as she closed the kit. "You also might end up with a little scar."

"That will just get me more girls, right?"

"Probably," she admitted.

He smiled and stood up. "Let's see where we are."

It took him a few minutes to get the plane door open and then he jumped down to the ground, a distance of about four feet since they had somehow ended up caught between a couple of trees.

"I'm going to take a walk," he said. "I want to see if I can get a signal if I can get away from all these trees."

"Wait," she said quickly. "I'm coming with you. The rain is letting up. It's not that bad anymore."

"Why don't you stay here and wait for me? You're going to get wet."

"I have a coat and boots on. I'll be fine. I want to see where we are, too." She grabbed her bag with her phone in it and then jumped down to the ground.

They walked for about ten minutes, but the terrain didn't change. They appeared to have landed in a forest. "I thought I saw a clearing right before we set down," she said to Jake. "Was I crazy?"

"No, that's what I headed for. It must have been the other way. I guess we got turned around when we came down."

As he finished speaking, thunder rumbled the air and lightning flashed over the tall trees. In the distance, she could see even taller mountains. "Did you see that?" she asked Jake. "We're near a mountain range."

"There are several that run down the center of the country, including one close to the airport in Tuxtla Gutiérrez, but considering the time left in our flight, I'd say we're at least a couple hundred miles from there."

She hoped he was wrong. "We need to get out of these trees and see if we can find some distinctive landmarks."

The rain suddenly increased, as if a cloud had burst over their heads.

"That's not going to happen now," Jake added. "Let's go back to the plane."

They ran through the trees and rain until they got to the plane. Jake helped her up, and she was more than happy to get inside. He pulled the door shut, but there was still rain coming in through two broken windows.

"We should cover those," she said.

He nodded, looking around. Then he turned over two of the seats and pulled out flattened life vests. He grabbed tape and she helped him cover the windows.

"That should work," she said, "but now it's pretty dark in here." There was still some dim light coming in through the cockpit window but when night came it would be pitch black.

"I've got a battery-operated lantern," he said, returning to the closet. He pulled it out and set it on the floor. "We should probably wait to turn it on until we really need it."

She nodded, crossing her arms in front of her chest as shivers ran through her.

"You should change, Katherine—get dry." He walked over to another compartment and pulled out her suitcase and another small black travel bag that apparently belonged to him.

"You packed a case—when did you do that?" she asked in surprise.

"I have a go-bag I keep at the airport. I tossed it in before we left, just in case..."

"Just in case you decided to take me to your great-grandmother's house?" she challenged.

"I wouldn't go that far. You can change first. I'll go into the cockpit, give you some privacy."

She waited for him to close the door between the cabin and the cockpit before reaching for her suitcase. She quickly changed, happy to put on dry jeans, thick socks and a sweater. When she was done, she called to Jake. "Your turn."

He came back into the cabin with a map in his hand. "I think we might be here, Katherine." He turned his cell phone light on the map so she could take a look.

She saw a lot of tall mountains, wide swaths of rainforest and very few cities. The airport closest to his great-grandmother's village looked very far away. Her heart sank. "You really don't think we're closer?"

"I won't know for sure until we can get outside in sunshine and daylight and take a better look around, but this is my best guess. First thing tomorrow, we need to find a village or a phone signal and find help."

She didn't like the serious note in Jake's voice. He'd been so calm and confident she hadn't felt too worried about their predicament—until now. "How soon will anyone start looking for us?"

"I'm not sure, probably soon. But they may not know where to look. We were blown off course, and the storm isn't going to make things easier." His jaw tightened as he shook his head. "I hate the thought of my mom getting that call again. It will remind her of the last time someone from the airport called to tell her that my dad was missing."

She hadn't even considered that someone back home would be notified that the plane was missing, but in her case her brother wouldn't be found and her mother probably wouldn't understand. At least her mom's illness would save her from worrying about her, but the reminder that she had no one who would really care that she was missing was depressing.

Jake folded up the map. "We'll take this with us tomorrow."

"I have guidebooks and maps in my bag, too. I picked them up at the airport. Maybe they'll give us more information."

He nodded.

She saw the shadows in his gaze and felt bad. No one would worry about her, but he was right; his mom would be devastated. "I'm sorry, Jake."

He met her gaze. "For what?"

His question made her realize how many things she had to be sorry for, but she settled for the easiest and the most current. "That your mom and your sisters will be worried about you. But we're okay, and eventually they'll know that. Hopefully, we'll be found before too much time passes."

"We'll see. I don't think we should leave the plane tonight." He glanced at the watch on his wrist. "It's already four o'clock. Even if the storm lets up, we'll lose light in another hour and a half. We need to stay put until morning."

She hated every word that came out of his mouth. She didn't want to spend the night with him, not in this isolated plane in the middle of nowhere, not when TJ's life was in danger, not when there would be no choice but to talk to Jake, but she couldn't argue against his logical reasoning. They could hardly wander around the Mexican wilderness in the middle of the night.

"It won't be bad," Jake continued. "We're dry. We're safe. We have some light. We have food and water on board, enough to last us for a day or two, so we'll be all right."

"You should change, too. I'll wait in the cockpit."

"You don't have to leave. It's not like you haven't seen me before," he said, a dark edge behind his teasing words.

She had seen him before. She'd explored his body with great eagerness, and that body had gotten even better with age. Her heart flipped over in her chest, and she knew she'd hesitated one second too long, because Jake gave her a slanted, speculative look.

"Katherine?"

Turning quickly, she bolted into the cockpit, closing the door on his question. She drew in a breath and let it out, trying to calm her racing pulse. She told herself it was the adrenaline from the crash that had her unsettled, but she also knew it had a lot to do with Jake.

How the hell was she going to spend all night with him in this plane?

She reminded herself that they were alive, and that was the important thing. Tomorrow, they would hike to the nearest village and get help. She just wished she knew how far away civilization was. At the moment, she couldn't see anything.

Rain splashed through the cockpit window in an endless

sheet of water. It was a lot colder in here, too. She was glad she'd put on a heavier sweater underneath her jacket.

Jake knocked on the door a moment later and said, "All done."

She took her computer bag into the cabin where it was warmer and sat down on one of the leather seats while Jake rummaged through the galley and closets.

"This wasn't an ordinary charter, so it wasn't stocked the way we normally do for executives," he said. "But we do have some food." He came back with two snack boxes filled with cheese, salami, and crackers. "Not much, but they're still cold. Might as well eat them now."

While she opened up the box, he went back to the galley, returning with bags of pretzels and chips and two bottles of red wine.

He gave her a proud smile. "It's going to be a party, Kat."

She reluctantly smiled at his words. She appreciated the fact that he was trying to make the best of a bad situation, but it was almost harder to be with him when he was being nice to her, because that just reminded her of the good times they'd had together.

Jake had always been lighthearted and easygoing. She'd been the one who was too serious, too worried about everything and for a while they'd complemented each other. She'd encouraged him to be more ambitious, to have bigger, long-term goals, and Jake had encouraged her to relax, let down her guard and have fun.

But Jake had changed with his dad's death, and she hadn't been able to handle his new personality—one that was angry and bitter and far too reckless. He'd scared her, and she'd run. He thought she'd abandoned him at the worst time in his life. Maybe she had. But she'd convinced herself that it was her or him and that if she stayed with him, she was going to lose herself. She chose to lose him instead.

She'd had regrets, more than a few, but she'd been too busy to allow herself to dwell on the past. Now, it was all coming back in bright, vivid colors, and she wasn't ready to handle it.

"What? You don't like red wine anymore?" Jake asked.

"No, I do. I was just thinking…" Her voice trailed away as she realized she did not want to tell him what she'd been thinking about.

Apparently, he didn't want to know, because he headed back to the galley to get glasses and a bottle opener.

A moment later they were sipping wine and snacking on cheese and crackers.

Jake sat in the chair across from her, which she'd originally thought was better than the chair next to her, but now she had nowhere else to look but at him. And looking at Jake made her heart flutter and dance around in her chest.

It had been so much easier to hate him and to stay away from him when he was hundreds of miles away.

"I found eight bottles of water in the closet," he said, breaking the silence between them. "That should last us for a while."

"We'll get help tomorrow." She hoped she was speaking the truth.

"I'm sure."

"How's your head feeling?"

"It's fine. Nothing to worry about." Thunder followed his words, and then a flash of light filled the cabin, as the storm once again pummeled the plane.

"We can't get away from the lightning," she murmured.

"Alicia would love this. She'd be outside in the rain, taking pictures and trying to figure out what the lightning was showing her." He drained his wine glass at the end of his sentence. "I don't know how she can love lightning when my dad died in an electrical storm, and she almost lost her life in one. But it still speaks to her. I find nothing intriguing or comforting about it, especially now that it caused me to lose control of my plane."

It was odd how much impact lightning had had on his

life, especially when she looked at the big events he'd just outlined. "Are you saying we crashed because the plane was hit by lightning? I thought planes got hit all the time."

"Not all the time and not as hard as we got hit. It short-circuited the instrument panel and did something to the steering. We lost radio contact. And the storm was too big to battle without instruments."

"I don't understand how we got caught up in it. Don't you have radar to help you avoid storms like that?"

"Of course we do, but this storm wasn't on the radar. It literally came out of nowhere. One minute there was nothing but blue sky, and the next we were inside a huge, thunderous cloud."

She'd been asleep when they'd hit the storm, so she had no idea if it was as sudden as he made it out to be.

"When it was happening, I have to admit I thought about my father," he said. "I wondered if the same thing had happened to him, that he'd suddenly gotten caught in a storm he couldn't go around. I wondered what he'd thought when he realized the plane wasn't responding, that he was going to crash. Only he had nothing but water beneath him."

She nodded. "What did you think, Jake—when it was happening? Were you afraid?"

He looked into her eyes. "No. I was determined. I had to save you. I couldn't let you down—again."

She sucked in a breath, her lips tightening at the look in his eyes, but she didn't want to talk about the past. "You've always been a good pilot. I knew you'd find a way."

"I hoped I would. It's strange, but…"

"What's strange?"

"Nothing."

"Come on, Jake. What?"

"I saw my dad in the lightning. He waved his hand in my direction, and I could have sworn he said, 'follow me'. Then he was gone, and we were going down. I'm sure my mind was just playing tricks on me. We'd been talking about him and lightning, so I just imagined him, right?"

"I would think that was the reason you saw him or thought you saw him. Unless you believe in ghosts or supernatural events."

"I don't, but Alicia does. She would tell me that seeing my dad was a sign, that the lightning hit the plane because it wanted to show us something."

"Like this tree we landed in?" she asked dryly.

Jake smiled. "Not the tree exactly." He set his glass down on the table between them and rested his arms on his knees as he leaned forward. "Maybe the lightning wanted to stop us in our tracks, give us time to think about what we're doing; it certainly did that."

"You're making a weather event sound like a person."

"My great-grandmother believes lightning is a god."

"You don't believe that, though."

"I didn't used to, but I have to admit a lot of crazy shit has happened over the years, all having to do with lightning."

"You can find coincidence wherever you look. You can spin anything to make it seem meaningful."

"That's true."

His speculative gaze made her want to fidget. "You're staring at me, Jake."

"Well, it's been a long time since I've seen you."

"You've been looking at me all day."

"Actually, I've been trying *not* to look at you all day. I kept thinking you'd be gone in a few hours, and that would be the end of it, but that's definitely not going to happen now. You and I are going to be here for a while, all night at least."

"I need some more wine," she said, pushing her empty glass toward the bottle.

"Me, too," he said, as he poured two more glasses.

"The wine takes the chill off," she said.

"There are some blankets in the closet. I can get them."

"I don't need them yet. Are we really going to be here all night?"

"Since we haven't seen anyone yet, I'm guessing no one nearby on the ground witnessed the crash, or they would have been here by now."

"Maybe not if they were far away."

"True, but far away means it will take them awhile to actually find us."

She sighed. "You're right."

"Nice of you to admit that I can occasionally be right."

She stared back at him, seeing a mix of complicated emotions in his eyes. It would be a long night if every sentence they spoke was filled with undercurrents. She couldn't go on ignoring the tension between them. "Okay, Jake, let's do it."

"Do what?" he asked warily.

"Have it out," she said, meeting his gaze. "We can keep trying to tiptoe around the elephant in the room, but it's not working, so let's talk. Let's put our cards on the table."

As soon as she made the suggestion, she regretted it. But it was too late to back down, and maybe she shouldn't. It was a risky choice she was making, but she couldn't stand the little digs he was dishing out, and if she'd learned anything in medical school, it was that she couldn't fix a problem if she didn't look at it.

"Are you sure you want to do this? Because there's nowhere to run if you don't like the way the conversation goes," he said.

"Nowhere for you to go, either."

"I'm not the one who runs; that's you, Katherine."

"I'm not running now." She squared her shoulders, preparing for what would surely be a painful assault. "You start, Jake. Say what you've been trying not to say since you saw me at the airport this morning."

Six

—➤➤➤➤➤—

Jake gave her a long look and then slowly shook his head. "I don't think so. You want to talk. You start. This is your show, after all."

"My show? I'd hardly call it that."

"I'm your employee. You hired me. That makes you the boss."

"Fine," she said, irritated by his attitude. "You hate me. How's that for a beginning?"

"It's not very good. Why don't you start with your own feelings instead of guessing at mine?"

He had a point. "All right. I feel..." She searched for the right words. "Angry and sad."

"Because..."

"Sad because I hurt you and angry because you put me in that position."

"Are you saying I made you hurt me?" he challenged. "That's a hell of an apology. I knew you'd make everything my fault. I don't think we need to talk, because clearly there's nothing new to say."

"We're not stopping now just because you don't like what you're hearing. You were in a bad place after your father died, Jake. Maybe you don't remember or you've rewritten history in your head, but you were drinking too much, skipping classes, and staying out until five in the morning with your friends."

"I was blowing off steam. Most people understood that."

"I tried to understand it. I tried to keep up with you, so you wouldn't be alone, but my grades started to suffer. I couldn't handle the late nights and the early morning classes. I missed a test. I fell asleep in the middle of a midterm."

"You're exaggerating."

"I'm really not. I told you all this before."

"I don't remember."

"Because you weren't listening to me back then. The school told me I was going to end up on probation if I didn't turn things around fast. I couldn't let that happen. I had to get good grades to get into medical school. I wanted to be a good girlfriend, but I didn't know how to help you." She paused, drawing his gaze to hers with her silence. "You were drowning, Jake. You were like one of those guys in the ocean who's flailing his arms and trying to swim, but he can't get anywhere, and when someone tries to save him, he starts fighting, and eventually both people go down. I couldn't let that happen."

"So you cut me loose. Hell of a choice for someone who allegedly loved me." Anger blazed through his eyes.

Maybe she had been ruthless, but she honestly hadn't known what else to do.

"You knew I was ripped up about my dad," Jake continued. "You knew my family was falling apart. My mom, my sisters—they were basket cases. They were crying every day. Everyone needed me, but I needed *you*. And you knew that. It wasn't going to be forever, but you couldn't give me a few weeks."

"It wasn't a few weeks; it was months. You were not yourself that year. You'd snap at the littlest thing I'd say. Every time I told you I needed to study, you made it sound like I didn't care about you. You think I cut you loose without warning, but the truth is you were pushing me away for weeks."

He jumped to his feet. "That's not true." He paced around the small cabin. "How could I push you away when you were already gone? You didn't swim out to help the drowning man. You looked at him from the shore. You called one of his friends to help, and then thinking you'd done your duty, you bailed."

She winced at the way he'd twisted her analogy. "I called Will that night because I thought you'd listen to him when clearly you weren't listening to me. You wanted to break into the university pool and skinny-dip in the middle of January. You were drunk, and I was afraid you'd dive into the shallow end and break your neck or do something equally stupid and dangerous."

"I was looking for a little fun with my girlfriend. That's it."

"We could have gotten kicked out of school."

"You worried too much."

"And you didn't worry enough, especially after your dad died. It was like you were daring the universe to throw more bad stuff at you. So I called Will, hoping he could make you see reason. But instead you talked him into going with you."

"It was fine. Nothing happened. We didn't get caught. It was all good."

"That time. I couldn't stick around to see when your dares would have consequences."

A frown turned down his mouth and there was anger in his green eyes. "I wasn't doing anything that bad, Katherine."

"You got arrested for fighting a week after the pool incident," she returned.

"That guy in the bar said something negative about my father. He called him *lightning man*."

"A lot of people called your dad that. He didn't care that people thought he was a little crazy for talking about lightning all the time. He told me plenty of stories."

"You don't know that he didn't care. He just didn't let on that the jokes bothered him." Jake paused. "My father was a Navy hero. I couldn't stand by and let someone make fun of him, not when he couldn't defend himself. And that fight was one punch. It was nothing, and I wasn't arrested; I was just sent home from the bar."

"By the police. You were scaring me, Jake. Maybe I could have handled what you were going through better if I'd been older, but I wasn't."

"So you split."

"I thought it was the best thing for both of us."

"You thought it was the best thing for you."

"It wasn't easy for me, Jake. I was in love with you. You were breaking my heart."

"That's not what you told me. You said, 'I don't love you anymore. It's over. We're finished. Don't call me again.' Did I leave something out?"

Her heart ached with the pain of that memory. "I think that was pretty much it."

"Did you have to be that cold, Katherine?"

"I had to say something so you wouldn't come after me, because if you had, I might not have been able to say no. I know I hurt you, Jake. And I probably could have done it better, but I didn't. I gave you a really good reason to hate me, which is where this conversation started. I thought ten years might have faded the pain, but when you saw me this morning, you looked at me with the same disgust I saw in your eyes the last time we spoke. Nothing had changed."

He didn't say anything for a moment, then sat back down across from her. "That's not completely true."

"It's not?" she asked in disbelief.

"No. A lot has changed. It's been a long time, Katherine. It's not like I've been pining for you for a decade."

"I never thought you would," she said, although the idea of Jake and other women had always been one she hadn't wanted to contemplate. "There have been other men in my life, too," she said, unable to resist making it clear that she'd also moved on.

"I have no doubt. I'm sure they're all very ambitious, successful, wealthy men, too."

"I'm not a snob, Jake."

"You've always valued achievement over everything else."

"I like when people follow their passion; it doesn't have to be about money. I respected your desire to be a pilot. But after your dad died, you didn't want to be anything. You were on the road to nowhere. I hoped you would get back to your dreams, but I didn't know if it would ever happen."

"You don't just get back to normal in one second after your father dies."

"It wasn't one second. You keep making it sound like you were grieving for a minute. It was months. You told me you didn't think you'd ever fly again, remember that?"

"Vaguely."

"Obviously that changed. How long did it take for you to get back into a plane?"

"About six months after you left. It was after I went to see Mamich. She told me that my father had loved flying and that I should honor his memory by flying for him. When I got back, I went down to the airport and I got into a plane. I was shaky as hell when I took off that day, but once I got up in the sky, everything shifted back into place."

She was glad he'd conquered a fear that would have prevented him from doing what he'd been born to do, but she couldn't help feeling a little sad that he hadn't been able to shift his perspective before their relationship fell apart. "I'm happy that you got back into flying, that you made it your career. It's what you always wanted."

"And you always wanted to be a doctor. Everything turned out the way it was supposed to."

She'd always thought she'd be a doctor *and* married to Jake. But she probably wouldn't have made it through medical school if she'd stayed with him. She might not have made it if she'd had a long-term relationship with anyone. She wasn't the kind of person who juggled well. When she wanted something, she went all in, and she didn't know how to balance things out. She didn't know how to do well at more than one thing at a time.

"Don't you agree?" Jake prodded.

"I guess."

"You don't sound as sure as you did a minute ago. Is it possible that your memories aren't as black-and-white as you'd like to think they are?"

"What does that mean?"

"I don't think you panicked back in college just because I was encouraging you to have some fun," he said. "You were struggling in your pre-med classes long before my dad died. You were questioning whether or not you could get through chemistry and biology, much less medical school. But after my dad's death, after I went a little nuts, you blamed it all on me."

"At least you admit you went a little nuts."

"Can you admit that you were floundering?"

She let out a breath. "The pre-med classes were difficult. I was struggling, yes; a lot of people were. That's why I knew I had to stay focused. I couldn't blow off classes to party with you. You were a big distraction for me."

"And when you got rid of me—of your distraction—what happened? Did you suddenly soar?"

"No. It was still hard. But I did better. I could focus on classes and not feel guilty about staying in the library until midnight, because then I wasn't being a good girlfriend. I could put all my attention on my work."

"You make me sound like a selfish, demanding asshole."

"At times you were," she said, meeting his gaze.

"And you've always been perfect?"

"I didn't say that."

"Good, because from what I can see, you've neglected

your family the past few years. Did they become too big of a distraction, too? Was your mom's illness blurring your focus? Was that why you stayed away?"

She sucked in a breath as his words stabbed her like a knife. "That was mean, Jake."

His jaw tightened. "I just don't understand why it has to be only one thing for you. Why can't you be good at school and work and still have friends and family and relationships? I know you said there have been other men, but really? Because I can't imagine that any other guy wouldn't have been just as big of a distraction."

"I dated other medical students. They were as busy as I was. They knew there could be nothing more serious than a casual relationship. And I didn't abandon my family. I offered to come home after my dad died, but my mom wouldn't hear of it. She wanted me to finish. She said it was important to her and to my father. I was doing it for them as much as I was doing it for me."

"Bullshit. That's just what you tell yourself so you can sleep at night."

"I haven't slept a full night in eleven years, Jake. And I do feel badly that I left TJ with more than he should have had to handle on his own. I kept thinking it's just a few more months, and then I'll be better able to help financially and also with time, but I know that wasn't fair to my brother. That's why I'm here now. I'm trying to help him."

"Would you be here today if you hadn't finished your last shift? Or would you have told TJ to solve his own problems when he called you?"

It wasn't a question she wanted to answer. She told herself she would have done the exact same thing, but there was a part of her that wasn't sure that was true. "I don't know," she said honestly. "I'd like to think I would still be here."

Their gazes met again, and the angry fire in Jake's eyes seemed to dim with her heartfelt answer.

"I get tunnel vision," she added. "I see the goal line, and all I can focus on is getting across it. I know it's a bad trait. I need to work on that."

"You miss a lot of things along the way, Katherine."

"I tell myself it's worth it."

"Has it been worth it? You're a doctor now."

"I haven't had time to absorb that fact."

"Are you staying in Houston?"

"I don't know. I have offers in several cities."

"Including Corpus Christi?"

She nodded. "Yes. It's not the best opportunity, but it's there if I want it."

"It doesn't sound like you want it."

"If I was thinking just about my career, I wouldn't want it, but I do love my mother, and I'm very aware that her condition has deteriorated far more quickly than I imagined it would. So, Corpus Christi has gone to the top of the list."

"I'm sorry about your mom. She doesn't deserve what she's going through. I always liked her a lot. She was incredibly nice to me when we were going out, and when my dad died, I remember talking to her more than I talked to my own mom."

"She's always been a great listener. Sometimes, I wonder if she had more to say than she ever got a chance to say. She always put herself behind my father, behind my brother and me. She was our supporter, but I'm not sure we were always hers."

"That's probably the way it is with parents. You take them for granted. You think of them just as Mom and Dad and not as people in their own right. When you said my dad had a whole life before I was born, you were right. I didn't know him as a young man. I didn't know him when he was flying for the Navy. There could have been lots of things in his life that he didn't talk to me about. And I'm sure the same is true for your mom."

"We both ran out of time to ask."

"Maybe you're not completely out of time. Your mom has some lucid moments."

"She does. And I really try to make those count." She finished her wine and set her glass down on the table. "So is the elephant gone?"

"He's outside in the rain," Jake said with a dry smile.

"Finally. He was taking up way too much room." She reached for her backpack and pulled out the guidebook on Mexico. "Maybe I'll read while we still have some natural light."

"Good idea. I want to take another look at the map. Perhaps between the two of us, we can figure out where we are."

"Okay."

"Katherine," he began.

She saw indecision in his eyes and wondered what else they still had to say to each other. "What?"

"Never mind. It doesn't matter."

He went into the cockpit and shut the door, leaving her wondering just what he'd wanted to say. Maybe it was better she didn't know. They'd spoken enough truth for one day.

She flipped through the guidebook. She'd always been good at researching, and learning more about the country gave her some small feeling of control. She doubted that feeling would last. She was smart enough to know that their situation was not very good. If they were truly lost in the middle of a rainforest, who knew how long it would take for anyone to find them.

A wave of fear ran through her, not just for herself but also for TJ, because he was still in danger, and she was even farther away from helping him than she'd been the day before.

But she'd accomplished one thing, she realized. There was no way Jake could drop her off at the airport and leave her on her own. For better or worse, they were stuck together, and hopefully they'd make it all the way to his great-grandmother's village together, too.

Seven

—➤➤◄◄◄—

Jake flipped every switch on the instrument panel, hoping to find some juice somewhere, but not only had the panel been blown during the lightning strike, everything was now soaking wet. It was clear they were not going to be able to communicate with anyone from the plane. They would have to find their way to a cell phone signal or the nearest town. He didn't have a good feeling about where they'd landed or how far away help might be. Their short trek through the forest had made him believe they had landed in one of several heavily forested and mountainous areas in central Mexico. There might not be a town for miles.

In addition to dealing with a possibly remote and hard-to-reach location, he had no idea what kind of people they would find on their way. Parts of Mexico were very dangerous, run by drug cartels and people who would not like the fact that they were trespassing, however inadvertently. Or they might see two American tourists as an opportunity for ransom.

With that thought, he unlocked a box by his feet and pulled out a handgun. It had become company policy to keep a loaded weapon in the cockpit in case of terrorist activity. He hoped he wouldn't have to use it, but he would keep it close just in case.

Setting the gun aside, he spread the map on the console

and circled several possible areas where they might be based on how long they'd been in the air before the storm hit and their flight plan. Unfortunately, his memory wasn't as clear as it should have been. He'd been deep in thought during the flight, memories and feelings about Katherine blurring everything else in his head. He'd never gotten so distracted in the cockpit. He should have let her sit in the cabin. They might not be in this mess if he hadn't insisted she sit next to him.

But he couldn't rewrite history.

His gaze turned back to the map. If he was right about where they were, then there might be a city about eight miles away. They could walk eight miles. Katherine was a strong, determined woman. She'd make it. When she wanted something, she didn't quit.

Too bad she hadn't wanted him the way he'd wanted her, because she'd definitely *quit* him.

Frowning, he thought about their recent conversation. While there hadn't been a lot of new information exchanged, today was the first time he'd realized how scared she'd been during their last few months together. He'd known she was annoyed with him for partying too much and keeping her out late, but he'd thought she was just being uptight, because she was always a little uptight. He was used to dragging her out of her shell and showing her a good time. He didn't know why she'd been resisting him so hard.

But maybe he'd been more intense than he'd thought. Had he really been *that* crazy, *that* out of control after his dad died? Had her worries been justified?

Or had she been floundering in school and turning her fear of failing her pre-med classes into fear about their relationship? Had she created a scenario where she could live with saving herself and leaving him in the dust?

He let out a sigh. Did it really matter?

As much as he didn't like the way she'd broken up with him, he couldn't deny that he hadn't been the best version of himself the year after his dad died. While it had felt good to blame her for everything, he had a lot to account for himself.

He'd definitely grown up in the past ten years. He wasn't that drowning, angry guy anymore, and he certainly wasn't looking for her to rescue him. He could take care of himself and he could take care of her, too. While he'd been reluctant to take her into Mexico, now he had no choice. Until he could get her to a safe place, they were going to stick together. He would never abandon her, no matter how much pain she'd caused him in the past.

Which made him a much better person than her.

He smiled to himself. He could spin things as well as she could.

The truth was they'd both made mistakes, but they'd also both grown up. The focus from here on out was to get to safety first and then on to Nic Té Há to rescue TJ.

It felt good to have a plan, like he was in control. It was a tenuous thread of hope, but he was going to cling to it as long as he could. But as he looked around the cockpit, he couldn't help thinking about what was going on back home.

Had Rusty gotten the news already? Radar would have shown their plane going off course, but those last few minutes he'd been unable to communicate. Anyone searching for them would have a wide area to cover.

It was just like his dad's disappearance.

His stomach twisted painfully. He could imagine the pain and horror his mother and sisters would go through when they heard his plane had gone missing.

Dani was going to DC tonight; she might already be on her way. Alicia was returning to Florida tomorrow, which meant she'd probably be with their mom when the news came in.

Just like his dad's disappearance.

Alicia had been the only one in the house with their mother that night, too.

One of his mom's friends had called him at school to tell

him to come home. He vividly remembered driving through the dark night to get to the brightly lit house, which had filled with family and friends since the first terrible call.

The hours that followed had been horribly tense, emotions soaring high with tiny seeds of hope, only to be crushed by disappointment and despair. The days had turned into weeks. The house had emptied out, leaving only a few to carry on the vigil. And then the search had ended.

He felt sick at the memories. He didn't want his mother and sisters to go through all that again. He had to find a way to get to a phone and let them know he was all right. He wanted to go right this second, but night was falling fast, and it would be stupid to leave the only shelter they had until morning. Hopefully, it wouldn't take more than a few hours to get to help tomorrow.

And maybe Rusty wouldn't rush over to his mom's house until the morning. Rusty had also gone through the search for Jake's father. He'd remember how hard it was to tell the family. Perhaps he'd wait until he had more definitive news.

It was a slim hope, but he hung on to it.

He got up and went back into the cabin.

Katherine gave him a wary look, as if unsure of his mood. He didn't blame her. He wasn't any more comfortable with her despite their recent clearing of the air. There was still an emotional and physical tension between them—anger and hurt but also attraction and desire.

He didn't know how he could want a woman who'd hurt him so badly and who hated his guts, but somehow he did.

He was lucky that she didn't want him…or did she?

Was that why her gaze was filled with so much confusion? Was she, too, feeling the conflicting emotions?

It wouldn't be surprising. There had always been a push-pull between them. Katherine had fought hard against her reckless desire for him. When they were seventeen, it had been easy to push past her barriers, but he had a feeling the past ten years had reinforced her barriers with steel.

Which was a good thing, he told himself. He didn't need to make this situation even more difficult or complicated.

He sat down in the seat across from her and tipped his head toward her guidebook. "So, what did you learn about Mexico?"

"It's a big country. Most of the larger cities are on the coast. The interior is vast and rugged, and I have a feeling that's exactly where we've landed."

"I would agree. But I think if we head south, we should run into a town about eight miles from here."

"Eight miles doesn't sound that bad. We can make that."

"I'm sure we can." He paused. "In the meantime, I have an idea on how we can pass the time until morning…"

The wary look returned to her eyes. "You usually have really bad ideas."

"Not this time." He smiled, then reached into a side panel and pulled out a deck of cards. "Gin rummy or crazy eights? I believe I still hold the title of champion in both games."

Her lips curved somewhat reluctantly at his boastful words. "I'm pretty sure I beat you at rummy the last time we played."

"Hmm, as I recall, the last time we played, you distracted me by unbuttoning your shirt and then making out with me." Heat coursed through him as that memory ran through his head. He could still see her beautiful breasts spilling out of her lacy bra under her buttoned-down blouse. He hadn't been able to think about the cards in his hands, only about how quickly he could get his hands on her breasts.

She must have read his mind, because she pulled the edges of her jacket more closely together. "That won't happen tonight," she said pointedly. "I'm only playing cards, nothing else."

"Too bad. We could have made this a lot more interesting."

"You and I don't need to get any more interesting," she said.

"Fine, cards only. What does the winner get?"

"I don't know...satisfaction at winning?"

He shook his head. "That's not enough of a prize."

"You're so competitive, Jake. Why does there always have to be a trophy?"

"Because it's more fun if there's something at stake. But you know that, because you are even more competitive than I am. I bet you were top of your class in medical school, weren't you?"

"I might have been," she said.

"Number one or top five?"

"The only position that counts is the first one," she retorted.

He laughed. "I knew it."

"Fine. What do you want if you win this game?" She immediately held up her hand. "And whatever you want cannot involve me getting naked."

"Really? That was always a good prize before. And I seem to recall that I got naked as much as you did."

"So now you're remembering that I did beat you quite often," she said.

He tipped his head in concession. "Fair point. What do you want?"

"If I win, I get the chocolate bar."

"You and chocolate—your greatest love affair outside of medicine," he said dryly.

"Your turn. What do you want?"

He thought for a moment. "If I win, you let me decide which way to go tomorrow. You have faith in me to lead us in the right direction. You give me the power to choose our path."

Her lips tightened. "Don't you think we should work together?"

"We should work together, but that will go better if you agree to let me lead. Otherwise, we'll spend half the morning arguing and debating the merits of each possible path."

"It's important to consider ahead of time what you're getting into."

"I promise to consider it."

"You could let me lead, and then we wouldn't have any problems."

"Too late. You already asked for chocolate as your prize."

She let out a sigh. "Fine. You're not going to win anyway, so I won't worry about it."

"That would be a first."

She made a face at him. "We're not just playing one game. It's five out of seven. That will prove the true winner."

He was fine with that. They had a lot of time to kill. "All right."

"Deal the cards," she said, a fighting light in her eyes. "And prepare to lose. Wait a second—never mind that, you don't prepare for anything. What was I thinking?"

"Insults are not going to distract me, but nice try, babe."

"And calling me your babe isn't going to annoy me enough not to concentrate," she returned as he dealt the cards.

"Calling you *babe* is a sign of affection."

"You don't have affection for me, Jake. I think we've clearly established that."

He shrugged, thinking that he wished they'd clearly established that fact, but for some reason he liked her better now than he had in a very long time.

As his mind went down that road, he lost his focus, and the first game was hers.

After that, it was all about the cards.

For the next three and a half hours, they jockeyed back and forth between winning games until they were tied at three-three. The dim light in the cabin had turned to black, and they finished their next two games by the light of the emergency lantern.

Tied again at four-four, they had one more game to go for the prize.

As Jake watched Katherine focus on her cards with absolute and complete focus, he felt both admiration and annoyance. He didn't like to lose and Katherine was good at cards. She wasn't just good; she also seemed to be lucky, getting the cards she needed at exactly the right time.

She smiled as she looked up from her hand. "You're going down, Jake."

"Second time today," he said dryly. "I used up my good luck when I was able to land without killing us."

"So that was luck and not skill?" she challenged, a teasing light in her eyes.

He laughed. "You got me there. So what's your play?"

She spread her cards face up on the table. "Gin."

"Damn."

"I win, Jake. That's five."

"Maybe we should go eight out of ten."

"Can't change the rules now."

"Then it looks like you get the chocolate bar."

"I'll save it for the morning," she said, settling back in her seat. "It will give me a good start to the day."

"Want to finish off the wine?" He lifted up the bottle. "There's at least one glass left."

"Let's split it," she said.

"Very generous of you."

"I've always been a good winner."

He smiled as he poured her wine. "Maybe in your head."

"How can you say that?"

"Because I've been on the losing side of your wins a few times. Your ego gets a little big."

"Not true. And if I'm a bad winner, then you're worse."

"Let's agree we both don't like to lose." He filled both of their glasses about half-full.

"I can drink to that," she said, picking up her glass. "That was fun. I got to forget for a while where we are and what's looming outside this plane."

"I'm glad."

Katherine glanced at her watch. "It's only ten. We still have a lot of hours to go until morning."

"Time will pass; it always does."

"That's true." She absentmindedly played with the necklace around her neck. He was surprised to see it was her locket from a very long time ago.

"You still wear that," he murmured.

Her hand abruptly fell to her lap, and she looked uncomfortable with his observation. "Not usually, but I put it on yesterday. It was my last shift, and I thought Hailey should be there with me. She was the one who inspired me to be a doctor."

"Can I see it?"

"You've already seen it."

"A long time ago. Come on, show me."

She hesitated, then unclasped the necklace and handed it to him. He opened the locket and saw Hailey's cute freckled face and toothy smile. "Cute girl." He looked back at Katherine. "Tell me about her again."

"Why?"

"Because it's only ten o'clock, and we have hours to go until morning," he reminded her.

"All right. We were best friends from the first day of kindergarten. Hailey came up to me at recess and put her hand in mine and said we're best friends now. That was it. We were inseparable. She was an only child, and I didn't have a sister, so we decided we'd be sisters. We did everything together: played soccer; sold Girl Scout cookies; took Irish dancing lessons—which I was not very good at; gymnastics—which I was better at; and we would make up imaginary games to play after school and on the weekends. She had an amazing imagination. I never knew what she was going to come up with."

He liked the way Katherine's voice and eyes softened when she spoke about Hailey. He'd heard about her childhood friend before, but back then there had been more pain in her voice as she'd been closer to the loss.

"Hailey was good for me, probably better than I was for her."

"I doubt she saw it that way."

"She shouldn't have died so young. It was so wrong."

Now the pain came back into her voice, and he frowned. "You weren't to blame, Katherine."

"It was my fault she got hit. I tripped on my costume. She had already crossed the street, but she came back toward me—to help me. That's the reason she was in the street when the car flew around the corner."

"It was a drunk teenager, wasn't it?"

She nodded. "He was seventeen years old. He didn't even stop. I ran to Hailey, and I screamed for help, but no one was around. It was five minutes before another car came down that road. Hailey was awake the whole time. She was so scared. I held her hand, and I told her it would be all right. I promised her that we'd be eating our candy in a few hours."

"That's good. You made her feel better."

"I lied to her. I think I knew it even as I said it. There was so much blood around her and the nearest hospital was thirty minutes away. She died ten minutes after we got there. They were still looking for a doctor to treat her when her heart stopped. It was a rural medical center and the only physician on duty had no experience with pediatric trauma. They had to call someone to come in. I remember the nurses running around trying to get someone on the phone." She paused. "By that time, I was in the waiting room all by myself. The police had called my parents, but they were at a Halloween party, and they hadn't answered the call. By the time they got there, Hailey was dead."

"I'm sorry. That must have been rough."

"It felt surreal at the time, and to be honest, it still does."

Katherine held out her hand, and he gave her back the locket.

She put it around her neck and added, "I hated how

helpless I felt that night. I thought if I'd known what to do, maybe I could have saved her."

"I know you've always felt that way, but now that you're a doctor, do you still believe that?"

"No," she admitted. "I don't believe that I, as a twelve-year-old girl, could have saved Hailey's life, but if there had been a doctor closer, if we'd gotten to the hospital faster, if there had been a pediatric ER physician, maybe she would have made it. I don't know for sure. Her injuries might have been too severe." She sighed and then took another sip of wine.

"You have to find a way to forgive yourself, Katherine."

She stared back at him with pain in her eyes. "You told me that before."

"More than once," he agreed. "But you still hold yourself responsible."

"It was my fault."

"It was an accident."

"Intellectually, I know that. And since I've become a doctor, I know it even more. Life can change in a second. I've seen a lot of accident victims. I've seen a lot of broken-hearted families. But when it's your own personal history, it's different."

"Does knowing that you're helping other families avoid the same tragedy help you?"

"Yes, a little," she admitted. "I always wanted to be a doctor, even before that night, but after that, I knew that was my destiny. I just didn't know how difficult it would be, but Hailey's memory got me through."

"Do you still hate Halloween?"

She nodded. "With a passion."

"I remember when you used to hide in the library on Halloween."

"I couldn't stand to see all those kids in costumes. It was just too hard. Even though we moved away from the town where Hailey died, the Halloween memories followed me."

"Do you think Hailey would be proud of you now?"

"Yes," she said with a smile. "When we were little, we used to talk about what we wanted to be when we grew up. She wanted to be a dancer; I wanted to be a scientist."

"You two obviously had different personalities."

"Very different. She was so outgoing and friendly, and she embraced life. She was fearless. In some ways, you reminded me of her."

"Wait, did you just compliment me?" he asked abruptly.

"I told you that before. Both you and Hailey brought me out of my shell."

"What about now? Are you out of the shell, or did you tuck yourself back in after we split up?"

"I don't know. I haven't had time to analyze myself."

As she finished speaking, she yawned, and even in the shadowy light he could see the exhaustion in her eyes. She'd only caught a short nap in the plane before the lightning storm had struck, and apparently she hadn't slept at all the night before.

"You should close your eyes," he said.

"It's way too early," she mumbled, another yawn following her words. "Let's keep talking—but not about me or our past."

"What does that leave us?"

"A lot. What do you do for fun these days?"

"I fly airplanes."

"That's your job."

"It's also the most fun I've ever had."

"What else?"

"I play in a basketball league in the winter and a softball team in the summer. I picked up the guitar about four years ago, and I jam with friends once or twice a month."

"Really? You always said you wanted to play the guitar—that musicians got all the girls. I thought you were doing fine, even without being able to play an instrument."

"It's more about the music now than the women," he said

with a small smile. "Maybe if we played somewhere other than Jeffrey Danforth's garage, I'd be able to tell a different story. Not a lot of women hanging out back there."

"You're still friends with Jeffrey?"

"I am." He'd been friends with Jeffrey since he was ten years old, and while Jeff had gone wild and crazy in college, he'd settled down since then.

"I thought Jeff was bad news," Katherine said. "He was very happy to point you in the wrong direction."

"He's changed. He's an accountant now, married with a kid, and boring as hell."

"That's surprising. I can't believe he even graduated from college."

"It took him six years, but in the end he got his act together, and so did I."

He realized now that Katherine really had seen the worst of him. He hadn't thought of it that way before. He'd always focused on her leaving him when he needed her, but he certainly hadn't been bringing a lot to their relationship at that point.

"Let's get back to the present," Katherine said. "Are you seeing anyone? Are you in a relationship?"

"There's no one serious at the moment," he admitted. "What about you?"

"Same."

He couldn't imagine that there weren't men who wanted her. Katherine was one of the most beautiful women he'd ever seen. She was also a woman who had never really known how pretty she was. She did have a wall around her heart, a cool air, and a hands-off kind of vibe that probably scared a few men off. He'd gotten past those walls a long time ago, but it would be impossible to do that now.

Not that he wanted to scale her walls. He already had enough scars from Katherine Barrett; he didn't need any more. He just wished they hadn't talked about Hailey, hadn't played cards the way they used to, because in the past few hours he'd seen the girl he'd fallen in love with a long time ago.

Katherine wrapped her arms around her waist and shivered.

"Time for the blanket?"

"Maybe."

"Close enough." He got up and retrieved the blanket, then handed it to her. Instead of sitting across from her, he took the seat next to her. "For body heat," he said, seeing her questioning look. He thought she'd probably be willing to freeze to death before using him for body heat. "Don't worry. I'll keep a safe distance," he added.

"Maybe you should take the blanket."

"Not a chance. You need it more than me. You're always colder than I am."

"All right," she said, throwing the blanket over her lap. "It does help."

"Good." He paused. "I'm going to turn off the light. Save what battery we have left."

"Okay."

They sat quietly in the dark for the next several minutes. Then Katherine said, "Do you think we're going to be okay, Jake?"

"I do," he said firmly.

"I feel so out of my depth. I don't know where we are, what's around us, or what we'll be facing when we leave the plane. I like to be prepared, but I don't know how to prepare for what's coming."

"We'll face whatever comes when we have to. We'll think on our feet. You're pretty good at that. I'm sure as a doctor you run into the unexpected."

"Yes, but I know what to do in the ER. Out here…"

"We'll figure it out. I won't say don't worry, because I know you will worry no matter what I say, but I feel confident we can get to a village and then find a way to move on from there."

"It's not just about saving ourselves, we still need to get to TJ as soon as possible. Who knows where he is or what's happening to him?"

"There's nothing you can do for TJ now. Why don't you try to sleep? You'll need your energy tomorrow."

"Good idea."

After a few moments, he closed his own eyes, thinking they were settling in for the night. Then Katherine said, "Thanks, Jake."

Her voice had a soft sweetness to it that tugged at his heart. "For what?"

"For—being you," she said slowly. "The *you* I remember."

He wanted to tell her that he'd only been that *other* guy for a year, and that if she'd stuck around long enough, she would have known that.

But what was the point? They'd already hashed out the past. They needed to move forward so they could work together and face whatever was waiting outside the plane.

He folded his arms across his chest and breathed in and out, trying not to think about how close Katherine was to him, how easy it would be to lift the armrest between them and pull her into his arms. They'd always slept well together. Probably because before they'd slept they'd made love until they were exhausted.

His body tightened at that unwelcome memory. He had a feeling it was going to be a longer night for him than for Katherine; her presence, her scent, and the memories of being with her were firing up his senses. He'd had a strong connection to her from the first minute they'd met, and that had never gone away. He'd felt things for other women over the years—attraction, affection, desire—but nothing really close to what he'd felt for her.

She was his first love. Maybe that put her in a special category. Maybe it would never ever be as good with anyone else.

That was a depressing thought.

With a sigh, he shifted in his seat and tried to think of something besides Katherine.

The storm played back through his mind; the huge towering clouds, the fierce lightning—his father's image.

He shivered with the memory. His dad had waved to him. He'd told him to follow. Follow where?

He reminded himself that he didn't believe in ghosts or any other kind of supernatural activity. Logic suggested his mind was just putting his dad in front of him because there was a mystery about his death. He didn't want to look at that mystery, because it hurt, but his mind was forcing him to go there.

He gave up on the fight to get his dad out of his head, instead silently saying, "If you've got more to say, Dad, say it now. And if you can throw in some directions, that would be helpful."

But there was no answer from his father now. No lightning either. It might take another storm for him to see what he needed to see.

⟶⟫⟪⟵

Jake stood at the edge of a cliff overlooking a sea of trees and valleys that went on forever. He beckoned her to come forward.

"You're too close to the edge," she said, stopping a few feet away from him.

"We have to go down the mountains. It's the only way we'll get to TJ."

"How do you know he's down there?"

"How do you know he's not?" Jake returned.

She edged forward, seeing a steep rocky mountainside that seemed impossible to get down. "We'll fall. We'll die."

"We don't have a choice. They're coming for us."

She heard shouts in the distance, or was it a rumble of

thunder? Who was coming? Was it an army or was it a storm?

"Take my hand, Katherine."

She looked at his outstretched hand. He was asking her to trust him. His green eyes implored her to take his hand, to believe in him.

Her stomach churned with doubts. Was it the new Jake? Or was it the old Jake who'd let her down? How could she tell? He'd said he'd changed. Had he? Had she?

"I will protect you," Jake said. "I love you."

"Not anymore," she told him, refusing to believe in the lie.

"Are you sure, Katherine?"

Wasn't she sure?

"You always make things harder than they have to be," he said. "You don't have to trust me; trust yourself—your instincts. What does your heart tell you to do?"

If she was just listening to her heart, there was no decision to make. She grabbed Jake's hand and his strong fingers tightened around hers. The connection was intense and powerful.

"I'm not going to let you fall," he told her.

"I won't let you fall, either."

He gave her the smile that always made her heart melt. "A kiss for luck?"

She moved into his arms, his warmth enveloping her. Every breath she took was Jake. Nothing had ever felt as right as his mouth on hers, his lips parting, his tongue sliding against hers. She tilted her head, allowing him greater access. He moaned, and she delighted in his response. She moved even closer to him, wanting to feel his hardness against her, wanting to take everything he had to give and then give it back to him.

They kissed like the lovers they'd been. Had time really passed in between? Or had it all been a bad dream?

His hand ran through her hair, holding her in place for

his kiss. She'd always loved the way he took charge, the way he made her feel so hot and so desirable. She put her arms around his neck as they shared another kiss and another, desire building with each touch of their lips.

It felt so real. There was so much heat. And the stubble on his jaw when she rested her cheek against his for just a moment was sexily familiar.

"Katherine?"

His voice was much louder than it had been.

She blinked her eyes open and met his gaze. He wasn't blurry anymore. His voice didn't sound far away. They weren't on a mountain; they were on a plane.

Jake was very, very real and very, very close. Oh, God, what had she done?

Eight

—➤➤◆◆◄—

"Good morning," Jake said, his voice husky, tender, intimate.

Katherine jerked backward and realized that at some point in the night one of them had lifted the armrest between their seats. They'd ended up in each other's arms, and they hadn't just been sleeping, they'd also been kissing.

She put a hand to her tingling lips. It hadn't been a dream, or at least not all of it.

"I haven't woken up that way in a long time," he added, his gaze still fixed on hers. "I'd almost forgotten how good it was."

She felt heat creep up her cheeks. "I was dreaming."

"About me?"

"Yes," she admitted, then instantly wished she hadn't been so honest, because an appreciative gleam had now entered Jake's eyes.

"About the way we were?"

She shook her head and moved as far away from Jake as she could get without leaving her seat. "No, it was about now. You were standing at the edge of a cliff, and you thought TJ was down below. You told me we had to go down there to get him, but I was scared. Of course, you talked me into it."

"What happened then? Did we get TJ?"

"I don't know. I took your hand, and then you said something about a kiss for luck...you know what happened next."

"You kissed me for real."

"I thought I was dreaming."

"I thought I was, too, for a minute." He paused. "It was always good between us, Kat. That hasn't changed."

"But everything else has." She got to her feet. At least she still had her clothes on. Things hadn't gone as far as they could have. She looked around, seeing light coming through the windows. "What time is it?"

He glanced at his watch. "Seven fifteen."

"We should get going."

"I agree. We'll leave our suitcases behind. I'll take the lantern, the first-aid kid, and the food and water supplies in my backpack."

"I'll take my computer and maybe a few other clothing items I can stuff in my small bag."

"Great."

She was happy when they started to gather their things together. She needed to catch her breath. Her nerves were still jangling from their kisses, her body aching a bit with unfulfilled desire. But she wasn't going to soothe that ache. She needed to keep her focus. She had to concentrate on getting to her brother. That was all that mattered.

—◆◆◆—

Hell of a way to wake up, Jake thought as he stuffed their supplies into his backpack. It was just too damn bad they hadn't gone a little further—or a lot further—before the dream ended.

Or maybe it was better that they'd woken up, because along with the long-smoldering desire he felt for Katherine, he also had a lot of painful memories still to deal with.

At times, she seemed like the old Kat, the one he'd fallen

in love with, but he couldn't forget the Katherine who had broken his heart and left him in the dust.

Who she was now was still a bit of a mystery. Not that he needed to solve that mystery. It was extremely doubtful that a relationship between them now would end up any differently than the first time around. They were very different people, and whatever trust they'd had ten years ago was long gone.

Katherine knew that as well as he did. She had her guard up, and he should do the same.

When he returned to the cabin, he found Katherine waiting and ready to go, but she couldn't seem to look him in the eye. It was good to know she was feeling just as unsettled as he was.

Opening the door, he was happy to see some sunlight streaming through the trees. The storm was over. It was a new day.

They got down from the plane and headed around the back of it, going in the opposite direction from the day before. He hoped this time they'd hit the clearing he'd seen from the sky instead of getting deeper into the woods. The air was cool and crisp, which also led him to believe that they had landed in the central, interior part of Mexico since the southern states and coastal areas were far more tropical and temperate.

While the rain had passed, water still dripped steadily from the tree branches, giving his head a nice soak. Just like a shower, he told himself, trying to stay positive despite the fact that the isolation and quiet of the area didn't seem like a good sign.

Katherine didn't appear to be interested in conversation, and since he had no idea what to say to her, he let the silence drag on.

Fifteen minutes later, they came out from under the thick canopy of trees and walked through a grassy area about two hundred yards wide. He paused in the middle of the clearing and did a slow turn. To the front and the left of them, he could see nothing but trees. To the right, small hills led up to a more impressive mountain range with peaks he'd judged to be at least ten thousand feet.

"I'm guessing that is the Sierra Madre Oriental Mountain Range," he said.

"How can you tell?"

"The range has really high peaks, and those seem to tower above the others. But to be honest, I'm not sure. There are at least four significant mountain ranges in the country."

"Mexico is bigger than I realized. The guidebook said it's the eighth largest country in the world. There are thirty-eight states, and like the US, the weather changes from region to region."

He smiled. "Good to know."

"If that range is what you think it is, where should we go?"

"I think we should stay to the east of it, head through those trees. Otherwise, we'll be climbing mountains. But..." He paused, considering their options.

"But you think we should try to get higher so we can get a phone signal," she finished.

"I do. We could also get a better view and see if we can spot any homes or roads. But it will take us awhile to get enough elevation to make a difference, and there are more likely to be people in the valley than on the mountain."

She frowned. "So it's risky either way."

"Do you want me to make the decision?" he asked.

"No."

"Then do you want to make it?"

"Not really."

"Well, we can't stand here all day. Pick a path and let's go."

"I'm considering our options."

He sighed. "This is why you should have let me win gin rummy. I'd be making the decisions, and we wouldn't be wasting time making a pro and con list."

"And where would you go?"

"Into the mountains. I'd give it two hours. If we can't get a signal, we come back and head the other way."

"All right. I can do two hours."

"This reminds me of the time we went camping," he said as they headed west toward the mountains.

"That was not at all like this. We were a mile outside of town. Our cell phones worked, and we had a car, a tent, and food."

"Ah, that tent," he said with a smile. "We made some good memories in that tent." He laughed as her eyes sparkled and her cheeks flushed. "I see you remember those."

"I also remember that you wanted to show me some hidden pool, and we went off the path and got poison ivy. I was itchy for weeks after that. And we never even found the pool."

"But we did end up at the highway, and we got to see that driver taking a leak behind his truck," he said, flinging her a grin. "So, it wasn't a wasted trip."

She laughed. "Yeah, that was a good time. Never a dull moment with you, Jake Monroe."

"Or you, Katherine Barrett. Does anyone ever call you Kat?"

"Nobody in Houston."

"Do you have a lot of friends there?"

"Some. I haven't had much time for friends, but I've gotten close with a few of the medical residents. We've spent some really long days and nights together. It's going to be strange when everyone scatters, but that's the way it is."

"Don't you mean sad...not strange?"

"I guess it will be sad, too."

He wasn't really surprised that Katherine played down the emotional aspect of leaving her friends and coworkers. She had perfected the art of locking her emotions away. It had started with Hailey. Losing her best friend in such a traumatic manner had scarred her for life. She'd probably never invested in a friend the way she had with Hailey.

She'd gotten close with him, but when things got difficult, she'd bailed. Maybe it was to save herself from drowning, or maybe she just wanted to be the one to leave first, so she could put the emotions away on her own terms.

He suspected she'd kept most of her friends in Houston at arm's length, too. He wondered about her patients. How did she handle working on people—on kids—who might not make it?

"How do you do it, Kat?" he asked.

"Do what?"

"Treat someone who might not survive?" He slowed down so they were walking side by side.

"That's an odd question to ask."

"Do you have an answer?"

"I think of them as their problem: broken arm, appendicitis, head injury, kid who swallowed a miniature car."

"That didn't happen."

"You'd be surprised what people, especially kids, put in their mouths."

"I don't think I want to know." He paused. "So it doesn't get to you? What happens when they're seriously ill, when you can't help them?"

"I never have a long time to think about it. It's on to the next patient. I work as a pediatric physician in the ER. Most kids I only see once—for a few hours. Sometimes I follow up, but usually they go back to their own doctors. I put out fires; I don't have long-term relationships."

That made complete sense. "Did you choose pediatrics because of Hailey?"

"She was definitely part of the decision, but I do like kids, and when you save them, you save all the life they have left to live, and that feels good. They can go on to accomplish all their dreams."

"I bet you're a terrific doctor."

She glanced over at him. "A compliment?"

"I've never questioned your intelligence, Kat, or your ability to be really good at something."

"I am good," she said. "It's not that I don't care about the patients—it's that I *can't* care. Emotions get in the way. I have to be the one focusing on fixing the problem. That's my job. That's what they need me to do. The recovery, the nurturing, the explanations—they come later."

"When the fire is out," he murmured.

She nodded. "Exactly."

And that was how she got through it. She kept moving and she didn't look back. It seemed that was the way she lived every part of her life.

He picked up the pace as they hit the foothills, leading the way up the slippery, rocky, wet hillside.

Katherine stayed close behind him. Occasionally, he reached back to offer her a hand, but she waved him away, saying she was fine. He hoped she'd remain that way because the hillside was getting steeper, and they still weren't high enough to see beyond the trees.

Half an hour later, he heard her breath getting a little rougher as they struggled through a particularly difficult stretch. Finally, they got beyond it and he paused to take a breather. "You okay?"

"Fine. I guess I need to get to the gym more often."

He pulled out his phone. "One bar," he said, excitement in his voice. His joy quickly faded when he couldn't get a call to connect.

"Maybe a text would get through," Katherine suggested, trying her own phone with the same results.

"I can send one and see." He debated on who he wanted to send a text to. He didn't want to alarm his mother if she hadn't heard anything yet, so he selected Rusty's number from his contacts and texted him the details of what happened. He pushed Send, but nothing seemed to happen. "I don't think it's working." He shoved his phone back into his pocket. "We're going to have to go higher."

"It's getting pretty steep, Jake."

"If we walk that way, it looks like a more gradual climb," he said, tipping his head to the east.

"All right."

He was about to turn back to the mountain path, when she grabbed his arm. "Wait. Look, Jake. I see something moving in the trees. Is that a car?"

He followed her gaze. In the forested area where they'd crashed, he could see flashes of metal in the sunshine and shadows moving through the trees. "Maybe we are going to be rescued," he said, somewhat amazed by that thought. "Someone must have seen the plane go down after all."

"Thank God. I was not feeling that optimistic about our plan to climb this mountain to find a signal."

They moved down the hill a lot faster than they'd come up. When they got to the bottom, they headed into the trees. They were probably fifty yards away from the plane when he heard men shouting. The tone of their voices gave him pause. Inexplicable shivers ran down his spine, and he stopped abruptly.

"What's wrong?" Katherine asked.

"Don't talk," he said quietly.

"Don't talk? I was just about to yell for help."

"I don't have a good feeling about this."

She stared at him in alarm. "What do you mean?" she asked, dropping her voice down to a whisper.

He didn't have time for an answer, but he did have time to pull her behind a tree as he saw shadowy figures coming in their direction. He wanted to see who was there before they showed themselves. He thought about grabbing the gun out of his bag, but he didn't want to make any noise. He should have had the gun out the whole time.

Katherine's fingers tightened on his arm as a man appeared a dozen yards away. He had a dark baseball cap on his head and wore a short-sleeved T-shirt and jeans. Both arms were heavily tattooed, and he carried a semi-automatic weapon in his hands.

The man paused as someone behind him yelled. He turned away and a man in a uniform joined him. They spoke in rapid Spanish and then headed back toward the plane.

"That second guy looked like a policeman," Katherine murmured.

"Yeah, but his friend didn't."

"If we stay hidden, Jake, we could be here for days. They could be here to rescue us. Could you make out what they were saying?"

He glanced back at her. "No." He was conflicted on whether or not to show themselves and ask for help or risk being discovered by the wrong people. Then he began to smell smoke.

"Oh, my God," Katherine said. "Fire."

He turned his head to see what had put the horror in her eyes and saw flames zipping up the branches of some trees not very far away.

"We've got to get out of here." He grabbed her hand and pulled her in the opposite direction of the plane. The smoke got stronger as they ran, and they were no more than a quarter of a mile away when an explosion knocked them flat on the ground. Rocks, dirt, and branches rained down around them.

Stunned, Jake struggled to catch his breath. Then, with ears still ringing, he scrambled to his feet and ran to Katherine, who'd landed a few feet away. She appeared dazed but not injured.

"Are you hurt?" he asked.

"I don't think so."

"We have to get farther away, Kat." He wasn't just worried about the men with the guns; the explosion had set off a blazing forest fire.

Katherine jumped up, and they took off running again.

They didn't stop for at least twenty minutes, staying on the edge of the forest, which gave them cover, and the nearby mountains, which he thought might provide an avenue of escape from the fire that was ripping through the trees. Finally, breathless, they paused for a moment to look back.

"What the hell happened?" Katherine asked in bemusement.

"They blew up the plane," he said shortly, fear turning his gut inside out. He'd been only semi-worried about surviving in the wilderness before. But now they didn't just have the elements to worry about.

"They weren't there to rescue us," she said. "Not if they blew up the plane. You don't think it could have happened on its own, do you?"

"No way. There was no leaking fuel. We were fine last night. Those men didn't want anyone to find the plane."

"Why? What did we do? Do you think this has to do with TJ? He told me if I tried to come after him, someone would know, someone might follow me. That's why I didn't fly commercial. But what if someone saw me get on your plane?"

"We don't know if this has anything to do with TJ. We could have trespassed on someone's very private property."

"Like a drug cartel?"

"Exactly. But it doesn't matter who we're running from. Right now we just have to make sure they don't catch us."

Nine

—→➤➤◄◄◄←—

Alicia zipped her suitcase and called out to Michael in the adjoining bathroom. "We should hurry if we're going to catch our plane."

Her soon-to-be husband entered the bedroom late Sunday morning with a smile and a sexy gleam in his eyes. Her heart skipped a beat as she looked at him. She wondered when Michael would stop taking her breath away. She had a feeling it would be a very long time from now, if ever.

"You're telling me that?" Michael teased. "I wasn't the one who decided to help your mom make blueberry muffins from scratch for breakfast."

"It was our tradition when I was little. It was one of the few things she and I did together. Everything else was usually her and Dani. I couldn't say no."

He walked across the room and leaned over to give her a tender kiss. "I'm glad you spent time with her. I'm happy that you're getting closer to your mom again. And to the rest of your family, too."

"But just when I'm ready to get close again, everyone else goes away," she said with a sigh. "Dani sent me a text. She said her apartment has a view of the White House. She's very excited to be so close."

"I think your sister has her eye on the White House for

her own personal ambitions."

"I'm sure. Dani always predicted she'd be famous and important one day. She's not quite there yet, but she's getting close. I do wonder how long she'll be content to work under other people, though. She has a tendency to like to run the show."

"She's smart enough to wait for the right opportunity. I don't think you have to worry about her."

"I'm not worrying about her; Jake is another story. Ever since he came by yesterday with Katherine, I've been thinking about him."

"He'll be in touch when he knows something."

"I just can't quite believe it's all still going on. Actually, I can believe it." She'd been frustrated for weeks at being shut out of the investigation into MDT. "I knew that this wasn't over. TJ's disappearance is directly related to Jerry's operation. I'm positive of that. I know Katherine asked us not to talk to anyone, but I'm thinking I should call Special Agent Wolfe. He, at least, was receptive to listening to my theories."

"Why don't you wait until you hear from Jake? This could all be over shortly."

"I guess."

Michael gave her another kiss. "As you said, we need to get a move on, so are you ready to head to the airport?"

"I am. Let's go." They were halfway down the hall when the doorbell rang. "I wonder who that is."

As she reached the bottom of the stairs, she saw her mom talking to a man on the porch. He was tall, with red hair. Her heart thudded against her chest. She'd seen this man before. He'd worked not only with Jake but also with her dad. He'd been the one to tell her mother that her father's plane was missing.

And now he was here—a day after Jake had flown to Mexico.

Oh, God!

She moved quickly toward her mother. "Mom?"

Her mother's face was stark white, and there was pure terror in her eyes.

"What's wrong?" Alicia asked, barely able to get the words through her tight lips. When her mother couldn't seem to answer, she turned to the man. "What's happened?"

"It's Jake," he said. "I'm sorry to tell you that his plane is missing."

She swayed from the shock of his statement. Michael came up behind her, and she leaned against his solid body as she tried to absorb what she'd just heard. "I don't understand."

"I'm Rusty Sampson. I'm the owner of Culverson Air Charters. Jake flew a charter to Mexico yesterday, but he did not arrive at his destination. There were a number of storms in his flight path, and he lost contact with air traffic control about two hours into his flight."

Her stomach turned over, and a wave of nausea ran through her. She grabbed her mother's icy-cold hand.

"It's just like before," her mother muttered in a dull, numb voice. "Just like your dad. It was Rusty then, too. He came to the door. He said the same thing."

She looked from her mother to the man who'd just delivered the terrible news. His eyes were bloodshot, his expression tense and worried. "It's not like the last time," she told him. "Jake is going to be all right. What are you doing to find him?"

"We've contacted Mexican authorities, and a search is underway. I've sent two planes down there to look for him myself."

She drew in a deep breath, feeling like she might pass out. Jake couldn't be dead. He couldn't be. He was too young, too strong, and he had way too much to live for. "You said he ran into a storm?"

"A severe electrical storm, yes," Rusty said, meeting her gaze.

"Like with my dad."

Rusty stared back at her. "Your father was over the Gulf

of Mexico. I'm fairly certain Jake was over land."

"What difference does that make?"

"It will be easier to get him help, and he has a better chance of survival," Rusty replied.

"Why didn't you call us last night?" she demanded, realizing that Jake's chance of survival went down with every passing hour. "We could have been in Mexico by now."

"We were hoping to have made contact with him so that we could give you good news," Rusty said. "We're doing everything we can to find him. I want you to know that Jake is like a son to me. I won't stop looking for him."

"You stopped looking for my father," she said, feeling herself getting lost in the past now, too.

"I can't do this again," her mother said abruptly. "I can't." She let go of Alicia's hand and ran up the stairs to her room.

"I'm very sorry," Rusty said. "I'll be in touch as soon as I know anything."

"You need to find him and bring him home."

"I will do everything I can."

Alicia nodded and then closed the door. She turned in to Michael's arms, needing his strength. She felt like throwing up or crying or running away—maybe all three.

Michael held her close. "He's going to be okay, Alicia."

She lifted her head. "I want to believe that, but last time—"

"Don't go there," he said, cutting her off. "Jake is not your dad."

"The circumstances are eerily similar." Another thought entered her mind. "I wonder if Jake's plane could have been tampered with before he left. Jake and Katherine came here before the flight. There was time in between Jake's decision to fly her to Mexico and when they took off. What if someone got to the plane?"

"I'm sure there's security at the airport."

"It was a charter flight. Security is not as tight at a private airfield. And I know that Jake flies executives from MDT all the time. They're very familiar with that airport and those planes."

"It's something to consider," Michael said carefully. "We need more information, Alicia."

"I should go to the airfield and talk to Rusty again, ask him the questions I should have asked. I was so shocked; I couldn't think." She glanced up the stairs. "But first, I should make sure Mom's all right."

"Does she have a friend who could come and stay with her while we're waiting for news?"

"I'll ask her."

"We'll make sure she's okay and then we'll go to the airfield. We're going to find Jake and Katherine, Alicia."

She wanted to believe him, but she had no idea how they would do that.

Katherine's lungs were protesting at their frantic run through the forest, and she had a pain in her side that was getting worse by the minute, but thinking about stopping with armed men in the area didn't seem like a good idea. She shifted her tote bag to her other shoulder. The computer, guidebooks, and maps as well as her wallet and cell phone were weighing her down, but she really didn't want to leave them behind.

Jake kept up a steady, fast pace, flinging her the occasional worried look over his shoulder, but he obviously knew her well enough to know she could keep up. She wasn't going to quit, not until she stopped breathing.

She didn't know if they were going in the right direction but staying in the trees seemed like the best idea. They hadn't heard or seen anyone come after them in the past hour, but the men obviously had transportation, and they did not, so she had no idea how long they could stay hidden.

Jake slowed down and finally stopped, his chest heaving

with exertion as he drew in quick, ragged breaths. "You okay?"

She nodded, not having enough air to speak just yet. She put her bag on the ground and rolled her aching shoulder.

"You need to drop some of that weight," Jake said. "Just take your wallet and phone and leave the rest."

"We might need the computer," she argued. "I can carry it."

Jake opened his backpack and pulled out a water bottle and tossed it to her. "Drink."

She was happy to soothe her throat with cool water. Between the smoky fire and the running, she felt parched. She drank about a quarter of the bottle and then handed it back to him. "Your turn."

"I'm okay. We'll save it for later."

"You need water, too," she insisted. "You don't drink, I don't move."

"You're so damn stubborn."

"And I know how to avoid dehydration. We have enough problems."

Jake took a long drink and then put the bottle into his backpack. "Let's keep moving."

"Aren't we going in the wrong direction, Jake? We should be heading south. We're getting farther away from Nic Té Há by the minute."

"That would have been preferable, but that direction had less cover, and we had to make a snap decision. We can't go back. At some point, we'll head east and then eventually south."

"At what point would that be?"

"When we feel like we're safe and no one is following us."

She couldn't imagine feeling safe after what she'd seen in the woods.

"When it gets later in the day, I'd like to head back up into the hills, but I want us to get far enough away so no one can spot us once we start to climb and don't have the trees for protection."

She couldn't argue with his plan. In fact, she was pretty damn happy to have him with her now. She didn't know what she would have done if he hadn't survived the crash, or if he hadn't kept her from running up to those men and announcing her presence.

It was the first time in their relationship that Jake had been the more cautious one. He'd done a good job at keeping them safe.

"How long do you think those men will look for us?"

"Impossible to say."

"I wish I knew if they were connected to TJ's situation."

"So do I. I also wish I could get a message to everyone back home. It kills me to think of what our families are going through, not knowing if we're dead or alive."

"Just keep reminding yourself that we are alive, that we're going to make it back," she told him. "Your mom and sisters are not going to lose you."

"I'd like to believe that," he said heavily. "But I have to admit I wasn't expecting anyone to come after us—to blow up the plane, for God's sake."

"I wasn't, either. If you hadn't stopped me from yelling out to those men, we might not be alive right now."

"I had a bad feeling."

"Your instincts were right. What does your gut tell you now?"

"That we're up against more than Mother Nature. It's not going to be easy, Kat."

"But we're going to make it." She reached for his hand and gazed into his eyes. "I need you to believe it, Jake. I need you to help me make it true."

He gave her a long look, then said, "I believe it. You don't have to worry. We'll be okay."

It was exactly what she'd wanted him to say. Whether it was true or not, she'd needed to hear his reassurance.

"Thanks."

He squeezed her hand. "Ready to run again?"

"Yes."

She jogged and walked behind Jake for several more hours. A few dark clouds soaked them with rain, but she couldn't worry about being wet. Every step forward could take them closer to safety.

They headed into the mountains around four o'clock, hoping the shadows thrown off by the taller peaks would shield their presence. The hillsides were steep and often slippery, making the journey that much more difficult. Aside from stopping to get water or catch their breath, they kept going, knowing that they had to make each minute of daylight count.

Finally, their climb brought them to a plateau. Katherine set her bag on the ground and shared the second-to-last bottle of water with Jake as they looked out at the view. She saw an endless sea of trees and some grassy areas that could possibly be farmland, but it was difficult to tell from this distance.

"There's a road over there," Jake said. "See that brown patch that winds through the trees? It looks like there's a river down there, too. A road and a source of water leads me to believe there might be people nearby."

"That road is at least a few miles from here."

"Should we try for it?"

She hesitated. "We won't make it before dark. And once we get down in those trees, it will be easy to lose our way."

"Maybe we should spend the night here and go at first light."

As much as she didn't want to spend the night on the mountain, she thought it was the best decision.

Jake pulled out his phone. "Hey, wait a second, I have two bars now."

"Really?" she asked hopefully. "That's the first piece of good news I've heard all day."

"I'm going to send a text to Rusty and Alicia. Maybe they

can trace the signal of the phone and that will help them find us."

"Can you have them check in on my mom? She may not be able to understand that I'm missing since I'm gone all the time anyway, but I just want someone to see if she's worried or upset about anything."

"Of course." He typed in a brief message stating what he knew about their position and asking them to send help as soon as possible. He hit Send and it seemed to go through. "I think it went."

"I hope so. We might finally catch a break." She sat down with a groan of relief. "I think I have ten blisters, one for each toe."

"My feet have taken a beating too." He gave her a smile as he sat down next to her. "Can I just say that you've been amazing today?"

"You can definitely say that."

"You haven't complained. You haven't slowed us down. And you haven't wasted time arguing with me."

"I only argue with you when you're wrong."

He rolled his eyes. "Just take the compliment."

"Thank you. You've been great, too, Jake."

"Today reminds me of when I used to think we made a good team. We complemented each other."

"At least part of the time."

"There was more good between us than bad. I don't think I remembered that until recently."

She nodded. "It's easier to focus on the end instead of everything that came before. We're going to need to be a good team for a while longer if we're going to get out of here."

"Agreed."

She reached for her bag and pulled out the candy bar she'd won the night before. "Time for chocolate."

"I thought you ate that hours ago."

"I never had time." She opened the wrapper and took a bite. "This is the best thing I've ever tasted. It's like a piece of heaven."

"Way to rub it in."

"I won it fair and square."

"I know you did; that doesn't make it easier."

She took another bite, then broke the bar in half and held out the other piece to him. "I'm willing to share."

"No way, it's yours. I was just giving you a hard time."

"I know, but it's *ours*. I wouldn't feel right eating the whole thing. Come on, take it."

"You should save it for later."

"If you don't take it, I'm going to throw it down the mountain."

"That would be a stupid thing to do," he said with annoyance.

She shrugged. "And not sharing it with me would be a stupid thing for you to do."

He took the chocolate. "Thanks."

"You're welcome."

He demolished the bar in two bites. "I have to admit that was good. The best thing I've tasted in years. I just hope you won't regret your generosity when you wake up hungry in the morning."

"The only regrets I've had involve moments when I was being selfish, not generous." She paused, her gaze on the view for a long moment. Then she turned her head to look at him. "I know I've been self-absorbed the last several years, Jake. I need to work on that."

"There's a flip side to every negative trait. That dedication helps you to accomplish your goals."

"But I don't want my accomplishments to be at the expense of others. When I get home, I'm going to make things right for TJ and my mom. I can't believe that her condition has gone downhill so fast or that she changed doctors without telling me. I wish TJ would have called me and told me to get my ass back to Corpus Christi sooner. I don't know why he didn't do that. If he needed help, he should have asked."

"He did ask; that's why we're here," he reminded her.

"I'm talking about before Friday."

"Is it possible you missed some phone calls or texts?"

She frowned. "It's definitely possible, but if there was a big problem, I would respond."

"Maybe TJ didn't want you to come home. He wanted you to finish what you started."

"It's possible. He's always supported me."

"Is there any chance your mom will get better?"

"The prognosis isn't great, but there are new drugs coming out that might slow the progression of her disease. I need to do some research. It's not my field, but I definitely need to become an expert in it. I asked one of my friends, who's a neurologist, to look in on my mom this week. Something is a little off with her care, and it needs to get straightened out."

"Then that's what you'll do. When you put your mind to something, you usually succeed, Katherine."

"Wow, another compliment. That chocolate must have gone to your head."

He grinned. "I just call it like I see it."

"You're like me in that regard, Jake. You go after what you want, too."

"Sometimes," he conceded. "Not always."

"What haven't you gone after?" she challenged.

His answering look sent a chill through her.

"You," he replied. "I should have gone after you, Kat. I should have tried to change your mind. I should have done better by you."

Goose bumps ran down her arms. "I don't think you could have changed my mind back then."

"What you said yesterday about me being the drowning man and you being the one who couldn't rescue me because I wouldn't let you…"

"Yes?"

He held her gaze for a long minute. "I didn't see myself

as drowning until you said that yesterday. I knew I was angry, reckless, a little out of control. I wasn't giving you enough attention, but I never realized that you thought I was in real danger or that you had to save me."

"I was afraid for you, Jake," she admitted. "You were so light and easygoing on the outside that most people didn't realize how deeply you cared, how intense your emotions could be. But I could see how much pain you were in behind the partying and the thrill-seeking dares, and it scared me. Of course, as you know, I scare pretty easily, so that's probably not saying much."

"The big stuff doesn't scare you," he said quietly. "Spiders, yes, you're a big baby. Riding on the back of a motorcycle, no way; you could recite statistics of motorcycle deaths in your sleep."

She couldn't believe he remembered that. "I didn't want you to be one of those statistics."

"I think you were more concerned about ending up a statistic yourself, and that's okay. Back then, sometimes I needed someone to pull me off the edge." He took a breath. "But sometimes I think you needed someone to get you to that edge."

His words reminded her of the dream she'd had the night before when he'd asked her to jump off a cliff with him to save her brother. She'd tried to say no, but in the end she'd taken his hand...

Jake had always gotten her to the edge, which was partly why she'd broken up with him and ran as far away as she could get.

"Nothing to say?" Jake prodded.

"What can I say? We're different people. We were good for a while, but when life got tough..."

"We were young, Kat. We didn't know what we were doing."

"I can't argue with that." She paused. "I'm glad we got a chance to talk things out."

"Yeah, I feel much better about crashing the plane now," he said dryly.

She grinned. "You always could make me laugh."

"I could make you do a lot of things," he teased.

She blushed. "We're not talking about any of that."

"I don't know. We have a lot of hours to kill."

"Well, we can talk about other things—politics, religion, movies, books, sports, whatever..."

"When's the last time you went to a movie?"

"Four or five years ago."

"And read a book that wasn't a medical textbook?"

"Maybe eight or nine years ago."

"Watch a sporting event?"

"I did see the Cowboys play the Seahawks three weeks ago," she said, relieved to be able to answer one question in the affirmative. "They won after a Hail Mary pass in the final twenty seconds. The bar I was in went crazy."

"That was a good game. They got lucky, though. They could have lost just as easily."

"See, we can talk about other things besides us."

He laughed. "Tell me about your life in Houston. Do you have a roommate?"

"I have three roommates, all medical residents. We live in an apartment next to the hospital. We had some fun in between all the work. But it's over now."

"Do you ever keep in touch with anyone from high school?"

"Just Rebecca Saunders, because we went to medical school together. She's going to look in on my mom while I'm gone."

"Becky. I remember her. Nice girl. Anyone else?"

She shook her head. "No, I lost track of everyone a long time ago. It will be strange to come back to Corpus Christi."

"Would you come back if your mom wasn't there?"

She sucked in a breath. "Probably not."

"Why not?" he asked, tilting his head as he gave her a

questioning look.

"I don't know who I am there."

"You're whoever you want to be."

"In Corpus Christi, I have a past. Going somewhere new would be a clean slate."

"Wouldn't you be lonely?"

"I think I'd be more lonely in a town where the people I once loved were either gone or slipping away." She was talking mostly about her parents, but Jake was part of it, too. At least he had been until now. Now, she wasn't so sure how she would feel living close to him again. They'd been in each other's pocket the last twenty-four hours. It was going to be strange to go back to never seeing him again.

"You still have TJ," he reminded her.

"Once I find him. Do you think I was stupidly impulsive to come down here?"

He glanced over at her. "Impulsive maybe, brave definitely. Stupid—not so much."

"I should have come up with a better plan. I should have told someone to come and find us if we didn't report back."

"Even if my texts don't go through, Rusty will come looking for me, and if he's told Alicia, I can guarantee she'll be a bulldog trying to find us. And Dani has political connections. She might be able to get someone in the government to work with Mexican authorities to find us."

"I wish I had some family or friends to contribute to the search effort, but I don't."

"I have enough for both of us." He stretched out. "As hard as this ground is, it feels good after all the walking and running. You should try it."

She lay down beside him, looking up at the darkening sky. Big, black clouds were creeping over the mountains. It was going to rain again, and she doubted the overhang of rocks would provide much protection, but it was better than nothing.

Jake closed his eyes, and she did the same. But as tired as

she was, sleep didn't come easily.

Opening her eyes, she rolled onto her side and looked at Jake. Her chest tightened as her gaze ran over his strong features. He really was a beautiful man. She'd always loved watching him sleep. His features were so sexy and so male with his strong jaw, stubbly cheeks, and his full but firm and often demanding lips. It would be so easy to lean over and kiss his mouth. He wouldn't push her away. He might not like her, but he still wanted her.

She rolled onto her other side so she wouldn't be tempted to touch him. She tried to sleep, but the wind picked up, making her feel cold and even more uncomfortable. It was going to be a long night.

She turned onto her back, wincing as she tried to get a rock out from under her hip.

"Come here," Jake said suddenly.

She jerked as his eyes flew open, and he looked right at her. "I thought you were asleep."

"With you tossing and turning like that?"

"There are too many rocks, and I'm cold." As she said the words, she realized she was quickly ending her great day of not complaining.

"Come here," he repeated.

She shook her head. "No."

"I've got a nice shoulder you can use as a pillow, and we'll warm each other up."

She vividly remembered just how nice his shoulder was, just how comforting it had been to fall asleep with the sound of his heartbeat under her ear. But she couldn't move. If she got closer, she didn't know if she could stop at just sleeping with him. Which was a crazy thought. They were lost in the wilderness, for God's sake. They weren't on some romantic date.

"Kat—"

"I'm fine."

"If you don't come here right now, I'm going to throw

you off the mountain," he said with exasperation, repeating her earlier threat about the chocolate.

"You don't have that much energy."

"You want to try me?"

She scooted across the ground and put her head on his chest as his arm came around her shoulder.

"That's better," he said. "You need to rest, Kat. We'll figure everything out in the morning."

She put her arm across his waist. "We're safe for now, right?"

He didn't answer. The soft whoosh of his breath told her he was already asleep.

"Yeah, we're safe," she whispered, hoping it was true.

—➤➤◄◄◄—

Katherine awoke to large drops of rain pelting her face. Damn! She sat up and scooted back against the rocks, but the overhang offered little protection from the massive downpour of water. Jake huddled next to her as their life quickly went from uncomfortable to miserable. The rain was coming down in sheets. She'd never seen so much water in her life.

Jake put his arm around her shoulders. There was no point in trying to resist the little comfort he was offering her. They sat there for almost an hour; wet, shivering and praying for respite.

Despite those prayers, the storm only seemed to get bigger. Lightning flashed, followed by more thunder. The strikes were minutes apart. The heavens had opened up with a vengeance.

"I'm beginning to think you're a lightning rod," she told Jake.

"Me, too," he agreed.

"Have you seen anything in the flashes? Is your dad sending us more messages?"

"I don't know," he said slowly.

She gave him a speculative look. "That sounds like you did see something. What?"

"Every time there's a flash, I feel like I see something round and gold."

"Like a coin?"

"Could be. It's not clear. And it's probably just the light bouncing off something that creates that illusion."

"Probably." As the rain increased, she felt like screaming or crying or both. "Is it ever going to stop?"

"Any second now," he said reassuringly.

"You used to be a better liar."

"I never lied to you, Kat. You might not have liked what I had to say, but it was always the truth."

She had to admit that brutal honesty had been more his style.

A loud roaring sound filled her ears. "What's that? It sounds like a plane. Would anyone really be flying in this weather?" she asked.

He stared back at her as the roar increased. "It does sound like a plane, but...Shit!"

"What's wrong?" She'd barely gotten the words out when a rush of water came over the rocks.

Jake jumped up, and she followed, but then stumbled as another huge wave of water took her legs out from under her. She tried to grab for her bag, but it was already gone.

She didn't know where the flood had come from, but the hillside had disappeared under the strong muddy current.

Jake grabbed her hand as they both lost their footing and were swept down the hillside that had taken them so long to climb.

Her body hit rocks and ground and trees. She felt like she was being battered and ripped apart, and there was nothing she could do about it.

"Hang on," Jake yelled, a wild light in his eyes.

She wanted to do just that, but the current was too strong. It was ripping them apart. "I'm slipping."

"Don't let go, Katherine."

"I'm trying not to," she screamed, but she couldn't fight the power of the flood.

Her hand slipped away from Jake's. She went under the water and came up gasping for air. "Jake?" she yelled, seeing him nowhere in the dark, rushing water. Terror ripped through her as another wave sent her head back under the water.

It would stop, she told herself. The water would slow down, or she'd find a way to grab on to something and hang on...any second now...

Ten

A dozen curses ran through Jake's head as he battled the current and the trees and the huge rocks that seemed to slam into him every time he came up for air. He couldn't see Katherine anymore, and that terrified him. She'd never been the strongest of swimmers.

But she was determined, he told himself. She wouldn't give up. She'd fight like hell to survive.

Finally, the rush of water began to slow as the trees split the current in dozens of directions, defusing the power of the flood. He managed to hook his arms around a tree, and then with all the energy he had left in his body he pulled himself halfway up the trunk. It was so damn dark, he couldn't see anything.

"Katherine," he yelled. "Katherine."

He could barely hear his own voice over the rush of water.

He didn't have his backpack anymore. No phone and no lantern to spill some light on the situation, which was no doubt going to present more problems down the road. But right now all he cared about was finding Katherine. He could not lose her.

"Katherine," he cried out again.

She didn't answer his call, but when the lightning lit up

the area around him, he could see her bobbing in and out of the water about ten feet away from him. He let go of the tree and swam in her direction, which was thankfully exactly where the current wanted to take him.

Katherine slammed into a tree and tried to find a way to hold on, but she was losing the battle. He knew he had about one second to get to her before she'd be gone again. He swam through the water as hard as he could, barreling into her, pinning her body against the tree. He wrapped one arm around the tree and the other arm around her.

She stared at him in shock and amazement.

"Hang on," he said. "Let's try to get on the other side of this tree. There's less water."

Together, they managed to edge around the tree. When they finally got to the other side, he saw a low hanging branch that could lead them to the safety of some rocks a dozen feet away.

"You need to grab that branch and use it to cross over to the rocks," he told her.

"I can't. I'm too tired. I can barely hang on to you."

"You can do this, Kat. I believe in you."

"It's too hard, Jake. Go without me."

"No way. Nothing has ever been too difficult for you. You like challenges, remember? And the bottom line is that I'm not going without you." She didn't say anything, but he could see the light coming back into her eyes. "I'm going to lift you up. You grab the branch and kick your way across. I'll be right behind you."

"I'll try," she said.

"On three. One-Two-Three." He used all of his might to help pull her high enough out of the water so she could grab the branch. She almost didn't make it, but Katherine used whatever energy she had left to grab on and then move her hands across the branch as she kicked her way through the water, finally landing on the rocks.

Once she was safe on the ground, he went across the

same branch, hoping it would hold his weight.

He was two feet short when he heard the branch crack, and his body sank deeper into the water.

"Jake," Katherine yelled, extending her hand to him. "Grab on."

"You can't hold me."

"I can do it. Come on."

He swung his legs as hard as he could and then jumped toward Katherine's outstretched hand. True to her word, she hung on as he landed half on the rocks and half in the water. She helped pull him to safety and then they both collapsed, gasping for breath.

They lay there for several long minutes as the flooding water ran past them.

Finally, he sat up. Katherine was on her side, coughing up water. He patted her on the back. "You okay?"

She nodded.

"So the mountains weren't a great idea," he said lightly.

"You think?" She shot him a dark look.

"I thought going up would be safer for us."

"It probably was. If we'd been on lower ground, we might have drowned before we even realized what was happening." She moved into a sitting position her feet tucked under her and her arms wrapped around her body. Her blonde hair was soaking wet and plastered against her face and back. When she turned to look at him, he could still see the fear in her wide eyes. "What are we going to do now? I lost my bag, my phone, my computer, my passport—everything."

"Me, too, but we're still alive. Still beating the odds."

"Barely." Her mouth trembled. "I thought I lost you, Jake. I thought you were gone."

"Hey, you know how hard I am to get rid of," he teased. "I'm like a bad penny; I keep showing up."

"I thought I was the bad penny." She tried to smile, but she couldn't quite get there as tears streamed down her face. He wrapped his arms around her. "We're going to be okay,

Kat."

She rested her face against his chest as her body heaved with sobs. He let her cry. She needed to release the tension, and he needed to hold her, to feel her body against his, because for a while there, he'd thought he'd lost her, too.

The idea of a world without Katherine in it seemed too painful to contemplate. She might not have been in his life for a decade, but he'd always known she was all right, and that was something.

The water around them began to recede about the same time Katherine's tears did. The storm had also passed, and in between the tall trees, he could see moonlight.

Katherine finally lifted her head to look at him. She rubbed her eyes. "Sorry. I never cry."

"I guess you were overdue. You don't have to apologize. That was terrifying."

"I don't know how you found me again, Jake. When I saw you coming toward me, I couldn't believe it."

"It was the lightning. It lit up the area and I saw you, so I went after you."

"You mean you were already out of the water and you jumped back in?" she asked in amazement.

"Not exactly. I had scrambled up a tree, but I wasn't on dry ground."

"But you still went back into the current to get to me?"

"I didn't want to be out here alone," he joked.

She shook her head, amazement in her eyes. "You are so much better than me, Jake. I let you drown all those years ago, but when you had the same choice—"

"It wasn't the same choice. Back then I was only figuratively drowning in my grief. Today, you were actually going under water, and like I said, I didn't want to be out here alone, not without a smart doctor telling me what to do next."

"I have no idea what to do next. We need shelter, and I'd love to get out of these wet clothes, but I think we're miles away from anything. And we could still run into those men again."

"You've once again clearly identified the problems in front of us."

"Sorry."

"I doubt those men are walking around in this storm. So I'm not going to worry about them right now. But I do think we should start walking again. Even though it's dark, we can't stay here. Let's head away from all this water."

"I wonder where we are now. I can still see that road in my head, but where did the water bring us?"

He shrugged. "I don't know." He got up and held out his hand to her. She stood up, holding onto him for a moment.

"I feel a little weak," she said.

"Me, too."

"But while my body might be worn out, I am mentally tough. I've been pushing the limits of exhaustion for years; I can do this."

He smiled at her mental pep talk and realized her words had imbued him with a renewed sense of purpose. He could push himself, too, and that's what he was going to do, because there was really no other option.

They walked for about a half hour. He honestly had no idea what direction they were going. He couldn't see enough of the night sky to use the stars to guide him, and he was more than a little worried that they were going to end up nowhere closer to civilization than they'd been before.

But then, to his surprise, they came through the trees and stepped onto what appeared to be a dirt road. Down that road about a mile, he saw lights.

"Oh, my God," Katherine said, putting her hand on his arm. "Is that a house, Jake?"

"I sure as hell hope so, and I hope the people inside aren't wearing uniforms or carrying guns."

"Right now, I don't know if I care who's inside."

"You care. We should stay on the side of the road, close to the trees, just in case we don't like what we see when we get closer."

"It has to be help, Jake—it just has to be."

"Let's find out."

They picked up the pace, their energy restored by the sight of lights. When they got closer to the property, he could see a house and a barn about fifty feet away.

"Look, a baby swing," Katherine said, pointing to the porch. "I think a family lives here, Jake."

Through the curtains, he could see a man and a woman in the living room, and he felt immensely reassured by that sight. He just hoped they'd answer the door and not be alarmed by their dripping appearance. His watch had stopped in the flood, but he was guessing it was about eight o'clock at night.

He knocked on the door.

A moment later, a man stood in front of them. He appeared to be in his fifties or sixties and had black hair tinged with gray, dark eyes, and weathered, ruddy skin. He held a rifle in his hands and judging by the look in his eyes, he wouldn't hesitate to use it.

"*Hola*," Jake said, giving the man a smile. "*Ingles?*"

The man stared back at them without replying, which wasn't a good sign.

"Didn't your great-grandmother teach you any Spanish?" Katherine asked him.

"Mamich always wanted to talk in English when I visited her," he replied.

"Let me try. I know some phrases from the hospital. *Nos puedes ayudar?*"

The man looked from Jake to Katherine. He hesitated and then glanced over his shoulder.

"What did you ask him, Kat?"

"If he could help us."

A woman came to the door. She had the same dark hair, dark eyes and olive skin as the man, but she appeared to be in her late twenties. "Papa?" she questioned looking from the older man to Jake and Katherine.

The man said something to his daughter in Spanish.

"What's wrong?" she asked them.

Relief ran through Jake. "You speak English."

"*Sí*. You are American?"

"Yes," Jake replied. "We're sorry to bother you, but we got caught in a flood, and we lost everything. We've been walking for hours, and we haven't seen another house. Do you have a phone?"

"The cell phone doesn't work out here," she said. "I am Gloria. This is my father, Eduardo Lopez."

"I'm Jake, and this is Katherine," he returned.

"*Hola*," Katherine said.

"Come inside. We'll get you some dry clothes to change into. It's been a terrible storm tonight."

"*Gracias*," he said, happy to have found a woman who spoke English and a house that was warm.

"You can leave your coats there." Gloria pointed to a line of hooks by the front door.

Jake was more than happy to shed his waterlogged coat and Katherine seemed thrilled to do the same.

Gloria's father said something to her, but she just waved a dismissive hand and led Jake and Katherine up the stairs.

While the older man didn't try to stop them, Jake was acutely conscious of his suspicious gaze following their every step.

Gloria led them into a bedroom. It was a small room, made even smaller by the double bed and the large dresser and desk in the room.

"This is my brother's room," Gloria said. "He doesn't live here anymore. You can stay here tonight. He left some clothes behind in the closet, Jake. Please use whatever you want." She smiled at Katherine. "I'll get you something from my room." She paused at the sound of a baby's cry, a frown crossing her lips. "I just put her down five minutes ago."

"I hope we didn't wake her," Katherine said.

"She never sleeps. Come with me, Katherine. You can rummage through my drawers while I get my daughter."

"I'll meet you downstairs," Jake said.

Katherine paused in the doorway. "Thanks for getting me here, Jake."

He tipped his head. "I'm glad we found some good luck for a change."

"Me, too."

When they entered the room across the hall, Gloria walked quickly over to a bassinet and picked up a very angry baby. The infant didn't appear to be more than a few weeks old. Gloria patted her daughter's back as she pulled clothes out of the dresser and tossed them on the bed. "You can change in the bathroom. I'm going to try to feed her again."

"*Gracias*, Gloria," Katherine said, feeling an overwhelming debt of gratitude toward this young woman who had taken two strangers into her house. She wondered if she would have done the same—probably not. Although, she would have called someone for help, but that was different than actually getting involved. Still, this was a very different world—a remote location and no phone. Maybe, strangely enough the lack of technology made people more willing to help each other.

"Bring your wet clothes out when you're done, and we'll put them in the dryer. And then we'll get you and your husband some food. You're hungry, *sí*?"

"Yes," Katherine agreed, her stomach rumbling at the thought of food. "Starving." She didn't bother to say that Jake wasn't her husband; she was far more interested in getting dry.

She took Gloria's clothes into the bathroom and indulged in a hot shower before drying off and changing into black leggings, a long-sleeved tunic, and thick socks. She felt so much better just being clean and warm and dry. But her good mood evaporated when she returned to the bedroom and found both the baby and Gloria crying.

"What's wrong?" Katherine asked, sitting down on the bed next to Gloria, who was propped up against the pillows, trying to get her daughter to nurse.

"She won't eat. I can't get her to take my breast. She's hungry, and I can't feed her. I keep trying, but it just doesn't work. She's not comfortable. I'm not a good mother."

Katherine felt a wave of sympathy for Gloria's obvious distress. "Your baby is just trying to figure it out, that's all. How old is she?"

"Ten days. The nurse is supposed to come tomorrow, but I'm afraid my daughter will starve to death before then. She sucks for a minute and then she starts to cry. I gave her some formula earlier, but she doesn't like the bottle either. She takes just a little and then she screams."

Katherine frowned. "Poor thing. It sounds like she's all mixed up. May I hold her?"

"Do you know about babies? Are you a mother?"

"I'm not a mother, but I'm a doctor. A pediatrician, actually."

Gloria's mouth dropped open. "A doctor? Do you know what's wrong with her?" she asked as she handed the squirming, screaming baby to Katherine.

"Let's take a look," Katherine said.

She checked the baby's skin color and eyes for jaundice and gently palpated her abdomen to see if she could feel any obstructions or masses, but aside from the baby's obvious distress, she didn't feel or see any abnormalities. "Was it a normal birth, Gloria?"

"*Sí*. I thought everything was fine. My friends said that breastfeeding would be easy, but I can't do it."

"Well, she's getting some nutrients; I can see that. First thing we need to do is try to calm her down."

"I don't know how to do that."

"Let's try something. One of the pediatricians I trained with showed me a little trick. There's a way to hold a very young baby to comfort them." Katherine pulled the baby's right arm to her side and then brought the child's left arm across her chest. Then Katherine held the baby's arms in place with her own hand, her fingers gently resting under the baby's chin. With her other hand, she held the baby's bottom and gently rocked her back and forth.

Almost immediately, the baby stopped crying.

"Oh, my God, how did you do that?" Gloria asked. "It's a miracle."

"Not a miracle—just a position that comforts her. Now that she's calming down, you can try breastfeeding again."

"She'll just start crying again."

"Let's try a slightly different position. First, I want you to take the baby and just hold her like I'm holding her. Bring her close to your body and just let her rest against your bare skin. Let her feel you for a minute. You both need to relax, to feel in touch with each other."

"All right," Gloria said, taking the baby. "I'll try."

"She's probably picking up on your worry and nervousness," Katherine added. "The calmer you can be, the calmer she can be. I know that's difficult, but try taking some deep breaths and just speak softly to her."

Gloria did as Katherine suggested, speaking in soft Spanish to the child who was now nestled against her bare breasts. Katherine piled extra pillows on Gloria's lap and encouraged her to shift the baby higher so they were both belly to belly, and Gloria didn't have to lean over or hold the baby up to her breast. Within a moment, the baby opened her mouth, and with a few more words of encouragement, she latched onto Gloria's breast and began to nurse.

"She's doing it. She's taking in milk," Gloria said in amazement. "I'm afraid to breathe."

"Don't be afraid. Just enjoy. And no crying," she added, seeing the tears gathering in the young woman's eyes. "This is a good thing."

"I've been so worried. I thought she hated me. She wouldn't eat; she wouldn't sleep. All she would do is cry. She has been driving Papa mad."

"It's hard to see your baby cry, but think of her cries as her words. You'll soon figure out what she really needs. You're going to be fine, Gloria."

"She doesn't usually stay on my breast this long."

"She's comfortable, and so are you."

"Thank you so much. I will be forever grateful."

"I'm the one who should be thanking you for taking two strangers into your home."

"I think you were sent here for a reason. You should go downstairs now. Papa is heating up some soup. You must be hungry."

"I am, but I can stay with you if you want."

"I'm fine now. If you take your clothes down to the laundry room, you can put them in the dryer."

"I'll do that."

"And Katherine, my father speaks English when he wants to."

She smiled. "Good to know."

Katherine left Gloria and went down to the kitchen. After putting her clothes in the dryer, she went into the kitchen and found Jake sitting at the table, studying a map. Eduardo stood at the stove, stirring something in a big pot. When he saw Katherine, he tipped his head toward the table.

"Whatever you're making smells delicious," she said as she sat down.

"Have some bread." Jake pushed the plate of what appeared to be freshly baked bread in her direction. "It's better than the chocolate bar we ate earlier."

She ripped off a piece, buttered it and devoured the bread in three bites. "You're right. I've never tasted anything so good."

"There's more coming."

Eduardo set two bowls of thick, spicy soup on the table.

"This is delicious," Katherine said, in heaven after one spoonful.

Eduardo sat down across from them and pointed to the map on the table. "You are here," he said.

Katherine followed his finger and realized they were farther south than she'd realized, which gave her hope. "We need to go to Nic Té Há," she said. "Do you know where that is?"

Eduardo frowned and shook his head.

"It's a small village," Jake said. "It's about thirty miles from the airport in Tuxtla Gutiérrez."

"Ah, *sí*," Eduardo drew his finger down the map and pointed to another area.

"How far?" Jake asked.

"Five hundred fifty kilometers."

"That's about three hundred sixty miles," Jake said.

"It looks closer on the map," she said with disappointment.

"Is there a bus or a train?" Jake asked.

"The bus makes many stops. You can get a car in Palenque."

"How far is that?" Katherine asked.

"Thirty kilometers. I can drive you in the morning," Eduardo replied.

"That would be wonderful," she said. "We're very thankful for your kindness."

"We are more than thankful for *your* kindness," Gloria said, walking into the room with her baby daughter now asleep on her shoulder. "Papa, she ate—finally. Katherine showed me how to calm her and feed her. I prayed for someone to help me, and God sent an angel to my door."

Eduardo gave Katherine a look filled with gratitude. "*Gracias*. Gloria has been so worried."

"It was nothing," she said feeling a little uncomfortable with their praise.

"Would you like more soup?" Eduardo asked her.

"If there's enough, I would love a little more," she admitted. "I think it's the best soup I've ever had."

"Papa is an excellent cook," Gloria said, sitting down at the table. "He's cooked for me since my mother died when I was ten years old. He's still taking care of me now. My husband is an American. He's in the Army. We were living in South Carolina until he got deployed. I didn't have any family there so I came home until he gets out in six months."

"That must be very difficult," Katherine said.

"Papa takes good care of us, but I miss my husband."

"I'm sure you do." Katherine paused, wanting to be honest with Gloria and Eduardo. "There's something we need to tell you. Jake and I were flying to see his great-grandmother when our plane went down on Saturday. We've been wandering around ever since. We thought we were getting help, but then we saw men with guns, and they blew up the plane. We ran for our lives. We don't know why they did what they did or if they're still looking for us. We don't want to put your family in danger, so if we need to go now, we will." She deliberately didn't look at Jake, knowing that she probably should have spoken to him first before giving up their safe house.

Eduardo's lips tightened. "I saw the fire, but it was quickly put out by the storm. I didn't see a plane go down."

"Do you know who would destroy our plane?" Jake asked.

"Probably the Montenegro cartel," Gloria said. "They control this area. They might have thought you were spying on their operation."

"We weren't doing that."

"I will take you beyond Palenque," Eduardo said. "I will get you safely away."

"What about money?" Gloria asked. "You said you lost everything."

"We did," Katherine said with a nod. "We were up in the

hills when a rush of water took us flying down the mountain."

"There is a river high in the mountains," Eduardo said. "It floods with the rains this time of year."

"We'll give you enough money to get a car," Gloria said, exchanging a look with her father.

"You're very generous," she said. "We'll pay you back."

"I'm not worried," Gloria replied. "When did you last see the men?"

"It was early this morning," Jake answered. "Do you know how far away the fire was? We've lost track of where we were."

"My guess would be about twelve kilometers," Eduardo put in.

"That's all? I felt like we walked fifty miles," Katherine said, thinking they really hadn't gotten that far for all the effort. Her sigh turned into a yawn. Now that she was warm and dry and her stomach was full, she felt overwhelmingly tired.

"You should go to bed," Gloria said. "You both must be exhausted."

"Let me help you clean up," she offered.

Eduardo waved her away. "Go. Sleep. We will leave in the morning. If anyone comes to the door tonight, you will stay in your room. *Si?*"

"Yes," Jake said. "We understand."

"Good night," Katherine added.

As they walked up the stairs, she glanced at Jake. "I should have talked to you before I suggested we leave. I just felt they needed to know we could be bringing them trouble. They were being so nice."

"It's fine. At least you waited until they thought you were an angel. Then they couldn't throw you out."

She smiled. "I didn't do that much."

"Whatever you did, I'm thrilled. We've eaten, we have a roof over our heads, and tomorrow we have a ride to town. All our immediate problems have been solved."

She nodded, but as soon as they entered the guest room and her gaze fell on the double bed, she realized that there might still be one problem...

Eleven

> ⇒⇒⇒⇐⇐⇐

Katherine looked over at Jake as he walked over to the bed. "What do you think?"

He shook his head. "No way am I sleeping on the floor, Katherine. We're sharing this bed."

"I wasn't going to ask you to sleep on the floor." She actually didn't know why she'd said anything, because all she'd done was bring attention to the fact that they were going to sleep together.

"Good, because I'm not going to, and neither are you."

She got into bed next to him, careful to keep some space between them, which wasn't easy in the full-sized bed. She rolled onto her side and tucked her hands under her head, facing Jake. "I have to admit, I can't quite believe we're safe. A few hours ago, I wasn't sure we would make it."

"I never had a doubt."

"Liar."

He smiled. "So, what miracle did you work with Gloria and her baby?"

"She was having trouble breastfeeding. I showed her a technique that usually calms a baby down and then helped her get into a better position. It wasn't a big deal."

"It was to her."

"She's a nervous young mother whose husband is

deployed. She just needed a little support."

"Well, I think you made a friend for life. Her father liked you, too. I had no idea he spoke English until you came downstairs, though. He didn't say a word to me."

"Gloria told me he spoke English, but that he's distrustful of strangers."

"Can't say I blame him, but I was happy when he put down the gun."

"I'm actually glad he has one, just in case those men come knocking on the door."

Jake frowned. "I had a gun in the backpack."

"You did? I didn't know that."

"We have them in the cockpit now. I put it in the bag before we left, but that's long gone."

"I know Gloria said she'd lend us money for a car, but how are we going to get around Mexico without passports?"

He sighed. "We'll figure it out. If we can get to my great-grandmother's, she'll be able to help us with all that."

"Okay. I'll worry about that tomorrow."

"Finally, an attitude I can get on board with," he teased.

She smiled back at him. "I guess you're rubbing off on me."

"About time." He paused. "You want to hear something crazy?"

He put his hand on her hip, and her pulse leapt. She was suddenly acutely aware of the fact that they were in bed together. "What's that?" she asked, her voice a little too breathy.

"I'm not as sleepy as I was downstairs."

"Really? How is that possible? We climbed a mountain, walked about a hundred miles, and fought our way through a flood. You should be exhausted."

He gave her the lazy, sexy smile that always sent butterflies dancing through her stomach. "It was quite a day, and we survived. I think we should celebrate."

"I'm not sure I like where you're going with this."

"Oh, you'd like it very much, Kat."

"Jake," she said, sighing a little. "We don't even like each other anymore."

"Don't we?" he asked, his fingers tracing a circle on her hip. "I told you earlier that I thought you were amazing today."

"You weren't bad, either, but it wouldn't be smart. We have enough problems to deal with."

"Do we always have to think about every possible outcome before we do something?"

"I usually do. You know that."

His grin broadened. "That's true. You and your very long pro and con lists. I sometimes wondered how I ever made the cut."

"You wouldn't go away. I tried to get rid of you more than a few times."

"But I kept coming back. You were too special not to fight for, Kat."

Her heart warmed at his words. "And you were too irresistible to fight against," she murmured. "You could talk me into anything. Sometimes it feels like a hundred years ago when we were together, and sometimes it feels like yesterday."

"If it feels like yesterday, does that mean I can still talk you into something?"

"You are *bad*, Jake."

"You used to like that about me."

She still did. "We should just sleep. We need to rest for tomorrow."

"I feel too wired at the moment. I think you do, too." He paused. "It doesn't have to mean anything, Katherine."

"It always seems to mean something with you, Jake." She looked into his beautiful green eyes. "Even when I don't want it to."

"Think of it as a celebration of life. We survived a flash flood, for God's sake."

She licked her lips, so tempted by his words. She needed to find some way to say no. "What about protection? I'm on birth control, but there are other issues to consider."

"I'm healthy. What about you?"

"I am, but to be absolutely certain, we should have a condom."

He laughed. "I love it when you talk dirty to me."

She punched him in the arm. "I'm a doctor. I know what is important."

"You're not a doctor tonight. You're Kat—the most beautiful girl I've ever seen with silky blonde hair, incredible blue eyes, and the softest, sexiest mouth I've ever tasted. You're the girl whose body I dreamed about every night for years, a dream that went on far longer than our relationship." The green in his eyes deepened with emotion. "I want you, Kat. Is there any chance you want me, too?"

His intimate, tender words stole the last of her resistance. "There's a chance," she whispered.

His answering smile made her pulse jump.

Jake slid across the mattress, putting his arm around her, snuggling against her so close his warm breath teased her mouth. She soaked up his heat with absolute delight. The mattress cradled their bodies, the pillows soft beneath their heads. Everything felt so good, and then even better when Jake touched her mouth with his.

Closing her eyes, she surrendered. She wanted his kiss, his touch, his body...everything. She wanted to escape from reality. She wanted to feel something other than pain and discomfort and worry. She wanted him, the boy she'd fallen in love with, the one who'd made her feel reckless and brave and desirable every time he looked at her.

She opened her mouth to him, welcoming the slide of his tongue against her teeth. She slid her hands under his T-shirt, loving the feel of his hard muscles under her fingers.

In her professional life, she could be detached and unemotional and keep her feelings locked deep inside, but now, with Jake, she was all emotion. Her brain had completely shut down. She wanted to be with Jake, and she didn't want to care about what would happen tomorrow or next week or next year. Tonight was all that was important.

Jake's hands crept up under her top, and she tore herself away from his kiss so she could pull her shirt up and over her head. Her bra and underwear were still in the dryer downstairs. Once she shed the clothes Gloria had given her, she was completely bare.

Jake made fast work of his clothes as well, and when they came together again, they were skin to skin.

It felt both familiar and incredibly different making love to Jake now. He was passionate yet restrained, in a needy hurry at times and deliciously, mind-blowingly slow at others. When she urged him to go faster, he gave her a steely-eyed look that told her he was going to make her crazy with want before he gave her what she wanted.

And what she wanted was *him*—all of him.

His body was beautifully mature; his chest broader than she remembered, his arms stronger, his touch more possessive, more knowledgeable. His hands were everywhere, his mouth following close behind, until she was writhing on the bed from an overwhelming surge of sensation.

She wanted to explore his body as much as he wanted to explore hers, to taste him, and to torture him in exactly the same way. But as much as she wanted to take control, Jake wouldn't give in. It was clear he was running the show, and it was exciting and sexy to surrender, to let him lead, because where he led felt amazing.

When he finally slid into her body, she cried out his name in absolute pleasure.

They moved in perfect sync, the rhythm between them matching their frantic breathing and racing hearts, until they came together in a passion that was both old and new, that touched her soul, her heart, and all the parts she hid away from everyone but Jake.

After a few moments, Jake rolled over onto his back, and pulled her into the crook of his shoulder. She rested her head on his chest and felt almost deliriously happy.

"I thought it would be like before," Jake muttered.

There was something in his tone that brought her head up. She gazed into his eyes. "But it wasn't?"

He shook his head. "It was better. How is that possible?"

She had to admit to sharing the sentiment. "I don't know. We got better with age?"

He laughed and stroked her back. "We did."

She settled back against him, throwing her arm across his waist as she closed her eyes, exhaustion sweeping back over her. "Time for sleep."

She waited for Jake to answer, but the steadiness of his breath told her he'd already slipped into dreamland, and she was eager to follow.

When Jake woke up, Katherine was gone. He stared at the tangled sheets in bemusement. He ran a hand through his hair and then glanced at the clock on the nightstand. It was eight o'clock and there was sun coming through the windows.

He hadn't planned on sleeping so late. He'd wanted to be on the road as early as possible. He wondered why Katherine hadn't woken him.

Katherine.

He smiled at the memories of last night. Making love to her had been better than he'd remembered. He just wished he hadn't fallen asleep. He also wished she'd woken him before she'd gotten out of bed this morning.

But he suspected Katherine already had her guard back up.

As much as that annoyed him, he had to consider that it might be a good thing. They had a lot of other things to focus on today. The night they'd shared was going to have to be a memory for now. He'd told her earlier that it didn't have to mean anything. He hadn't really believed it when he said it, but he'd wanted her more than he'd wanted to speak the truth. Being with Katherine had always meant *something*, and being without her again was probably going to bring back a boatload of pain.

But the way he felt right now...he had to believe it was worth it.

He got out of bed and went into the bathroom. When he returned to the bedroom wearing nothing but a towel, he caught Katherine putting his dry clothes on the bed.

Her eyes widened, and her mouth parted when she saw him. The remembered intimacy between them flashed through her eyes in a way that made his body immediately harden.

"I brought your clothes," she said quickly.

"I can see that. I'm not necessarily in a hurry to put them on."

"You should be, because Eduardo is almost done making breakfast for us, and it looks spectacular."

"You look spectacular."

"Your vision is obviously not that great. I'm pretty beat up."

"Even beat up, you're the most beautiful woman I've ever seen."

"You shouldn't keep saying things like that, Jake."

"Even if it's true?"

"You said it didn't have to mean anything, Jake, so all these compliments aren't necessary."

He'd known she'd retreat, put her walls back up, but knowing it and experiencing it were two very different things. Katherine always had to make things hard, but maybe that was part of the appeal. She'd always been a challenge, and she still was.

"So get dressed, and I'll meet you downstairs," she

continued. "I want to get on the road as soon as possible, Jake. We still need to find TJ."

He grabbed her by the arm as she turned to leave. "I know what we need to do, Katherine, and we'll do it," he promised. "But I'm not going to regret last night."

She stared back at him for a long second. "I don't regret it, either."

"Good." He let go of her arm, and she practically sprinted to the door. He wanted to believe her speedy escape was because she was fighting her own desire to stay with him, but that might just be a nice story he was telling himself, he thought dryly.

Dropping his towel, he got dressed and went downstairs.

An hour later, they said good-bye to Gloria and squeezed onto the bench seat in the cab of Eduardo's pickup truck.

As they drove down a very long and lonely road, Jake kept an eye out for any sign of the men they'd escaped the day before, but there were no other vehicles in sight.

Twenty minutes into the trip, Eduardo pointed out the area where he'd seen the fire.

Jake nodded but had no interest in slowing down. He wanted to get as far away from the area of danger as possible.

Several miles down the road, they passed a few other farms and small houses and then eventually a village that was little more than a couple of streets and a half dozen houses. But Eduardo kept going, telling them a bigger city would offer more transportation options.

"Do you think your phone will work now, Eduardo?" Jake asked.

"*Sí*," Eduardo said, handing over his cell phone.

Relief washed over him as he saw the bars light up on the phone. He punched in Rusty's number. "It's Jake," he said.

"Well, it's about damn time," Rusty said. "Where the hell are you? I texted you back a dozen times yesterday, but you didn't answer after that first one you sent. I thought you fell off a cliff."

"That's about right. I wasn't getting a signal. I didn't know if the text even went through. Does my mom know I'm all right?"

"Yeah, Alicia was actually with me when you texted. She was hounding me every second about the search."

Jake smiled to himself. "I have no doubt. I actually thought she was already back in Miami."

"I caught her and her fiancé right before they were going to the airport. She texted you too, but you didn't answer. She said if I heard from you to let you know that she would make sure Katherine's mother was all right."

"That's great."

"We pinged your phone for your location, but the storms kept the searchers on the ground. Where are you now, Jake?"

He hesitated. "I'm not sure. I don't have my phone anymore, but Katherine and I are all right. We're getting a ride into some town. You can call off the search now."

"How are you getting home?"

"I'm not sure yet. Katherine has something she needs to do down here. When that's done, we'll be on the first plane out, although, I may need you to fax a copy of our passports to the airport down here."

"You don't have your passport anymore?"

"No, it's a long story."

"I'd sure like to hear it. What happened to the plane?"

"Lightning took out the instrument panel. It was a monster storm."

"It grew bigger and moved faster than we expected," Rusty agreed. "I couldn't believe what I saw on the radar."

"Me, either."

"You can never do this to me again, Jake. I can't go to your mom's house one more time and say those words."

"I wouldn't want you to."

"It was rough. Your mom was really shaken up, but she's all right now. She'll feel better when you're home."

"Yeah. Look, you're starting to cut out. I'll call you as

soon as I know my plans to get home."

"Make it soon, Jake."

"As soon as I can."

He handed the phone back to Eduardo. "*Gracias.*"

"Were they searching for us?" Katherine asked.

"Yes."

"It's funny that we never heard or saw any planes."

"They were probably miles from where we were."

"But they traced your cell phone."

"He said the storms grounded them soon after he got the text."

"That makes sense. Thanks for not mentioning my brother to Rusty."

"I know what I'm doing. One of these days you're going to believe that," he said with a smile.

"One of these days," she echoed, smiling back at him.

It was after eleven when they reached Las Flores, a city boasting a population of 6,024 people. Eduardo rented a car for them, provided them with a small amount of cash and wished them well on their journey.

Jake assured Eduardo that he'd return the money when he got back home.

After buying some snacks and bottled water for the trip, they got on a two-lane highway that would hopefully take them to Nic Té Há. Jake anticipated the trip would take five to six hours, which should get them there around six. He didn't look forward to spending another cold night outside, and with their limited cash, he didn't think a hotel would be an option.

Katherine turned on the radio, and the car was flooded with Latin music. He didn't know if she just wanted a barrier to any personal conversation or if she was in the mood for some music, but he was happy enough to listen to the radio and try to enjoy the drive. There was a lot of open space along the highway, and most of it was green and quite beautiful. The storm had ended, and while there were still clouds passing across the sky, the worst of it was over. He hoped that was true for them, too.

Over the next two hours, his confidence grew. They were making good time. He hadn't seen anyone following them, and in the old Chevy that Eduardo had rented them, they didn't stand out, either. No one gave them a second look.

Their luck had finally changed.

That thought had no sooner crossed his mind than the back tire popped and the car swerved out of control.

Katherine gasped in alarm.

He hit the brakes hard, trying to steer in the direction of the skid, and they eventually ended up on the side of the highway. Thankfully, the empty road had prevented them from running into any other cars on their sixty-second wild ride.

As he shut down the car, he hit the steering wheel hard. "Dammit." Then he got out to look at the damage.

Katherine scrambled out of the passenger side and joined him by the back right tire, which was as flat as a pancake.

"We must have run over something," she said.

"Or the old tire just burst." He opened up the trunk in search of a spare, but there was nothing in the empty space but the jack. He squatted down to see if the spare was under the car, but there was nothing. "No fucking way," he muttered. He jumped back to his feet. "There's no spare, Katherine."

She stared back at him in dismay. "Well, what are we going to do?"

"How the hell should I know?"

The flat tire was suddenly the last straw. He kicked the tire with his shoe, not once, but twice, then three times and a fourth for good measure all the while shouting every swear word that came to mind.

He hit the back of the car with his fist, making sure both his foot and hand were aching with pain before he finally backed off from assaulting the vehicle.

Katherine had moved away from him and stood with her arms crossed as she waited for his anger to cool down.

"Are you done?" she asked. "Do you want to smash a window? Maybe pull the door off and throw it across the road?"

"How can you be so calm? Do you realize that we are once again stranded with no transportation, very little food, and even less money? We haven't seen a car in the last thirty minutes."

"Someone will come along."

He eyed her in amazement. "Really? That's what *you* think? You, the biggest worrier of all time, are going to just wait for someone to come along?"

"We don't have a choice, and we're on the highway. I'm sure there will be another car soon."

"Maybe, maybe not." He slammed the trunk shut. "I thought our luck was changing. How stupid was that? We either have no luck or it's all bad."

Every stress-filled moment of the past two days fueled his anger. He did want to smash a window, and if he didn't have to keep the car intact to use as possible shelter, he would have done just that.

"I hate Mexico." He leaned against the car and folded his arms across his chest.

Katherine walked over to him and surprised him by putting her hands on his shoulders. She looked into his eyes. "It's going to be all right, Jake."

"You sound so sure."

"I am. And you'll think that, too, as soon as you get over wanting to kill the car."

He reluctantly smiled at her words. "That tire was the last straw."

"I know. I get it. I might have done the same thing if you

hadn't gone off like an angry rocket."

"Who doesn't put a spare in a rental car?"

"Maybe that's why the rental was so cheap. How far away from your great-grandmother's do you think we are now?"

"Three hours. We were making good time until this. I thought we'd get there before dark."

"We might still be able to do that."

"You're being surprisingly optimistic."

"After what we've been through, things don't seem as dire as they did yesterday."

"Not yet anyway," he said darkly. "So what's the plan, Miss Calm, Cool and Collected?"

"Stay with the car until we get a ride."

"We're going to be an easy target if anyone is looking for us."

She frowned. "We're pretty far away now, Jake. I think we've lost them."

"Really? I have no idea what to think. My brain is blocked."

"That's because you're pissed off. We need to get you in a better mood so you can start thinking again."

"Oh, yeah? How do you intend to do that?" His heart pounded against his chest when he saw the answer in her eyes. "Seriously? Here?"

"Just a kiss. No big deal, right?"

He didn't have time to answer because her sweet mouth was on his, and every bad feeling slid out of his head. He didn't really care about anything except the fact that Katherine was kissing him. The rest of the world could go to hell. He'd just stay in this moment, with this woman.

But, of course, as luck would have it, the rumble of a car broke them apart.

Despite the bad timing, he was thrilled to see a farm truck lumbering down the road in the direction they needed to go. There was a man and a big dog in the cab, and several crates of chickens in the bed of the truck.

Katherine stepped out in the road and waved the truck down. The driver motioned toward the back of the truck.

"I guess he's giving us a ride," Katherine said. "But not in the front."

"I'll take it." He grabbed their bag of food and water and then helped her into the back of the truck. As the truck lurched forward, they sat down in the middle of the bed, surrounded by crates of squawking chickens.

He smiled at Katherine, and she grinned back at him.

"So, what do you think—best ride ever?" she asked, having to speak loudly to be heard over the chickens.

"I couldn't have asked for more," he said dryly. "You, me, an ancient truck and some pissed-off chickens."

"It's an adventure. At high school graduation, you told me that we were going to have an adventurous life. Do you remember that?"

"Vaguely," he grumbled. "I said a lot of stupid shit back then."

"Stupid or not, I'd say you achieved that goal."

"The last thing you wanted was adventure, Kat."

"You're right. I didn't want to take any risks. I just wanted to be safe and for everyone around me to be safe. I didn't want to make a friend and lose them the way I did with Hailey. After her death, I worried all the time. It became a habit as familiar and as necessary to me as breathing."

He nodded. "I get that, but you sound like something has changed."

She laughed. "Everything has changed. Over the last few days, my life has gone upside down, spun around, and turned inside out. I have absolutely no control over anything that is happening right now. I think I finally just realized that."

"You don't seem as upset about it as I would expect."

"I've finally let go. I've surrendered."

He smiled. "Surrender has always looked good on you."

She laughed again. "That is the worst line you have ever

said to me, and you've said some really cheesy lines, Jake."

He shrugged. "It wasn't a line; it was the truth."

"Right."

"I'll give you some more truth. You look a lot like the old Kat right now, and I'm happy to see her back."

She shook her head. "I don't want to be the old Kat or even the old Katherine. I want to be someone new—someone who doesn't worry all the time, who doesn't have tunnel vision, who lives more in the moment and less in the future or the past. I just don't know how to change."

"You'll figure it out," he said, meeting her gaze. "And I like the sound of that woman."

"Me, too."

The truck jerked, and he put his arm around her to protect her from slamming into the side. "You okay?" he asked.

"I'm fine. Where do you think we're going to end up, Jake?"

"You mean today or forever?"

She stared back at him. "I'm trying to live in the moment, remember, so let's stick with today."

"We'll know when the truck stops, and he tells us to get out, but I'm hoping that won't be for a while since we're going in the right direction."

The truck jerked again and the chickens started a squawking roar. "Damn," he muttered.

Katherine grinned. "Like I said, best ride ever."

Twelve

Forty-five minutes later, the old truck turned off the highway, kicking up a cloud of dust that sent Katherine into a coughing fit. She wiped her teary eyes as the dust cleared enough for her to read a sign.

"Looks like we're in Valle Verde," she said.

"It doesn't look like a green valley," Jake commented as the truck came to an abrupt stop.

He was right. It looked more like a desert pit stop. While she was happy to see a town of any sort, Valle Verde did not appear all that impressive. There was a bank, a market, a liquor store, and a couple of cafés all within reach of a courthouse and medical clinic.

Jake helped her off the truck. He was always such a gentleman, she thought. Even when he hated her, he was still very conscious of making sure she was all right. She hadn't really appreciated that until this trip.

"Thanks," she said.

Jake let go of her hand to reach into his pocket and pull out what little money they had left to offer to the driver of the truck. The man waved the money away and pointed to a building across the town square that was obviously an auto repair shop.

"*Gracias*," Jake said.

She added her thanks as the man got back into his truck and drove away.

"Are we really going to the auto shop to see if someone can fix the tire on the rental car we left miles back on the side of the highway?" Katherine asked. "That will take way too long."

"I agree. Let's see if we can find a bus station."

She tipped her head toward an old bus making its way down the street. "Let's see where that's going."

They found a small bus depot a couple of blocks away. The clerk spoke enough English to tell them the next bus to cities in Chiapas would leave at three o'clock, in approximately ninety minutes. They could exit the bus at Guadalupe and take another bus into Nic Té Há as there was no direct connection to the village.

With that information, they bought tickets and then wandered down the street to a café. "Do we have enough money for food?" she asked hopefully.

"Just enough."

They ordered tamales and rice and sat down at a small table in the front patio to wait for their meal. Looking around the square, Katherine was reminded that there was a normal world going on and that they were finally back in it. The last few days had been surreal, but they were getting back on track to what they'd come here to do.

The waitress brought them their food and for the next ten minutes they concentrated on eating. "That was the best tamale I've ever had," she told Jake.

He grinned. "Let's see—you've had the best chocolate, the best homemade bread, the best soup and now the best tamale. You're on a roll."

She wadded up her paper napkin and tossed it at him. "I'm just more appreciative of food because it doesn't appear very often. But even if I wasn't starving, that would have been good." She sat back in her chair. "I feel better now. By tonight we should be at your great-grandmother's house, and hopefully she'll be happy to see us, or at least you."

"No one is ever unwelcome at her home. I'm glad you're going to finally meet her."

"Finally?" she queried.

"I told her a lot about you when I was here last. You were fresh on my mind."

She frowned at that piece of information. "So she's going to hate me on sight. Great."

"No, my great-grandmother sees past everyone's outer wall. She sees their heart. She's going to know instantly that you're a good person. She'll probably wonder why the hell I was ragging on you all those years ago."

It was nice to know that he thought she was a good person now, even though he hadn't always thought that.

"We should get back to the station," Jake said. "I don't want to miss the one and only bus to the end of the world."

She would have said he was being dramatic calling Nic Té Há the end of the world, but at this point it certainly felt that way.

They paid the bill, used the café restroom and then headed to the bus. They waited in a line with a large family; a mom, dad, grandmother, and six children under the age of ten. The kids were obviously excited at the prospect of a trip. Katherine couldn't make out much of what they were saying, but it was clear by their expressions that they were very happy.

She couldn't help thinking how different life was in this part of the world, how the simplest of pleasures meant so much—even when that simple pleasure was getting on a dirty, stinking bus. She wrinkled her nose as the bus lumbered into the station.

Jake laughed at her expression. "Hey, it's better than riding with the chickens."

"We'll see," she said darkly.

"As long as it has wheels and goes where we want it to go, I'm good."

"I think it's good you've set your expectations low."

"I've surrendered...just like you," he reminded her.

She reluctantly smiled. "Right. I gave up control. Whatever will be will be."

"Right now, it's going to be this bus."

They found a seat toward the rear of the bus as many of the passengers did not get off at the stop. It was clear most people were making a long journey as they had suitcases and pillows, and some were sleeping on the uncomfortable seats.

As the bus rambled down the road, Jake put his arm around her shoulders, and she couldn't resist leaning her head against his chest and closing her eyes. Maybe when she woke up, a miracle would have occurred, or the nightmare she was living in would have ended. She'd be safe, back in her room in Houston, her brother TJ working at his job like a normal person and Jake...

Frowning, she realized there was one thing wrong with waking up from the nightmare—she wouldn't be with Jake anymore. They'd be strangers again.

Maybe she didn't want to wake up just yet...

"Wake up," Jake said. He straightened his arm, wincing a little at the cramp in his bicep, but holding Katherine had been worth a little pain.

She gave him a sleepy blink of her blue eyes. "Where are we?"

"Our stop. Come on, we have to get off."

She straightened. "Oh, we're still on the bus."

"Yeah, where did you think we were?"

"For a moment, I thought this was all a dream."

"Or a nightmare, but it's not."

"I feel like we just got on."

"You fell asleep fast. I, on the other hand, watched a man cut his toenails for at least a half hour."

She smiled. "Sounds like fun. Sorry I missed it."

He got up and led the way out of the bus. There was no bus depot—just a bench and a sign—but fifty yards away there was a gas station and a convenience store, a motel with adjoining restaurant and bar and a dozen or so houses.

He walked over to the sign. It listed the bus schedule. The next bus to Nic Té Há would be at seven o'clock, two hours from now. Damn. He really didn't want to wait that long.

"What do you think?" Katherine asked.

"The clerk at the depot said this stop was only four miles or so from the village. We could walk that in the two hours it will take the next bus to get here."

"But we don't know where we're going."

"We've got the map."

"It's not on the map."

"True. But there must be some road signs. How difficult could it be?"

She frowned. "Don't ask that question. You're just begging the universe to show us exactly how hard it could be. Why don't we go over to that convenience store and ask them if the bus is usually on time and/or if there's any other way to get to the village? I have to use the bathroom anyway."

"All right. Are you game to walk if it comes down to it?"

"Sure. Four miles is a piece of cake these days."

"Maybe we can buy a flashlight at the store."

They walked across the street, past the empty gas pumps and into the store. A middle-aged man sat behind the cash register. A very old TV played a Spanish soap opera on the counter next to him.

While Katherine went to use the restroom, Jake used his limited amount of Spanish to ask for directions and get the clerk to draw the route on his map. Then he used what was left of their cash to purchase a flashlight, two bottles of water and a big chocolate bar for Kat.

As he finished the transaction, he saw a Jeep pull up in

front of one of the gas pumps. The man who got out of the driver's seat had on a baseball cap. His short-sleeved shirt revealed heavily tattooed arms. Jake's heart jumped against his chest. It was the same man he'd seen by the plane right before it blew up. Had they been followed all this way?

There were two other men in the car, and one of them had a gun in his hand.

Shit! He moved quickly toward the back of the store. Katherine was coming out of the restroom. He grabbed her hand. "We have to get out of here."

"What's wrong?" she asked in alarm.

"I just saw the men from the woods."

"What?"

He ignored her gasping question, thankful there was a way out of the building that allowed them to leave without being seen. Once they were through the back door, he moved quickly around the wall of the motel next door, pausing in the shadows to see if they were being followed.

Katherine was plastered against his side, and he could feel her fear, but he didn't want to talk or move or do anything to draw attention. It seemed to take forever until he heard an engine. He carefully peeked around the wall and saw the Jeep pull out of the gas station and continue down the highway.

"They're gone," he said, blowing out a breath of relief.

"Are you sure?"

"Yeah. They didn't see us. Thank God I saw them before they came into the store."

"I'm glad we weren't sitting at the bus stop." Her worried gaze met his. "Do you think they're tracking us? Was it just a coincidence that we're on the same road?"

"I don't think it was a coincidence."

"But how could they follow our trail? We've been in a car, a truck, a bus. We haven't talked to anyone since you called Rusty and that was from Eduardo's phone."

"We've been seen, Kat. At the rental car place, the bus station, and the café where we had lunch." He paused. "They might have been following the bus and were far enough behind that they didn't see us get off."

"That would be a break. Did you get directions to Nic Té Há?"

"The clerk drew some lines on the map for me. He didn't speak much English, but I think he understood where I wanted to go. I just hope whoever went into the store to pay for gas didn't ask him if he'd seen us."

"If that had happened, they wouldn't have left. The guy would have told them we were in the store minutes ago, and they would have searched for us."

He cupped her face and kissed her mouth. "Sometimes I love your logical mind."

"I'm going to remind you of that," she said dryly.

"I'm sure you will. Let's start walking. With any luck we'll be sitting down with my great-grandmother in a few hours."

"Remember when you asked me how bad could the walk be? And I said you were tempting the universe to show us?" Katherine asked, as they took a break from walking three hours later. "Shouldn't we have gotten to the village by now?"

He pulled out one of the water bottles and took a swig, then handed it to her. She was right. They should have reached the village by now. "I followed the directions exactly. See for yourself."

She traded the bottled water for the map and the flashlight. After a moment, she said, "I actually can't make any sense of this, Jake. It's a bunch of lines and squiggles. Obviously, when we picked one of the paths off the main road, we made a mistake."

He frowned. "Yeah, but that was an hour and a half ago. Do you really want to walk all the way back there and pick the other path?"

"What's our other option?"

"Keep going."

She let out a sigh. "There's one good thing about this trip, I'm getting a lot of exercise." She pulled off her jacket. "It's a lot warmer tonight."

He nodded. "We're a lot farther south than we were. We're getting into a more tropical climate."

"Well, I'm happy not to be cold." She handed him back the flashlight and map. "Let's go."

They walked for another ten minutes and then stopped abruptly as a large cement structure came into view. It was at least twenty feet high and fifty yards long.

"What's this?" Katherine murmured.

"It must be one of the Mayan ruins. They're all over the place down here," he said. They walked the length of the wall, then turned the corner and stepped into what had once been some sort of a courtyard with long cement steps overlooking a moonlit pool.

"Wow," Katherine said. "It's beautiful."

"It's called a cenote or a sacred well. The Mayans believe these wells to be portals to the gods. The water is purified by mineral-rich algae that can nourish the skin, so they sometimes believed the wells to also be similar to fountains of youth."

She gave him a surprised look. "You know a lot about them."

"There's one by my great-grandmother's house. She told me many legends about that pool of water. I suspect there are lots of stories to be told about this one, too." He felt a strange sense of reverence to the water, to the site that had been built so many years ago, to the people who had come before him. "It's strange to think I'm descended from the people who built this monument."

"It is strange," she agreed. "I never thought much about the fact that your heritage was mixed. You were an American Texas boy to me."

"But I have the blood of the Mayans running through my veins, too."

"Do you feel closer to that side of your family down here?"

"I do," he admitted. "Especially here." He pointed to the far end of the pool. "It looks like the water flows into that cave. The Mayans thought that if you dove into the water and swam into the caves, you would find your way to the underworld. The men who tried and didn't come back were believed to have passed through a portal to another time and place and were raised to godly status."

"Maybe they just drowned."

He smiled at her practicality. "You're probably right, but don't tell my great-grandmother that."

"I wouldn't do that."

He looked around, thinking that the structure provided some protection from the elements in case the sky opened up again. He'd wanted to get to the village tonight, but he didn't see that happening, and they were both getting tired. "I think we should spend the night here, Kat. I messed up on the directions. We need some sunlight to help us find the village."

"As much as I'm not looking forward to sleeping outside again, this place seems like our best option."

"Yeah," he said roughly, frowning at the map once again.

"It's not your fault, Jake. He could have misunderstood where you wanted to go."

"I just wish the village was on the damn map. Maybe he did think I was talking about another place."

"The good news is that I don't believe anyone is following us—at least I hope not."

"I think we're safe."

Katherine walked over to the steps under an overhang and sat down on the top step, stretching out her legs.

He sat down next to her and pulled out the candy bar he'd been hoarding. "Look what I saved for you."

Even in the shadowy moonlight, he could see the flicker of joy in her eyes. "You spent our last dollar on chocolate?"

"You bet, just so I could see you smile."

"You know me too well. Let's split it."

"It's all yours if you want it."

"I'd rather share it with you."

He broke the candy bar in two pieces and gave her one.

They slowly savored each bite. Katherine even licked her fingers as she popped the last piece of chocolate into her mouth. "That was..." She stopped and laughed. "I really can't say that was the best chocolate ever, can I?"

"Why not? You're on a roll."

"You definitely appreciate food more when it's in short supply."

"Mamich will cook us a feast when we get there. She can take herbs from the garden and turn a potato into something magical."

"It's too bad you didn't get to spend more time with her in your life."

"My dad brought us a handful of times when we were really young, but my mother was grounded in Texas. She didn't like Mexico, and she didn't think my dad's family liked her much. Maybe that was true. My mother can sometimes be harsh and judgmental, and she certainly didn't have anything in common with my dad's side of the family. There was a huge cultural barrier."

"Well, your great-grandmother will be happy to see you now. How old is she?"

"Let's see, I think she's eighty-nine, maybe turning ninety this year. When I saw her ten years ago, she was very sharp, but that was a long time ago."

"You haven't spoken with her since?"

"I wrote to her a few years ago." He shook his head. "I should have kept in better touch. I know Alicia writes to her more often."

"You said that you always spoke English with her; that's

surprising, isn't it?"

"Not for my great-grandmother. She was a teacher for many years, and she taught English to the villagers. She felt the children would need it as they moved away and went to the bigger cities and eventually perhaps to the States. I think it also always reminded her of her husband."

"I'm glad she's fluent in English. It will be easier to communicate with her."

"Definitely."

Katherine looked up at the sky. "The moon is bright tonight—the stars, too."

"No other light to block them out," he agreed.

"It's beautiful here with the tropical trees, the majestic ruins, the water sparkling in the moonlight."

He was surprised she could find the beauty in the moment. Katherine really had changed. She was usually worrying about the next potential problem, but apparently she had surrendered. "I agree."

"Kind of romantic, in fact."

He smiled. "You think so?"

"Don't you?"

"I suppose."

"Come on, Jake. This is like a film set for a romantic movie."

He laughed. "If you say so. It's beyond me to know and understand what women find romantic."

She cocked her head to the right. "Tell me about the last woman you dated. How did you meet? How long did you go out?"

"I don't know."

"Yes, you do."

"Fine. That would be Hannah. We met at a friend's birthday party a couple of months ago. We went out three times, and the third time was not the charm. I thought she was hot at the party, not nearly as interesting on the second date, and a bit of a mean girl on our third outing."

"What did she do?"

"We were at a bar with some of her friends, and she couldn't stop talking about how that one was too thin and the other one was a secret binge drinker and how she was sure they all talked about her behind her back. She was, in fact, the biggest gossip in the group. I knew she was going to be way too much drama. So that was the end of that. It was not a sad event. Your turn, Kat. Who was your last date?"

"Harrison Carmichael. He was another resident. His family was Texas royalty. Not Houston, but Dallas."

"Was he as pretentious as his name?" he teased.

"No, he wasn't a snob; he was a nice guy. But I soon realized that he was as driven and anxious as I was. We revved each other up in a bad way. We didn't bring out the best in each other but rather the worst."

"So you broke up with him?"

"I was going to, but before I could do that I saw him having sex in an empty hospital room with a lab tech. I was shocked that he would do something like that. It was out of character. But you know what—he was so happy with that woman. I think he needed someone to push him in a different direction."

"Where's the most interesting place you've ever had sex?" he asked curiously.

She stared back at him. "You mean since we had sex in the car and at the beach and in your friend's boat?"

"Yeah, since then," he said, her words arousing all kinds of beautiful memories of the passion they'd shared.

"Well, let me think."

"It should stand out in your mind. It should be one of those crazy moments that just happen without a lot of thought, so if you can't remember any, then—"

"Hold on," she said, putting up her hand. "I don't have to remember, because…"

"Because what?" he asked, his pulse taking a leap as she stood up. She tossed her jacket to the ground and then peeled off her top and bra.

"Holy hell, what are you doing?" he asked, unable to tear his gaze away from her breasts.

"I'm going for a swim in the sacred well."

"No you're not. That would be crazy. There could be—things in there."

She paused as she was about to unzip her jeans. "Things like what?"

Now he was sorry he'd stopped her. "Fish, snakes, I don't know—creepy stuff."

"You said the ancient Mayans bathed in these wells because the water was pure and rich in nutrients. I think we should try it."

He stood up. "You didn't want to skinny-dip in a pool with me; now you want to jump into a dark pond in the Mexican jungle."

"Yes. The old Kat was way too scared of nothing." She slid her jeans down over her legs. "I'm going in the pool. Are you coming with me?"

"You're seriously going to do this?" His tongue felt thick in his mouth as he tried to make sense of what she was saying.

"I seriously am. And if you want to join me, then the most interesting place I've ever had sex will be in a sacred pool by a Mayan ruin somewhere deep in Mexico." She turned and walked toward the water and the sight of her bare body in the moonlight had him shedding his clothes as fast as he could.

"It's cold," she said as she waded up to her knees. "How deep do you think it gets?"

"Deep enough to take you to the underworld."

She shot him a dark look. "Not your best line for foreplay, Jake."

"I'd be happy to have sex right here. We can use our clothes for a blanket. It will be awesome."

"Or..." She drew in a deep breath and plunged into the

water up to her waist. "I can still touch the bottom."

"What does it feel like?"

"Come in and find out."

He quickly found out the water was very, very cold. "What the hell? How are you not running out of here?"

"I'm waiting for you to warm me up," she said, standing up in the pool so that the water came just above her hips. "What are you waiting for?"

That was a very good question. He scrambled across the water, almost tripping in his haste to get to her.

She laughed as he put his arms around her. "About time."

"Hey, give me a minute to catch up. This is not the Katherine I know. I feel like I'm dreaming."

"It's not a dream," she said, pressing her breasts against his chest. "It's what you always wanted to do—skinny-dip. I was just too afraid to do it, but I'm not anymore. I don't want to be that boring girl who never did anything exciting."

"After this trip, I don't think you could ever say that."

She gazed into his eyes. "Feel like helping me make a good memory?"

"I think you can feel just how much I want to do that." He pulled her body even closer, so she could feel every hard inch of him. "Even in this freezing water, I still want you."

"Then have me." She threw her arms around his neck and kissed him with a passion and a fervor that was a mix of the old Kat and the new Katherine.

Then something splashed in the water next to them. Katherine screamed, and he jerked backward as he saw the water rippling toward them.

He didn't know what the hell it was, but he didn't intend to wait around to find out. He grabbed Katherine's hand, and they ran out of the water.

When they were away from the pool, they looked back to see a bird fly out of the water and land on a tree branch.

Katherine looked at him and then burst out laughing. "It was just a bird. So much for being a fearless skinny dipper. I guess we won't be having sex in a sacred pool."

"Then I guess a Mayan ruin will have to do," he said, walking her backwards toward their pile of clothes.

"I guess so," she said a little breathlessly.

He gave her a hard, hot kiss as his hands cupped her breasts, then he trailed his mouth down the side of her jaw and swirled his tongue around each of her nipples. Dropping to the ground, he delved into the heat between her legs.

It was the hottest experience of his life. It was everything he'd imagined all those years ago when he'd begged her to go skinny-dipping and she'd always refused. Now, he was glad they'd waited. Because now it was her idea, and when Katherine wanted something, she went all in.

Tonight she was all in on him. They savored each other's bodies, making love once, twice and three times. He couldn't imagine a better memory. Only he didn't want it to be *just* a memory...

Thirteen

—➤≫≪◄—

"Will this forest ever end?" Katherine muttered as she and Jake walked through another swath of trees late Tuesday morning. "I had no idea Mexico had so many trees and so much wilderness. You could get lost here forever. TJ was right. This is a good place to disappear. Survival is another story. Why couldn't he hide out in a nice little hotel by the sea? Or he could have flown to Houston, and I could have hidden him somewhere there. But, no—he has to decide to go to the end of the world…"

Jake smiled to himself as Katherine's angry, frustrated ramble continued. She was due for a little complaining. She'd been stoic and calm and determined the past few days. While his breaking point had been a flat tire, apparently her constant irritation was the number of trees in the forest.

"There are so many trees that their branches actually embrace each other. It's like some X-rated orgy fest of trees," she said, grabbing a branch in her way and tossing it to the ground. "I'm sure that branch will somehow bury itself somewhere in the dirt and spring forward another tree, a tall tree, with thick branches to block out the light and the idea that there is any other world outside of this damned freaking forest!"

"Want to kick a tree?" he asked. "It might help. Go a few

rounds with one of them?" He made a boxing motion; a step, a jab with his left, then with his right. "Take this. Take that."

She stopped walking and flung him an irritated look. "Very funny."

"Seriously, kick the tree. You'll feel better."

"I won't feel better; I'll probably break my toe. Then you'll have to carry me out of here." She tightened the sleeves of her jacket, which she had tied around her waist.

"I could do it. You've probably lost a few pounds since we've been walking."

"Are you trying to tell me that I needed to lose weight? Do you really think that's a smart thing to do? If I killed you right now, no one would find your body. In fact, you'd probably turn into a tree."

He started laughing and couldn't stop, and after a moment, she smiled and threw up her hands. "All right, my rant against the forest is over."

"Thank God. I was beginning to worry that you might piss off the tree gods, and we'd never get out of here."

"There aren't really any tree gods are there?"

"There definitely are. In the Mayan culture, there are gods for just about everything."

"Well, right now, I wouldn't mind if the lightning god struck down some of these trees so we could get some light and see where the hell we're going."

"Please, don't call down the lightning god. I've seen enough rain for a while." He held up the last water bottle. It was a quarter full. "Want a sip?"

"I'm fine. You can finish it."

He knew better than to waste any water unless they were desperate. "I'll hang on to it then. It's getting hot. The climate definitely feels more tropical, which means we're getting close."

"You've been calling us close for days, Jake, but I do agree on the heat. I'm already sweating and wishing I wasn't wearing a sweater, jeans, and boots."

"They were helpful a couple of days ago," he reminded her.

"We have to be near the village, don't we, Jake? We've been walking for hours. I thought the bus was dropping us a few miles from Nic Té Há. We've walked twenty miles since then."

Which was why he was worried. They should have been at the village long before now. They could be walking in completely the wrong direction.

"I don't like that look on your face," she said with a frown. "What are you thinking?"

"I've never gone into the town from this direction. I've always landed at the airport on the west side of the village."

"But you've explored some of the ruins around the area, so…"

"I wish I could say any of this looks familiar, but I can't. So let's keep walking."

"In circles?"

"What's our alternative?"

"We have none," she said, sighing at the end of that statement. "Let's go."

They didn't speak for the next half hour. He was as tired of the trees as Katherine was, but the last thing he wanted to do was spend another night outside. Being with Katherine had been amazing, but the cement ground had been another story. They had to find better shelter today.

Finally, the thickness of the trees began to diminish. There were patches of grass, rocks, an abandoned home that at first gave them hope, then quickly turned to disappointment when they realized most of the roof was gone and the house was falling apart.

"It's possible it could provide some shelter," Jake said, giving the structure a critical eye.

"No," Katherine said with a definitive shake of her head. "It's too early to stop and look for shelter. If this house is here, then maybe others are nearby."

"I agree."

They passed by another crumbling stone structure, walked through a grassy meadow and made their way onto what appeared to be a dirt road.

"Tire tracks," Katherine said, a gleam of hope in her eyes. "This road has to go somewhere."

"Let's keep heading south," he said, taking a look at where the sun was in the sky. "I feel like I've seen this road before."

"Really? You've seen this particular dirt road before?" she asked dryly. "That sounds optimistic."

"It's a gut feeling." As they moved around the bend, a small house came into view. "I've seen that house, too," he said with excitement coursing through his body. "It belongs to my great-grandmother's friend. We went there to visit her."

They ran down the road and up the steps. Unfortunately, their knock was not answered, and the door was locked.

"They're not home," Katherine said with disappointment, looking around. "Damn. We can't catch a break."

"I can see furniture inside. Do you want to wait?"

"Do you?" she asked, meeting his gaze.

He shook his head. "The village is down this road, maybe another mile or two."

She groaned. "Every mile turns into five."

"Look, if we don't find it in the next hour, we'll come back."

"All right." As they started walking again, she said, "Tell me more about the village again. How big is it? How many people live there?"

"Last time I was here, the population was around fifteen hundred. It might have grown since then."

"So, not that small."

"Or that big," he countered. "Not everyone lives in town. Many people have farms around the area. The commercial part of the community is about six blocks long and four blocks wide. There's one building that serves as a post office, a bank, and a police station all at the same time. There are other small businesses: a market, a café and bar, an inn, a shop with crafts, furniture and clothes. There is some tourist traffic because of the Mayan ruins nearby. So, while it's isolated, it's not completely cut off from civilization. I might have exaggerated when I used to tell you and TJ about it. Of course, when I visited as a teenager, I did feel like I'd gone to the end of the earth."

"Having walked through miles of wilderness to get here, I can see why you'd think that. Has your great-grandmother ever wanted to live anywhere else?" Katherine asked. "Did she never consider moving to America with her husband?"

"Never. She loves the land, the people and the culture. She's the town wise woman, the teacher, the herbalist and the seer."

"That's a lot of jobs."

"All interrelated. She preserves the traditions of the past but also teaches the young children to dream big, to think about the bigger world outside the village. She's very well respected, although I doubt you'd appreciate her reliance on herbal medicine, but she seems to have some success with the pharmacy of herbs in her backyard."

"I have no problem with herbs. A lot of medicines are rooted in plants."

"You should keep that thought when she recommends some vile-tasting herb for whatever ails you."

"I think I'm safe. Nothing is ailing me, although I do have some blisters on my feet."

"I'm sure she has the perfect salve. It might stink, though. Last time I was here, she made me get into a bath that she filled with yellow tea water. I had to sit there for thirty minutes."

"Why? What was wrong with you?"

As soon as Katherine asked the question, he realized he'd made a mistake to share that piece of information. "I forget. I think it was a headache or something," he said vaguely.

Katherine shot him a speculative look. "You came here after we broke up and after your father died. She tried to help you through your grief, didn't she?"

He didn't want to tell her that his great-grandmother had told him she could cure his broken heart, so he shrugged. "Something like that. The Mayan people believe that the mind and the body are intensely connected. Emotions play a big part in health issues."

"Stress can weaken the immune system. Maybe after we find TJ, I can spend some time with her and learn more about her herb garden."

"I'm sure she'd be happy to share."

They walked around another bend and then stopped abruptly as a cluster of buildings came into view about a half a mile away.

"Oh, my God," Katherine murmured. "Tell me that's not a mirage. Tell me that's *the* village or at least *a* village."

"That's it. That's Nic Té Há. We're here. We've arrived." He threw out his arms. "Ta-da!"

She laughed. "That ta-da would have worked better if we hadn't spent three days trying to get here."

He grinned. "Well, we're here—finally. Come on." He grabbed her hand and they ran down the street.

As they walked toward the town, the area reminded Katherine of rural Texas. The weather was hot and sticky, and the small homes were spaced apart with lots of land in between. There were chicken coops next to houses, the occasional horse or cow grazing in a small pasture. And there were people; kids kicking a ball across a yard, an old woman planting flowers in front of her home, and a man putting red tiles on a roof.

"If TJ came here, where would he go?" she asked Jake.

"He might stay at the inn, or if he wanted to lay low, he

could be camping out somewhere nearby and coming into town for food. That would probably make more sense. I don't see him just sitting in a hotel room."

"I can't really imagine what he's doing. He's a smart guy. He has to know he can't hide out forever. If he's in trouble, he can't just run; he has to figure out a way to fix the problem."

Jake shot her a smile.

"What?" she asked.

"I just don't know if TJ thinks the way you do."

"He might. He's an engineer. He's logical, super intelligent, and used to finding solutions. He would analyze his situation and from there figure out his next move." She paused. "Maybe he's not even here anymore. It's been four days since I spoke to him. He could have moved on. He could have called me again and didn't know why I didn't answer my phone."

"Hopefully, you'll find out very soon whether he's here or not. But I have a suggestion. Instead of knocking on doors, let's start with my great-grandmother. She's the heart of this town. She knows everyone and everything that's going on. If TJ has been in the village, she'll know."

"Okay, let's go there first. Do you remember where her house is?"

"I do."

They walked another quarter mile, passing by a fairly magnificent-looking church. Katherine had to stop for one second to take a look at it. "What beautiful architecture."

"It's very, very old," Jake said. "It's been rebuilt several times, but there's one wall inside that still has Mayan carvings on it. If we have time when this is over, I'll take you inside."

She nodded as they walked toward a home surrounded by a multitude of trees. Tucked inside all the greenery was a white adobe-style house with red roof tiles and arched windows.

"That's Mamich's house," Jake said, excitement in his voice.

They jogged the rest of the way, both eager to finally get to their destination.

Jake knocked on the door and a young woman answered. She wore white, cropped pants and a colorful gauzy top, and her long, dark hair hung in a thick braid halfway down her back. Her eyes widened when she saw Jake, and she muttered something to herself in Spanish.

"*Hola*," Jake said. "I'm Jake Monroe, Sylvia's great-grandson."

"*Sí*. She said you were coming." She waved them inside and motioned for them to follow her down the hall.

Katherine caught a glimpse of the interior of the house, red tiled floors, white stucco walls, colorful throw rugs and paintings on every wall, but there was no time to really look around as the woman took them out the back door.

The yard was large and heavily planted with vegetables and flowers. At the far corner was a wooden shed. The woman opened the door for them and said, "Sylvia. He's here."

As they stepped into the shed, Katherine saw tables covered with small pots of herbs, and in the middle of the tables was a dark-haired, dark-eyed woman who stood about five feet tall. Her long hair was also pulled back in a thick braid. Her skin was a dark brown and there were a multitude of age lines around her eyes and mouth, but when she smiled, it was very clear that her heart was still young.

"Jake. My boy." She opened her arms, and he walked into her embrace.

"Mamich," he said, giving her a loving smile. "It's good to see you."

Her gaze swept his face. "You are all right? You have many bruises."

"I'm okay." He glanced back at Katherine, and she stepped forward. "Mamich, I'd like you to meet Katherine. This is Sylvia, my great-grandmother."

"*Hola*," Katherine said.

"The girl with the golden hair," Sylvia said, her eyes gleaming. "I thought you were an angel watching over Jake, but you are real." She opened her arms once again, and this time Katherine stepped into a hug that was far stronger than she would have expected coming from this thin, somewhat fragile-looking woman.

As they broke apart, Sylvia turned to the young woman. "Will you make us tea, Carmen? We'll be in soon."

The young woman nodded and left them alone in the shed.

"I can't quite believe you're actually here," Sylvia said to Jake. "I've been worried the last few days. I dreamed of you both. You were running and scared. I hoped you would find your way here, but I was afraid someone might stop you."

Sylvia's words sent a shiver down Katherine's spine. How could this woman have known they were coming? How could she have dreamed about them? Jake had said his great-grandmother was a seer, but she hadn't really believed it. "Did Alicia tell you we were coming?" she asked, thinking that had to be the explanation.

"No. She didn't mention it in her last letter."

Sylvia studied Katherine with an intensity that made her want to shuffle her feet or look away or something.

"So this is *your* Katherine," Sylvia said, her gaze finally moving from Katherine to Jake.

Jake licked his lips. "Katherine and I are looking for her brother TJ. We think he may have come here or be on his way based on some things I told him about the village a long time ago."

Katherine noticed that Jake didn't answer his great-grandmother's comment. It certainly seemed that Sylvia knew something about her from Jake's visit ten years ago. If that were true, Sylvia probably wasn't going to like her very much. On the other hand, the woman didn't appear to have any animosity toward her. She was smiling even now as her gaze kept moving between them.

"TJ is about six feet tall with brown hair, and I think he has a beard now, or he might have shaved it off," Katherine said. "Has anyone been around town who looks like that?"

"We will have to find out. I am recovering from a cold. I haven't been out in the village much the past few days."

"Are you better now?" Jake asked.

"Of course." She waved her hand toward the plants surrounding her. "The earth provides the best medicine." She paused. "Did you become a doctor, Katherine?"

"Yes, I did," she said. "How did you know that?"

"Jake told me that was your plan, your heart's desire."

She nodded. "I just finished my training." She paused. "Jake told me that you're a healer. Do you use these plants?"

Sylvia nodded. "These herbs, those in the garden and the fruit of the trees that surround me. This area is rich in natural healing elements."

"I would love to learn more about it," she said, genuine in her interest.

"But first you must find your brother," Sylvia said.

"Yes. I'm very worried about him. He thinks he might be in danger. I came here to help him."

"And Jake came to help you," she said, with a nod.

"I flew Katherine down here," Jake said. "But our plane went down in a storm, and we've been trying to get here for the last three days."

His great-grandmother nodded, understanding in her eyes. "The lightning was fierce this week. The mountains breathed fire. There are more storms on the way."

Sylvia certainly had an ominous way of speaking, Katherine thought.

"I have known this time was coming for many moons," Sylvia continued. "But not until a few days ago did I realize that you would be the one, Jake."

"What are you talking about?" he asked.

"Your father. This is about him, too."

"No, this is about TJ, Katherine's brother," Jake

corrected.

"Not entirely. The world is connected in complicated ways; one person seems to have no relationship to another until it all becomes clear."

Jake gave his great-grandmother an exasperated look. "I don't know what you're talking about, Mamich."

"Your father is caught between worlds. He calls for help, but I am not the one who can help him. I thought it might be Alicia, because she can sometimes hear his call. But it is you. And it is time."

Jake paled at her words. Despite his natural cynicism toward the supernatural, his great-grandmother's words had obviously hit him hard. They'd hit Katherine hard, too. She didn't know how TJ and Jake's father could be connected, but there did seem to be a lot of odd coincidences, like two planes being taken out of the air by lightning ten years apart.

"I came here for Katherine," Jake said firmly. "For her brother. I don't know what you're saying about Dad. He's dead. He's not coming back, and there's nothing I can do to help him."

"He can't move on until the truth is revealed."

"What's the truth?" he asked in confusion.

Sylvia met Jake's gaze. "All I can tell you is that his bones are not where they're supposed to be."

Jake sucked in a quick breath. "I don't understand."

"Yes, you do."

"I don't," he denied. "I know that Alicia thinks that Dad's crash was not an accident. She's hired an investigator to look into it. If anyone is going to find the truth, it will be her, not me."

"She may not be in the right place to help. Did you see nothing in the lightning that struck your plane and sent you crashing to the ground?"

"I didn't tell you that lightning struck the plane," Jake said.

"Did it not?" Sylvia asked.

His lips tightened. "As a matter of fact, yes, it did."

"You saw your dad," Katherine interjected.

Jake's eyes darkened, and he didn't look like he appreciated her comment, but she hadn't been able to stop herself.

"You saw Wyatt?" Sylvia asked. "What did he tell you?"

Jake hesitated. "It was just my imagination, Mamich. We'd just been talking about Dad's accident, and I was in a similar situation."

"What did he say?" Sylvia repeated, not giving up on her question.

Jake let out a sigh. "I thought he might have said *follow me.*"

Sylvia nodded. "And you followed."

"No. I didn't follow him. I crashed."

"You landed where you were supposed to."

"I don't think so, because if Dad wanted me to get here sooner, he wouldn't have sent my plane down. Katherine and I have been on the road for days. We weren't even sure we were going to survive."

"And yet you did, and you are here. You fight so hard not to believe, Jake. What you must do is fight to see the truth," Sylvia said, urgency in her voice. "Don't be afraid of it. Don't turn away. It's too important. Not just for your father, but for you and your family."

"Okay, we've gotten off track," he said, running a hand through his hair. "We need to find Katherine's brother. That's our first priority. Dad has been gone for ten years, so whatever that truth is can wait a little longer."

"Of course. That is important, too. Let's go into the house. Carmen cleans at the inn every morning and helps me in the afternoons. If there is a guest in town, she will know."

They followed Sylvia back into the house.

"I have your tea ready," Carmen said, greeting them in the kitchen.

"We will have tea later," Sylvia said. "Carmen, Jake is

looking for a man. Have there been any American visitors at the inn the last few days?"

Carmen nodded. "A young man. I saw him yesterday. He said he was taking pictures of the ruins."

"Yesterday?" Katherine echoed in amazement. She looked at Jake. "We have to go to the inn right now."

"Yes," he agreed with a nod.

"Carmen will go with you," Sylvia said. "She speaks English better than those at the inn. She is one of my best students. She will help you."

"We'd appreciate that, Carmen."

The young woman nodded. "*Sí,* I will help you."

"We'll be back soon, Mamich," Jake told his great-grandmother.

"Yes. When this is over, we will have a long talk," she said. "There will be much to discuss."

"I forgot how spooky she is," Jake muttered as they followed Carmen into town.

"She seems very wise and very convincing. Maybe there is something more to know about your dad's death."

"Well, right now I just want to focus on TJ."

She nodded, feeling in complete agreement and also a little more hopeful. "I think he's here. The man Carmen spoke to has to be him."

"I really hope so, Kat."

"Although, it feels a little—easy."

"Easy?" he asked, shooting her an amazed look. "You call the last few days easy? Because, if so, you and I have a very different definition of *easy.*"

"Not then—*now*. We're just going to walk into the inn, and he'll be there? It doesn't seem possible."

"He has to be somewhere. Why not there?"

"I just have a bad feeling."

"That's because Mamich spooked you, too, but all her talk was about my father, not your brother."

"She said they're connected."

"How could she know that?"

"I have no idea. But I hope this does turn out to be easy. I want to give TJ a big hug and then punch him in the face for getting all of us into this mess."

Jake laughed. "That sounds about right for a sister." He took her hand and gave it a squeeze. "This is almost over, babe."

She wanted to believe that, but she couldn't shake the worried feeling as they entered the inn. Carmen spoke with the innkeeper in Spanish, then she grabbed a key from behind the desk and told them TJ was staying in room number two at the top of the stairs.

They went up to the second floor, and she knocked on the door. When there was no answer, she used the key.

The guestroom was furnished with an iron-framed queen bed, a nightstand and a desk. But her gaze went immediately from the décor to the T-shirt lying in a crumpled heap on the bed. She picked it up. It was warm to the touch, as if someone had recently taken it off. As she shook it out, she saw the logo on the back for the Houston Astros. Her stomach turned over.

"This is TJ's shirt," she said, looking at Jake. "I sent it to him last Christmas. This is his room."

"Okay," Jake said carefully. "Now we just need to find him."

"He has to be close by. Maybe he went to the market or the café." She moved over to the window.

The room looked out over the street. There were only a few people in sight; two old men sitting in chairs in front of the market and three little girls standing on the sidewalk sucking on Popsicles and kicking a ball between them. As her gaze moved down the street, she saw a man come out of the bank. He wore jeans and a forest-green T-shirt. He had a baseball cap on his head, and sunglasses over his eyes, but there was no denying the familiarity of his walk. She'd recognize that lazy, loping stride anywhere.

"Oh, my God, there he is," she cried. "There's TJ." She

tried to open the window, but it wouldn't budge. Jake added his muscle, but the window didn't move, so she turned and ran out of the room, hurrying down the stairs and through the front door.

When she hit the sidewalk, she was surprised to see a black van flying down the street, almost running over one of the kids who had gone into the street to grab their ball.

The van came to an abrupt stop when it reached TJ and before she could take her next breath, two men jumped out of the back of the van, grabbed her brother and threw him inside the vehicle.

"No," she screamed, running down the street after them.

But it was too late. The van was gone in a cloud of dust, and so was TJ.

Fourteen

"No, no, no!" She stopped at the end of the block. The road disappeared into the trees, and there was no way she could catch up to the van on foot. She couldn't believe her brother had been taken right before her eyes. "He's gone. They got him," she said as Jake put his arm around her.

"I know. I'm sorry."

She jerked away from him, adrenaline still coursing through her body. "How could we get so close and not reach him in time? If we'd come into town and gone to the inn right when we got here, this might not have happened."

"You don't know that."

"Neither do you."

"Look, Katherine, we don't have time for the blame game right now."

"We don't have time?" she asked, waving her hand in angry bewilderment. "What else do we have to do? We're in the middle of nowhere. We have no way of going after those men, and they could be hurting my brother right now." As her imagination leapt to the worst possible scenario, her stomach heaved and she had to bite down on her bottom lip to stop herself from throwing up. "Oh, God, I feel sick."

"Let's focus on making a plan to rescue him."

"What plan would that be?" she asked, feeling hopeless.

They'd been battling for days, and she was exhausted. She'd really thought she'd get to TJ before the worst happened, but she'd been wrong.

"We'll walk back to the inn and see if anyone on the street recognized the van or the men who grabbed your brother. This isn't over, Katherine. We won't stop looking until we find him. We didn't come all this way to fail. As long as we keep trying, we have a chance. Don't quit on me now."

She stared at him, the determination in his voice inspiring her. "You're right. I didn't come here to fail. Okay. Let's do it. Let's talk to people and find out who took my brother."

Despite Jake's plan to identify her brother's kidnappers, they had little success getting information from anyone on the street. Most of the people disappeared inside their shops when they approached and the few people they did speak to either said they didn't understand or didn't know what they were asking.

Carmen was their last hope. She stood in front of the inn, a worried expression on her face. "What happened?"

"Some men in a black van grabbed my brother and drove away. We've asked around, but no one claims to have seen anything."

Carmen's face paled. "A black van?"

"Do you know who drives a black van?" she asked.

"*Sí. Los hombres de el diablo*—the devil's men."

"Who's the devil?" Jake asked. "What's his name?"

"We must go back to the house—quickly now." Carmen practically ran down the street, not slowing her pace until they were inside Sylvia's home. She greeted Sylvia with a barrage of Spanish and then left the room.

"Did Carmen just tell you what happened?" Katherine asked. "My brother was taken off the street by three men in a black van."

"Did they see you?" Sylvia asked, concern in her dark eyes.

"I don't know. I don't think so."

"Katherine and I were running after them," Jake put in. "But the van kicked up a lot of dust, and the windows in the back were blacked out. I'm not sure they could see anything, but it's possible they did."

She suddenly realized that she might have put TJ in more danger by running after the van. "Do you know anything about this van?" she asked. "Carmen said it's driven by the devil's men, but that's all she would tell us."

"Come and sit." Sylvia led the way into the small living room. "I will tell you what I know."

Katherine sat on the couch with Jake while Sylvia took the adjacent chair.

"There is a large ranch in the mountains about ten miles from here," Sylvia said. "Years ago, it was a working cattle ranch owned by Jose Calderon. He was a good man. He lost his wife during the birth of his third son, so he raised his boys on his own. Unfortunately, without a mother's touch, the boys ran wild. When Jose died, he left the ranch to all of them, but the sons turned the ranch away from cattle and began running drugs. The oldest, Martine, was in charge for the next few years. Then his younger brothers waged war against him. In the end, Martine and the middle brother, Hector, were killed by the youngest—Rodrigo."

"He killed his brothers?" Katherine asked in shock. "Why?"

"Greed, evil," she said. "Rodrigo has been in charge the last two years. The ranch became off-limits to the locals. Anyone who trespassed was killed, their body left in the road as a warning to others. The villagers began to call him El Diablo—the devil."

"Oh, God," Katherine murmured, putting a hand to her mouth as she thought about her brother in the hands of this evil man. "Why hasn't anyone arrested him? Where are the police?"

"It is complicated," Sylvia said.

"How is it complicated?" Jake challenged.

"The Calderons always took care of this community—as well as others in the area. Even after Jose died, Martine carried on the tradition. For years, once a month, the black van came to town. It stopped at the bank. The driver went inside and left money for electricity, water, and road repairs."

"So the Calderons bought the silence of the locals," Jake said with a disgusted shake of his head.

"*Sí.* The money was desperately needed and happily accepted for many years," Sylvia replied. "But since Rodrigo took over, many people have been hurt, not just those who got too close to the ranch. Last month a child was run down by the van. The little boy barely survived. We want someone to stop Rodrigo from hurting anyone else, but we have nowhere to turn. The police look the other way."

"Maybe they can't look the other way this time. Rodrigo has kidnapped a US citizen, an employee of a powerful corporation," Jake said.

"Perhaps his company should get involved in his rescue," Sylvia suggested, giving Katherine a hopeful look.

"I'm not sure who I would ask at MDT," she replied. "My brother didn't know who to trust at his company, and I don't, either."

"Maybe that doesn't matter anymore," Jake said. "You witnessed your brother being kidnapped. MDT can't try to tell you you're wrong. They'll have to send someone to investigate."

"Or they could make sure TJ dies before he's found."

Jake's lips tightened. "I guess that's possible."

"I don't understand why a drug lord would take my brother. He's an engineer. He doesn't deal in drugs."

"TJ is an engineer who works on weapons systems," Jake reminded her. "Some drug cartels have the weapons of a small army. Perhaps they wanted some of the technology that TJ has been working on. Hell, maybe Jerry's contacts were in Mexico. They were never able to find his co-conspirators.

They thought he was selling technology to Middle-Eastern countries, but maybe he was selling to drug cartels in Mexico. That actually would have been easier, given the proximity of Texas to Mexico."

"That makes sense," she said slowly. "When TJ called me, he did say something about he didn't know why they'd sent him to Mexico, but he thought he'd figured it out. I didn't know what that meant at the time, but maybe that's when he realized Mexico was a partner or something..." She paused. "But if TJ knew a local and powerful drug lord might be after him, why would he stay in Mexico? Why would he come to this village? Why not go back to Texas or somewhere else?"

"It's possible he couldn't get out of the country. He might not have known exactly who was after him, either, so he thought buying some time by disappearing into the wilderness would work."

"But they found him." She thought about that. "Did we lead them here, Jake? Those men we saw on the highway—maybe we didn't lose them after all."

"It wasn't the same guys, Katherine. Those men were in a Jeep. They were wearing different clothes."

"They could have switched cars, or they could have still been working for this Rodrigo. Maybe it was the call back home that triggered something. You talked to Rusty. Did you tell him where we were going? I can't remember."

"No, I didn't tell him. I just said you had business to take care of, but even if I had told him, who would he tell?"

"Someone from MDT who went to the airfield asking questions."

"That's a long shot. And I'd trust Rusty with my life. He's been like a second father to me."

His words sent a shiver down her spine. "That's right. Rusty knew your father. He was around when your dad disappeared, and he was around when your plane suddenly lost power and steering capabilities."

"What are you getting at, Katherine?" he asked tightly.

"Just saying it's a coincidence."

"Rusty didn't sabotage my plane," he said, anger in his eyes.

"But lightning doesn't normally take down a plane. You told me that."

"It can. It's been known to happen."

"To two people in the same family ten years apart?"

He shook his head. "Why the hell would Rusty want to kill me or my father?"

"Rusty's charter service caters to MDT executives flying around the world. They could have paid him to sabotage our plane."

"Okay, you're way out there, Kat. I know you're upset, but—"

"What about Alicia?" she interrupted. "Alicia has a private investigator looking into your father's accident, researching MDT. Maybe she did something to send someone in our direction. I shouldn't have spoken to her before I came down here. That might have been a mistake."

"Well, maybe you shouldn't have come to me at all," he said, clearly pissed off. "If you'd flown to Mexico on a commercial jet, I wouldn't have spent the last several days running for my life. So if you want to blame someone, maybe look in the mirror."

"Jake—Katherine," Sylvia interrupted. "Stop. Fighting with each other won't help. You need to be partners, work together. You are on the same side."

Sylvia's words made her realize that she was taking her frustration out on Jake. She let out a tense breath. "You're right, Sylvia. I'm sorry, Jake. I'm just really upset."

Jake didn't look like he wanted to accept her apology, but he finally nodded and said, "Fine. Let's move on."

She turned to Sylvia. "We have to get to Rodrigo's ranch and figure out how to rescue my brother. We'll need to borrow a car. Are there any men who might be willing to come with us?"

"I don't know," Sylvia said slowly. "We don't have any local police. The nearest station is ten miles away, and those officers are in Rodrigo's pocket. As for some men, it will be difficult. Everyone is afraid."

"How many people are usually at the ranch?" Jake asked. "Do you have any idea? Have you ever been there?"

"I was there many years ago. At the time, there was a large house, a stable, pastures for cattle and horses as well as farmland."

"So it's big," Katherine murmured, not happy about trying to rescue TJ from some massive compound.

Sylvia nodded.

"Does anyone go in or out on a regular basis?" Jake continued. "Do they have food delivery? I'm looking for a way to get onto the property without arousing suspicion."

"What will you do then?" Sylvia asked before Katherine could fire off the same question.

Jake hesitated. "We'd need to create a distraction of some sort, focus attention away from whoever is guarding TJ."

"And then what?" she asked. "I don't know how you and I can do this alone, Jake. We don't have weapons. We're not soldiers. How can we possibly rescue TJ from a fortress controlled by a drug lord?"

"We'll use something as deadly as a gun—fire. Fire makes people run."

She nodded, thinking about the plane explosion that had sent her and Jake racing through the forest. "That could work. But they might throw TJ in the van and drive somewhere else."

"Maybe we can disable the vans before we set the fire. I know enough about engines to pull some wires, but everything depends on us getting onto the property."

"I will ask my friend Paolo to help us," Sylvia said. "Paolo used to work at the ranch when it was run by Rodrigo's father. He knows many ways onto the property. I'm sure he would be willing to lend you a vehicle. I will send

Carmen for him now." Sylvia got to her feet. "While we are waiting for Paolo, you will eat. I will make you lunch, and you will gather your strength for what lies ahead."

"Thanks," Jake said. "But don't go to any trouble."

"It is no trouble to cook for my great-grandson and his Katherine," she said with a smile.

Katherine blew out a breath as Sylvia left the room. "Do you really believe we can do this, Jake? Are we crazy to try on our own? Should I find someone with a phone and call someone at MDT? I could contact TJ's girlfriend, although I don't have her number anymore; it was in my phone. But I'm sure someone could connect me to her."

"I'm not against involving the company," Jake said. "But it will take time to get anyone down here."

She hated to wait another second knowing that TJ was in the hands of some very bad men. "You're right."

"We can do both. We can call MDT and then also go out to the ranch and see what we're up against."

"I just don't want to make this worse. What if I call the wrong person and then they make sure that TJ never gets found?"

"That's the risk. You're really good at pointing out the problems."

"I just wish I was better at fixing them."

"Well, you thought it was going to be too easy," he reminded her.

"Yeah, that was stupid." She paused. "I am sorry that I snapped at you. None of this is your fault."

"I know. You were just angry. I was a good target." He met her gaze. "But Mamich was right about one thing—we need to work together."

"I agree. To be honest, I can't quite believe you're still with me. You didn't even want to get off the plane and set foot in Mexico when this all started."

He smiled. "And look where I am now. Which, according to my great-grandmother, is exactly where I'm supposed to be."

"I wish Sylvia could look into the future and tell me TJ is going to be all right."

"Maybe she can, but I don't think you'll believe it until TJ is with you, and you can see for yourself."

"You're probably right."

"Let's get some food, Kat. Then we'll take another look at our crazy, half-assed plan and decide whether or not we want to talk ourselves out of it."

Their late lunch was a modest meal of chicken, rice, and beans, but every bite was savory and delicious, seasoned well by the herbs in his great-grandmother's garden.

"You were both so hungry. I should have fed you as soon as you arrived," Sylvia said.

"This is delicious, Mamich, but I noticed that you're not eating," he said.

"I'm glad you like it. I am not as hungry as I used to be. I eat enough to sustain me. That's all I need."

He wished she'd eat a little more. She was very thin, and despite her steely will and sharp mind, she had a fragile quality to her, as if she could break at any moment.

"How is your mother, Jake?"

"She's well. She works at the university."

"Did she remarry?"

"No. She lives alone and seems happy enough. Not that she'd probably tell me if she wasn't. She keeps her thoughts to herself, unless those thoughts are critical of what I'm doing. Then she's very vocal."

"As a mother should be. Alicia writes to me often, but I haven't heard from Danielle in years."

"She just got a new job in Washington, DC. She's going to be working for the US senator from Texas. She moved a few days ago."

"It sounds like an important job."

"I think it is."

"Danielle always needed to be seen, the burden of the middle child."

"I guess. She worked hard at being popular, that's for sure. She has more professional ambition than Alicia and I put together."

"But you are happy flying airplanes?"

"Yes. It's always been my dream job."

"It was the same for your father. Even as a little boy, he would look to the sky whenever he heard a plane. He told me once flying was his way of getting close to the heavens."

That sounded a little like his father but even more like his great-grandmother. "You were really close to him, weren't you?"

"After my daughter died, I looked at Wyatt as if he were own my child. I was very sad when his father took him to Texas, but we had forged a bond that was too strong to break. He came back here as often as he could, and he wrote me many letters." She paused. "I have them in my room. One day perhaps you'll want to read them."

She'd made that offer before when he'd been here ten years ago, but then it had seemed far too painful to consider looking at his father's handwriting, seeing his words. But now, maybe it would be cathartic. "One day," he said, knowing that he needed to keep his emotions about his father and the past at bay. He needed to concentrate on the huge task ahead of them.

Glancing over at Katherine, he saw her staring out the window, lost in thought. She was worried and scared, and he wished he had the power to make her feel better. But that wouldn't happen until they found TJ.

"Would you like more to eat, Jake?" Sylvia asked.

"No, that was enough."

"Katherine?"

Katherine started. "What?"

"Would you like more food?" his great-grandmother inquired.

"No, thank you." She pushed her empty plate away so she could rest her arms on the table. "That was very good. Jake was right. He told me you were a good cook."

"It is easy to cook when the food comes from your garden."

"I can't even imagine," Katherine said. "I barely use my spice rack, not that I have much time to cook."

"You were meant for more than cooking," Sylvia said. "The gift of healing is precious. You must treasure it."

Katherine nodded, but she looked a bit taken aback by his great-grandmother's words. "I never really thought of it as a gift. It's always been a goal that I had to strive for."

"And now that you have it, you will use it wisely."

"I will definitely try."

An odd expression crossed his great-grandmother's face. "You were meant to change the world—both of you. That is why you are here. Why I have dreamed of you these past nights."

"I don't know about the world," Jake said. "We're just trying to find one man."

"One man who is important to this world. I don't know how, but I know that he is. The saving of his life will save many others."

"Can you see if he's okay?" Katherine asked. "Do you have that ability?"

"I feel that he is waiting for you, but his destiny is still to be written."

Katherine nodded. "Okay." She pushed back her chair. "Would you excuse me? I need to use the bathroom."

"It's down the hall by the back door," Sylvia told her.

When Katherine left, she gave Jake a smile. "Your Katherine is as beautiful as you said. I am happy that you are back together with your soul mate."

He wanted to say he didn't believe in soul mates, but he

had to admit that if there was such a thing, then Katherine was probably it. "We're not exactly together. She needed me to help find her brother. I don't know where we're going to end up when this is over."

"No one knows the end, Jake."

"Not even you? You seem to have visions of some things."

"Some things become known to me—not all. I know Katherine wanted more assurance from me. I wish I could have given it to her."

"She probably wouldn't have believed you anyway."

"Her mind and her heart are always in battle," Sylvia said.

Jake was surprised that his great-grandmother had read Katherine so well. "Yes, they are. She's afraid of feeling too much."

"Or loving you too hard."

"I let her down a long time ago. I didn't realize it at the time. I thought she was abandoning me, but since we've talked again, I see things I didn't see before."

"I'm sure she does as well. Perhaps now is your time."

A very big part of him wanted to believe that. "I wonder," he said. "But how could I trust that she wouldn't run again?"

"Is she not worth the risk?"

"I don't know. I honestly don't think I could go through that pain another time." He'd never admitted that to anyone— not friends, his mother or his sisters—but somehow here in this small kitchen in the middle of nowhere, the words poured from his lips.

"You have no decision to make, Jake. You think you have a choice, but you don't. Katherine is already inside your heart. Even if she leaves, she'll always be with you."

"I don't want her to leave and take my heart. I couldn't be like you, Mamich. I couldn't love someone and let them go."

Sylvia smiled with the wisdom of the ages in her eyes.

"You are thinking only of yourself, of what you need, how you feel. What does she need from you? Love looks outward, not inward." A knock came at the door. "That must be Paolo."

Jake got to his feet, relieved at the interruption. The last thing he needed to be thinking about right now was love.

After washing up in the bathroom, Katherine headed outside. She needed to get some air, to think about what to do next. She had mixed feelings about whether or not to contact MDT or the police or anyone in a position of power versus trying to save her brother on her own. Her logical brain told her she was insane to think she and Jake could infiltrate the headquarters of a drug cartel and rescue TJ. On the other hand, it was doubtful anyone in the local area would help them.

The Calderon family had been running this territory for years and the deaths of innocent villagers hadn't inspired the local government to do anything that would stop the funnel of money coming from the cartel to the town. So why would anyone want to help them? In fact, if they asked too many people around town for help, there was a good chance that someone would relay that information to the Calderons, and they'd have no chance of saving TJ.

If they were going to take anyone by surprise, they would have to do it fast, before too many people knew they were in town or could get the information to the men in the black van.

She wandered through the garden as her mental debate continued. Stepping into the shed, she stopped to sniff some of the herbs. Sylvia had jotted down some names by some of the plants, and she knew enough about plant properties used for medicine to recognize some of them: agave, acacia, chamomile, lemon grass. Sylvia really did have an herbal pharmacy behind her house. She wished she had time to talk to Sylvia about what she used for what symptom and how she used it.

But first she had to find a way to save TJ, and distracting herself with the science of herbs wasn't going to get her any closer to that goal. She needed to go back into the house and hope that Sylvia's friend Paolo would be able to help them put together a better plan to get onto the ranch property than the one they'd come up with so far.

As she stepped out of the shed, she heard a footstep behind her.

She was just about to turn when someone grabbed her from behind. She opened her mouth to scream, but someone shoved a rag into it, gagging her. A bag came down over her face. She kicked out her feet, but someone picked her up and tossed her over their shoulder. A moment later, she landed on something hard. An engine roared and she suddenly knew exactly where she was—in the back of a black van.

It looked like she'd found her own way onto the ranch or to wherever TJ was being held. He had to be alive, she thought desperately. They wouldn't kidnap her if he wasn't— would they?

Fifteen

---⇒⇒⇒⇐⇐⇐---

Paolo Garcia was a lean, wiry man somewhere in his mid-sixties who'd known Jake's father and claimed a long friendship with Sylvia. He'd also known the Calderons and had worked at the ranch for several years while Rodrigo's father, Jose Calderon, was in charge. He'd told Jake that there was only one way onto the ranch without using the main road and that would require him to climb down a rather steep hillside. He also said that Rodrigo had put a lot of ex-soldiers on his payroll in recent months. There was talk that Rodrigo was planning a takeover of some territory, perhaps the state to the north that was run by another family cartel.

Everything Jake heard reinforced the doubts he'd already had. He needed to find Katherine and make her listen to Paolo. He knew she would run into fire for her brother, and he wanted to help TJ, too, but he also didn't want to lose Katherine in the process.

"Where is she?" he muttered.

"I think she needed a moment to herself," Sylvia said, meeting his gaze.

"I was happy to give her the space, but I need her in this conversation." As he finished speaking, he heard the slam of a car door, the roar of a motor, and through the living room window, he thought he saw a flash of black. He jumped to his feet. "Did you see that? It looked like the van from earlier today."

He walked over to the window and saw nothing but a dusty street in front of the house. That dust cloud also reminded him of the van.

Turning away from the view, he called out, "Katherine?"

He walked down the hall. The bathroom was empty. The bedrooms were empty, too. His heart flipped over in his chest as he saw the back door ajar.

"Katherine," he yelled again, as he ran outside.

The door to the shed was open, but the building was empty.

"She's gone," he said as Sylvia and Paolo came into the yard.

"Maybe she took a walk," Sylvia began.

He gave a definitive shake of his head. "She wouldn't leave without telling me." He knew without a doubt that Katherine had not left the yard voluntarily. "They took her— Rodrigo's men. She must have come outside, and they grabbed her. Dammit."

He wanted to put his fist through a wall. How had he been so stupid? He should have realized that whoever had grabbed TJ had seen Katherine running after the van. They'd come back to get her. And apparently, she'd given them the perfect opportunity when she'd stepped outside of the house. There was no more time for planning, no option for second thoughts. "I need to go to the ranch now, Paolo."

Paolo nodded, his expression grim. "You can take the truck. We will make a plan together."

"They may expect you to come," Sylvia said, concern in her dark eyes. "It will be more dangerous now."

"I don't care. I'm getting Katherine and TJ out of there tonight."

"I understand. We must speak for a moment first," Sylvia said. "Paolo, will you wait in the house?"

The older man nodded and left them alone.

"Don't try to talk me out of this, Mamich."

"I wouldn't do that," she said quietly. "I have been thinking while you and Paolo were talking. I can help you, but only if you choose to believe."

"Believe in what?" he asked, a little frustrated by her cryptic words.

"In me. Come with me."

He followed her back into the shed. She walked over to a box in the corner and pulled out a three-foot-long iron rod. "I have six of these. When you get to the ranch, you must plant them a dozen feet apart, as close to any brush or trees as you can get. I will call down the lightning. The rods will show it where to go and the flashes of light will lead you to Katherine."

He stared at her in bemusement. "You're going to call down lightning? How are you going to do that?"

"It doesn't matter. I have done it before, and it has worked—when the gods are willing to listen. They are listening now. I didn't understand why you and Katherine were coming. Even when you said it was to save her brother, there was something missing, but now I know that you are here to save the world from the evil at the ranch." She gave him a tired smile. "I am not explaining it well, and I know you have trouble believing in what you cannot see, so all I ask is that you believe in me. Can you do that? Can you trust me, Jake?"

"If whatever you're going to do will save Katherine and TJ, then I can believe. I can trust you." Here in this world of Mayan culture, his own reality seemed very far away. He was going to need a miracle to rescue Katherine, so why not hope the lightning gave him one?

"Good. Rodrigo fears the lightning as many do in this area. He believes in the gods. He will be afraid. The lightning will be his weakness, and it will be your strength." She put her hand on the side of his face. "Be careful, Jake."

"I was going to say the same to you. If Rodrigo's men

took Katherine from this yard, you may be in danger. You might want to stay with a friend tonight."

"I'm not afraid. The devil has been ruling our world for too long. Tonight, good will triumph over evil."

"I hope so."

"I have something to give you." She led him into the house, into her bedroom. Walking over to her dresser, she opened her jewelry box and pulled out a gold medallion.

He recognized it immediately. "Dad had one of those."

"Yes. So did your great-grandfather and your grandfather. They were made especially for the men in the family. This one belonged to your great-grandfather." She handed it to him. "The gold comes from the earth. The bird in the middle will remind you to look to the heavens. When you see the flutter of birds that I see in my dreams, you will know it is time. You will wear this medallion, and it will protect you. It is blessed."

"All right," he said, slipping it over his head. "I'll take anything that will help: medallions, birds, lightning, dreams..." He paused, looking into his great-grandmother's eyes. "I have to find her, Mamich. She's..."

"I know," she said, taking his hand and wrapping her fingers around his. "She's *yours*. Bring her home."

"I will," he said, knowing he would die trying to keep that promise. He just hoped it wouldn't come to that.

Katherine felt bruised from the bumpy road and sick to her stomach from the motion of the vehicle and the blindfold that prevented her from getting her bearings. The men had tied her hands behind her back, so she couldn't reach for the blindfold or protect herself from the jarring dips in the road.

She knew there were two men nearby. They'd spoken in Spanish only once to each other, words that she didn't understand. But aside from throwing her into the vehicle, they hadn't touched her or hurt her.

She had to be in the van, because there were no seats or seat belts, not that anyone would have worried about buckling her up.

Hopefully, they were taking her to TJ, and together they could figure a way out. But it felt like they'd been on the road at least half and hour. Were they going to the ranch that Sylvia had told them about or somewhere else?

If it was somewhere else, Jake would never find her, but she knew he would try.

That thought was both reassuring and terrifying. She wanted Jake to rescue her and her brother, but she didn't want him in danger. There was no way one could happen without the other, unless she could find a way to escape and take TJ with her.

She inwardly winced as her hip hit the floor hard. She prayed the trip would end soon.

Finally, some ten minutes later, the road became smoother. The vehicle stopped. A rush of cold air came into the van.

One of the men got her to her feet and walked her forward. Then he lifted her up and set her on the ground. Another man grabbed her arm and pulled her along what felt like a dirt path.

They walked for longer than she would have thought, at least a few minutes. Then they stopped.

A door opened, and she was shoved inside a room. The light behind her bag brightened.

"No," a man said, his voice deep and tortured. "Oh, God, Katherine."

Her eyes filled with tears. "TJ?" she asked. "Let me see him. Let me see my brother," she yelled.

The bag was ripped from her head. She blinked against the suddenly bright light.

It took her a moment to figure out where she was. She appeared to be in some sort of computer lab. She didn't know what she'd been expecting, but it wasn't this. She'd thought she'd end up in a barn at a ranch, but this looked like a high-tech lab.

Her brother stood in front of three computer screens. He was being held in place by the two beefy males who'd grabbed her. His face was bruised, his shirt ripped. He'd fought to get away, and they'd hurt him. She reminded herself that he was still alive and that was what mattered most.

She turned her head to the left and saw another man, one she didn't recognize. He was dressed differently than the others, wearing gray slacks and a buttoned-down light plaid shirt. His hair was styled. There was a heavy gold ring on his hand, and he stood tall and proud. Was this Rodrigo? El Diablo? He wasn't dressed like the devil, but there was an evil smile lurking in his eyes. He was enjoying their fear, their discomfort.

"Welcome," he said. "A beautiful unexpected guest."

"Where am I? Why are you holding my brother? Why did you kidnap me?"

"Ah, so many questions. You're here because you wanted to be. Did you not try to catch up with your brother earlier today?"

So they had seen her chasing the van.

"Why did you take him?" she asked, ignoring his question.

"Because he is needed."

She looked at TJ. "What's going on?"

"I don't know," he mumbled.

He was lying. Was it because he didn't want to speak the truth in front of his captors? She had to believe that was the reason. "What is he needed to do?" she asked the man in charge.

"Your brother has information and skills that others do not have. He has a job to do, but he has been reluctant to do it. Perhaps now that you are here, he will change his mind."

"Let her go," TJ said. "She's not part of this."

"She is now. It's up to you. If you want your sister to leave in the same condition she arrived in, then you will do as we ask. You have two hours to show me progress. If not, your sister will spend some time alone...with my men."

Katherine's heart thudded against her chest, and she saw TJ turn white at the threat.

"Two hours," the man repeated. He looked at Katherine. "It would be a pity to scar such a face, but I do not play games, and I am weary of this one your brother is playing. If you want him to live, you will offer your encouragement."

He motioned to one of the guards to untie her hands. Then the three of them left the room.

As soon as the door closed, Katherine rushed toward her brother. She threw her arms around him and gave him a tight hug. "Are you all right?" She stepped away to take a better look at his bruises. "They've hurt you."

"I'm fine. It's you I'm worried about. What the hell are you doing here? I told you to take care of Mom, not to come running after me."

"I couldn't stay away. You sounded terrified and desperate. I had to try to help you."

He shook his head, a somber expression on his face. "They're going to kill both of us, Katherine."

"What do they want you to do? Why are you here?"

"They brought me here to fix the algorithm behind the weapons system that Jerry Caldwell sold them. He used to work at MDT. I thought he was selling secrets, but he was selling actual weapons."

"I've heard about him. I talked to Jake's sister, Alicia, before I came here."

TJ ran a hand through his hair. "Alicia knows, too? I told you not to talk to anyone."

"I had to try to find out what you were involved in. You were so cryptic on the phone. You should have given me more information."

"I was still putting it together in my head."

"So what have you figured out?"

"I was set up by a woman in the company—Jasmine Portillo. I thought she liked me. Stupid."

"Jasmine?" she echoed in surprise. "I met her. I stopped at Mom's house before I came down here, and she was there. She said she was your girlfriend, and she was worried about you."

"She was at Mom's house?" he asked with alarm. "Damn."

"What? Tell me how she set you up."

"She came on to me. She flirted. It was nice. It had been a while. I didn't realize that she had a more important reason to get close to me. She was part of Jerry's operation. She'd been told there was a problem with the weapons, and that they needed an engineer to fix them; otherwise, they're unusable."

"And you're the only one who can do that?"

"One of a few. I realize now I was stupid when it came to her. She was interested in me, and she'd had a relative with dementia so she knew what I was going through. She told me that she knew of some freelance work I could do that would help cover Mom's expenses."

"Oh, TJ," she said with a frown. "You should have told me that you were getting round-the-clock care."

"I knew you were close to finishing. I was trying to keep things afloat until then. But as tempted as I was to make some extra cash, I told Jasmine no. I had a bad vibe. In fact, I started to wonder if someone else had picked up where Jerry had left off. I dug around a little, but the next thing I knew, Jasmine had put me on a list to go to a conference in Cancun. She said she was going, that we could have some fun on the side, and I thought why not? But when I got to Cancun, she wasn't there. And the conference people didn't seem to understand why I was there. I got the feeling someone was following me around. I called Jasmine, but she never called me back. I contacted one of my other coworkers, and he said he'd seen Jasmine in my office, trying to get on my computer. That's when I knew something was really wrong."

"What did you do next?"

"I checked out of the hotel. I took a taxi to the airport, and a truck rammed the side of the cab. Two men got out. I instinctively knew that it hadn't been an accident. I managed to get away and hide in the city. I was trying to figure out how I could leave the country, but there was no way I could just get on a plane. They weren't going to let that happen."

"So you went inland?"

"I remembered all of Jake's stories and I asked at the library if anyone new where the village was. A woman gave me directions. It was farther than I thought, but I thought I'd done a good job of hiding until earlier today when that van came out of nowhere."

"I saw them take you, TJ. I had been at the inn—in your room. I looked out the window and I couldn't believe you were walking down the street. But when I got outside, those men were throwing you into the van."

"And you ran after us."

"It was stupid. I wasn't thinking."

"I should have never called you. I was worried about Mom. I needed you to know I might not make it back. I'm sorry I got you into this."

"It's not your fault. We just have to figure a way out of here."

"There's no way out. There's at least one guard on the door."

"What about those windows?" she asked, thinking they could reach the windows near the ceiling if they climbed on the tables. "We must be in the basement."

"That's what I figured. We could break the window and try to get out, but I suspect we'd be caught before then. They're obviously not that worried about us escaping since they untied you and left us alone together."

"Jake's great-grandmother thinks that we're at a ranch run

by Rodrigo Calderon, the leader of a drug cartel."

"He said that was his name, the guy in the nice clothes," TJ said.

"Have you seen any other people besides the three who were just here?"

"Several in the barn where they have the weapons." He paused. "They're going to kill both of us as soon as I fix their problem."

"That's why you can't fix it."

"I wasn't going to, but I can't let them hurt you, Katherine," he said, pain and worry in his eyes.

She didn't want them to hurt her, either, but she knew their odds of survival were low either way, and she couldn't let herself drown in the fear of what might happen to her. "How long would it take you to do what they want?"

"Probably about a half hour. I have an idea what might be wrong."

"Is there a way to make them believe you've fixed the problem but actually haven't?"

He nodded. "That's what I was thinking. The program will look like it's working until it doesn't."

"What exactly are they trying to get to work?"

"It's called a railgun—an electrically powered electromagnetic projectile launcher."

"Okay. That sounds advanced."

"A railgun relies on electromagnetic forces to achieve a high kinetic energy. It can deliver destructive force with the absence of explosives and has a range that far exceeds conventional weaponry."

"Sounds like Rodrigo wants to control all of Mexico."

"I think his ambitions might be even bigger than that," TJ said.

"So someone at MDT sold him this gun?"

"He has two smaller versions of the gun. I have no idea how he could get the weapons without the company noticing that they were missing. There has to be high-level company involvement."

She had to agree. The technology TJ was talking about was extremely advanced. The security on it would be high, so how had a Mexican drug lord gotten his hands on the weapons?

"I can't believe you came here, Katherine. This past year I've barely seen you."

"I know. I've had my head down. I thought if I looked up for too long, I'd never make it to the end. But I let you down. I let you carry the burden of Mom's illness. If—when—we get out of here, that's going to change."

"If something happens to both of us, who will take care of her?" he muttered, despair in his eyes.

"Don't give up. We still have one secret weapon."

"We do? What's that?"

"Jake."

"Jake Monroe?" TJ asked in surprise.

She nodded. "He flew me down here. You told me not to get on a commercial plane, so I went to his charter company and asked him to take me to where his great-grandmother lives. I had figured out that's where you were going. It took us longer to get here than I imagined. I won't go into all the details, but Jake and I were going to try to rescue you tonight, but I left his great-grandmother's house to get some air, and Rodrigo's men grabbed me. I know Jake will come on his own."

"And do what?"

"I'm not sure, but I think it will involve fire. We need to be ready for anything."

TJ looked at her like she was crazy. "You think Jake can break us out of here on his own?"

"There's no one else to help, TJ. Rodrigo's cartel owns this part of Mexico. No one will go against him."

He suddenly smiled.

"What?" she asked, surprised by the change in his expression.

"You still think Jake is some kind of superhero."

"No, I don't."

"Yes, you do." He tilted his head. "I thought the two of you hated each other."

"It was more of a matter of him hating me. I let him down when he was hurting after his dad died. I thought he was bad for me. I saved myself, instead of trying to save him. I've been really selfish, TJ."

"I don't think that's true. You can get tunnel vision, but you have a big heart. You care about people. I think that's why you ran. You got scared. He meant too much to you."

"Maybe he did."

"What does he mean to you now?"

"I'll let you know after he rescues us."

He smiled. "I hope he can do it."

"He can."

"Then we better be ready. I'm going to rewrite the code. I just hope Jake hurries, because I don't think time is on our side."

Jake carried the heavy crate of iron rods up a thirty-foot incline and down a steep rocky hillside just behind the Calderon ranch. The sun had slipped behind the mountains ten minutes earlier, providing him with the welcome shadows of dusk.

Setting down the crate, he picked up his binoculars to get a better view of the property. He was directly behind the two-story house. A large stable was to the right and west of the house. Another smaller shed was beyond that. There were lights blazing on the first floor of the house, but the second story was dark. He could also see some light coming from what appeared to be windows along the bottom of the structure, implying some sort of a basement.

Away from the house, he could see lights in the stable

area, and a few men standing in the doorway carrying automatic weapons.

Another sweep of the property revealed a helicopter sitting on a helipad about a hundred yards away. No doubt that was how Rodrigo got in and out of the remote location quickly. Maybe he could use the chopper to get them off the mountain, although he hadn't flown a helicopter in a very long time.

He watched the property for several long minutes, wanting to see if anything changed, if he could figure out where TJ and Katherine might be held.

A man stood guard on the porch of the house, his stance and attitude more serious than the others who were walking around the stable area. That led Jake to believe that Katherine and TJ might be in the house.

He kept a silent vigil for another ten minutes. He wanted the night to get darker before he put his plan into action.

A sudden breeze brought his head up. Clouds were blowing past the moon, blocking out the light.

A shiver ran down his spine at the sight. Mamich had told him that she would call the lightning. He didn't believe she could actually do that. But there did appear to be a storm brewing. Of course, there had been storms the past few days that had had nothing to do with his great-grandmother. At least, he didn't think they had.

He set his binoculars on the ground and pulled the rods out of the crate. As instructed he set them up about a dozen feet apart, although it seemed to him that the tall surrounding trees would provide more attractive targets than the rods. But he wasn't going to question it.

When that was done, he took another look at the ranch. Nothing had changed.

He needed to make a move. He didn't know how long Katherine had, but his gut told him that the more hours that passed, the less chance he had of getting her out alive.

A distant light streaked across the sky, followed a

moment later by the rumble of thunder.

Shit! Maybe Mamich was going to bring the lightning.

A minute later, another jagged streak, closer this time.

The thunder grew louder.

But there was no rain. It was a dry electrical storm—perfect for what he needed.

He waited another minute, then pulled out the box of long matches.

Fear ran through him along with a mighty rush of adrenaline. He might only have one chance. He had to get this right.

"*Watch the sky,*" his great-grandmother had told him.

He looked up and saw the flutter of birds flying away from the area.

Just like she'd said. His stomach clenched. He touched the medallion around his neck for luck.

"It's time," he muttered aloud.

The next lightning flashed so close it lit up the hillside. For a moment, he thought he might be seen by those at the ranch, but then he was distracted by the image in front of him. It was his father again. He seemed so real that Jake's breath caught in his chest.

His dad held up a medallion, much like the one he wore around his neck. He said something like "*Get it back for me*" and then he was gone. The hillside was dark once again.

Jake looked back toward the house, seeing shadowy figures looking up at the sky.

"*Rodrigo fears the lightning,*" Sylvia had said. "*That's his weakness.*"

"Bring it, Mamich," he muttered.

The next strike hit a tree close to the house. He heard a yell and saw the men duck back into the house.

That was not the result he wanted.

He lit the first match and ran ten yards down the hill. He set one branch on fire, then another and another.

The next strike of lightning hit the rods he'd so carefully

placed.

He watched in amazement as the lightning literally jumped from rod to rod, each spike setting off fires that zipped up the trees and exploded the brush.

More lightning came down from the sky, the next jagged spike hitting the roof of the barn. It burst into flames.

Now the men came running out of both the house and the barn, yelling, panicked, cursing the sky. There were two vans that he could see, and one pulled out almost immediately, but he didn't see Katherine or TJ on board. Great! Any chance to decrease the number of people at the ranch was to his benefit.

The next lightning flash lingered for what seemed like minutes but was probably seconds. It shone like a beacon coming down from the sky, and where it hit the ground, it rested on something metallic, shiny, beckoning.

He took it as a sign.

He ran through the bushes toward the back of the house and prayed that Katherine was somewhere inside.

Because now he realized that he didn't just have Rodrigo and his men to worry about. The fires were already blazing out of control. He had to get Katherine and TJ out before the flames reached the house.

The lightning flashed again, showing him that shiny piece of metal that had called to him. It was peeking out of the dirt. He took a quick second to pull it out, shocked and amazed at what it was. For the first time ever, he felt like a true descendant of the Maya, and he believed as they believed.

Sixteen

—➤➤⫷⫸←—

"It's happening," Katherine said, getting to her feet. Lightning flashed outside the windows. Thunder roared through the air. She could hear shouting. So far no one had come in to get them, but that wouldn't last long.

TJ jumped up on the desk. She handed him the metal chair he'd been sitting on. He smashed the window, and she covered her face as the glass shattered and rained down around him. Then she climbed onto the desk and scrambled out the window with TJ's help.

As TJ came out of the window behind her, she saw men running and fire blazing in the woods. Jake had come through big time.

She ducked behind a bush as a man came toward them. When she realized it was Jake, she started to get up, but TJ dragged her down as another man with a gun came around the house from the opposite direction.

Jake was right in the line of fire. Before she could shout a warning, the guard took a shot.

Jake stumbled and fell face first to the ground. She had to bite down on her lip to stop the scream from coming out of her throat. To aid in that effort, TJ clapped a hand over her mouth.

The guard prepared to take another shot. She had to stop

him. She jerked out of TJ's grip, ready to rush forward and tackle the man when a huge explosion knocked her down and a shower of wood, rocks and dirt came down around her.

Dazed, it took a moment for her to realize that the building behind her was blazing, flames leaping twenty to thirty feet into the air. The man with the gun was gone. She didn't know if he'd run or been knocked out, but she didn't care. TJ was slowly getting up. He was okay. But Jake still lay on the ground. She scrambled to her feet and ran over to him.

She turned him over, seeing no blood on his face. "Jake, Jake," she said urgently. "Wake up. Please wake up." She put her head next to his ear and heard the soft whoosh of breath. He was still alive.

TJ came to her side. "We have to get out of here."

Jake groaned and blinked his eyes open, wincing at whatever pain he was in. It was hard to see where he'd been shot, but he reached toward his leg, and then she saw the blood soaking through his pants.

"He's been shot," she said.

"Let's get him up," TJ said decisively. "We may not have long."

"Okay. We're going to help you up," she told Jake.

He nodded, then grimaced as they somehow got him to his feet, although he immediately took the weight off his left leg and started to sag back down. "Can't," he muttered.

"Yes, you can," she said forcefully. "We're going to help you. How did you get in here?"

"Truck—trees—"Jake tipped his head to the right. "Up the hill."

They followed his clipped directions and half walked, half ran toward the mountain, dragging Jake along with them. She had no idea how badly he was hurt, or if she was making it worse, but she didn't have a choice.

Jake passed in and out of consciousness, sometimes finding the energy to take a step, sometimes not.

"Where now?" she asked as they got up the hill and started down the other side. "Jake. Stay with us," she ordered. "We need you to find the truck."

Her sharp tone brought his eyes back open. She wanted to nurture him not yell at him, but her doctor instincts were running high. This was no time for emotion. She had to fix the problem.

He pointed toward some bushes, and she followed his lead, hoping they were going in the right direction. She didn't know how many minutes passed before she saw the dark truck parked behind some trees. She felt an overwhelming rush of relief. Any minute, she'd expected to hear shouts or gunshots from behind her.

"Address," Jake muttered. "Safe house. Map. Paolo."

She quickly deciphered what he was trying to tell her. He'd set up a place to go after rescuing her—one less thing to worry about.

The door was unlocked, and they got Jake onto the passenger seat. She slid in next to him while TJ took the wheel. The keys were in the ignition.

TJ started the engine, and they headed slowly down what appeared to be more of a dirt path than a road.

"Why aren't you turning on the lights?" she asked.

"There's enough light from the fire. I don't want to alert anyone to our presence if I don't have to. You need to figure out where we're going."

She looked at Jake but his eyes were closed. "He said there was an address in here." She saw a piece of paper on the floor and picked it up. There was a roughly drawn map that used the village of Nic Té Há as one point and the ranch as the other. Since both she and TJ had been blindfolded on the way to the ranch, she was happy to get some perspective. There was an address marked halfway in between, with some short directions of where to turn and a few key landmarks that hopefully she could spot, but half of a brick wall and a tree with three trunks didn't give her a lot to go on.

"I think I've got it," she said. "Hopefully, it's not too far. I'm worried about Jake. I need to see his injury."

She touched Jake's hand, and her concern grew at the coolness of his skin. He was probably in shock. God knew how much blood he'd lost.

As she rubbed his hand, her gaze caught on a gold chain looped around his fingers. She pried his fingers open. Even unconscious, he had an intense grip on what appeared to be a gold medallion. She wondered where he'd gotten that and why he didn't seem to want to let it go. But he couldn't hold on any longer. She took the medallion and slipped it into the pocket of her jeans.

The truck hit a bump, and she lurched forward, bracing her hand on the dashboard. As she looked to the right, she saw the fire blazing higher and brighter than before. "What do you think exploded, TJ?"

"Probably the weapons in the barn."

She felt a wave of satisfaction. "Good, then they won't be able to use them."

"They weren't going to be able to do that anyway. I made the code look like it would work, but at the last minute it wouldn't. I was hoping it would be enough to convince them I was willing to work with them." He shot her a look. "I thought I could tell them I wanted to go to their side, work for them. They obviously needed me. I was going to trade for your life."

She was immensely touched by his words, even though she wasn't sure they would have made that trade. "Thank you, TJ. I'm glad it didn't come to that."

"Looks like Jake, the superhero, saved the day after all," he said with a smile. "When you told me he was going to set a fire, I had no idea the magnitude he was aiming for. He turned the entire forest into an inferno."

"He got some help from the lightning. Amazing timing," she said, wondering if Jake's great-grandmother had used some of her witchery to help them.

"Yeah, lightning with no rain. Weird, huh?"

"That's the least weird thing about this night," she murmured. "Do you think they're dead, TJ?"

"I don't know. They could have escaped, at least some of them."

"I hope Rodrigo was in the barn when it blew up."

"So do I."

They drove in silence for another fifteen minutes, and then TJ switched on the lights. She kept her eye out for the landmarks drawn on the map and eventually she saw the trio of tree trunks and the half-built wall. "Turn left there," she said.

A half-mile down the road was a small cabin. TJ jumped out of the car and ran up to the door. He was able to get inside, and a moment later he turned on a dim light and then came back to help her get Jake out of the car.

"It's just one room, but it will do," he said.

Jake woke up enough to stumble into the cabin and collapse on the bed. There was a small couch in the room next to the bed, an adjacent bathroom with a sink and a toilet, and a counter that held a small microwave and a mini-refrigerator.

"I'm going to park the truck behind the cabin," TJ told her. "I'll be right back."

While TJ went to do that, she brought the lamp closer to the bed and held it over Jake's leg. His jeans were covered in blood and there was still more coming out of the wound. She grabbed a towel from the bathroom and pressed it hard against the wound, eliciting a moan of pain from Jake.

When TJ came back, he helped her strip Jake down to his boxers so she could inspect the injury. The bleeding had slowed down, which was a good thing. She couldn't see an exit wound, so the bullet was still in his leg. That might be a good thing; it could be acting as a natural plug against a bigger bleed.

TJ brought her a sheet he'd found in a closet, and she

stripped off a piece of fabric large enough to wrap several times around Jake's leg. With the pressure, Jake groaned again, blinking his eyes open.

"Sorry," she told him. "I'm trying to stop the bleeding."

"What bleeding?" he asked dazedly.

"You were shot in the leg. But you're going to be okay," she reassured him as she knotted the bandage. She took one of the extra pillows from the bed and slid it under his leg to keep it elevated. After that, she pulled the blankets from the bottom of the bed and covered him up. He was already starting to chill from the shock.

"Where are we?" Jake asked.

"The cabin that Paolo told you about."

"What happened? I remember fire and explosions."

"You did what you said. You set the forest on fire with a little help from some lightning. The guards went running, and TJ and I climbed out a window and saw you get shot. Then the barn blew up; they had weapons inside. We dragged you into the woods and here we are."

He gave her a painful smile. "Sounds easy enough."

"It was not easy at all. You got hurt. I'm so sorry, Jake."

"Hey, I'm alive, and so are you. Where's TJ?"

"Right here," TJ said, stepping forward. "Thanks for the help."

Jake nodded. "You're welcome. Glad to see you. Your sister has been driving me nuts for days."

TJ smiled. "I'll bet."

"You need to go to the hospital," Katherine told Jake. "We just have to figure out where that is."

"Not now. Too dangerous."

She couldn't deny that there might still be danger, but she was worried about Jake. "We might have to take that chance."

"No, we'll wait for Paolo. He'll come tomorrow. He'll tell us what's happened. Said we'd be safe here."

"It was smart of you to get a place to take us to. You thought of everything."

"It wasn't just me. Paolo set up the house and gave me the truck. Mamich said she would call the lightning, and she did. I couldn't believe it."

"I couldn't believe you came after us by yourself," TJ said. "But Katherine had no doubts."

Jake met her gaze. "Really? You knew I'd come?"

"Yes, you've always been stupidly brave."

He started to laugh, then groaned again. "Yeah, that's me—stupidly brave but apparently incredibly lucky."

"Not lucky—smart. You provided a huge distraction. If you hadn't, we wouldn't have been able to get past the guards. They would have killed us." She shivered a little at that thought, still not quite able to believe they were safe.

"Mamich said Rodrigo's weakness was lightning. He's always been afraid of the god of lightning. Did you see Rodrigo?"

"Yes. He was there. He wanted TJ to do something on the computer to fix the weapon systems they bought from someone at MDT. We haven't had time to figure it all out yet."

"You will." He lifted his hand toward his neck and that's when she realized he wore another gold medallion around his neck. He touched the metal and glanced at her in confusion. "Mamich gave me this. It was my great-grandfather's. She said it would protect me. But in the lightning I saw my dad. He had the same medallion in his hand, and he pointed to the land behind the house. I saw something sparkle in the lightning. And I thought I found another medallion, an exact match."

"You did," she said. "You had it in your hand." She reached into her pocket and pulled out the second medallion. She held it next to the medallion around his neck. "It does match—almost."

She touched the medallion he was wearing and felt a deep indentation in the metal. "Oh, my God, Jake, I think a bullet hit this."

"I guess it did its job then," he said wearily.

Overwhelming emotion ran through her as she realized how close he'd come to being shot in the chest.

"And it led me to you," he added. "It put me right where I needed to be so I could see you, so you could see me." He grimaced as he moved his leg slightly. "Damn, my leg hurts."

She couldn't imagine how he was even speaking through the pain. "I wish I had something to give you."

"I'll be fine. I'm tough."

"I know," she said, as she tenderly brushed a strand of hair off her tough guy's face. "You should sleep."

He stared back at her. "Will you be here when I wake up?"

"There's nowhere else I'd ever want to be," she said, making a promise that went far beyond what he was asking her.

He gave her a painful smile and closed his eyes.

"Is he going to be okay?" TJ asked.

"I hope so. I wish I could get him to a hospital or a clinic."

"He said his friend would be by in the morning."

"That's hours from now."

"If you think we need to go, I'll risk it."

"Thanks. If anything changes, I'll let you know."

"So are you and Jake back together?" TJ asked curiously.

"I don't know what we are," she replied with a helpless shrug. "The last few days have been a whirlwind. We've shared some intense experiences, and we've talked a lot about the past, but this isn't real life you know."

"It's felt pretty real to me," he said dryly. "I always liked you and Jake together. I thought you both just needed to grow up."

"You're pretty smart, little brother."

"If you come back to Corpus Christi, you could make Jake a part of your real life."

"I am coming back, TJ, not just for Jake—for Mom, and

for you, and for myself." She paused. "Oh, and I wanted to ask you something. I saw the doctor's name on Mom's prescriptions changed. And when I called her old doctor, they said she was no longer a patient. Why did she switch?"

"She said something about insurance. I added her to my policy when I started at MDT. I thought we had coverage for any doctor she wanted, but I guess that wasn't true."

She frowned. "It doesn't sound like you took her to the new doctor."

"One of her friends did, but I gave her the name of a doctor that—"

His abrupt pause drew her brows together. "What?"

"Dammit, Katherine. Jasmine gave me the name of a doctor to take Mom to. That's who she switched to."

"That's weird," she said slowly. "Why did you get her involved?"

"I told you. She had a relative that went through something similar, at least that's what she said. Now I wonder if that was true, or if she was just using Mom in some way."

"Now I'm even happier that I asked one of my friends to look in on her."

His troubled gaze met hers. "They wouldn't have done something to Mom."

She really hoped he was right, but she didn't have a good feeling. "You said they were using Mom's illness as leverage to get you to consider doing some freelance work. Maybe it was to their benefit to make her a little worse."

"If she's sicker because of me, how am I going to live with that?"

"It's not your fault, TJ, and we don't even know if that's the case. We'll figure that out when we get back."

"I'm going to kill Jasmine."

"If she's guilty, I'm going to help you," she said. "But we both know she wasn't doing it alone, so you have to be careful how you play it. Do you have any idea what you're going to do next? Because I think you need to talk to the police, the

FBI, Homeland Security, the CIA, the president...whoever you can get to. They're going to want to hear about the fact highly advanced weapons technology was in the hands of a Mexican drug cartel."

"Now that I know actual weapons were involved, I have better information to offer," TJ said.

"And I think the more visible you are, the less easy it will be for anyone to go after you. They can't keep you from talking if you've already talked."

"I should have thought of that before I ran into the jungle to hide."

"You didn't know what you were up against. You did what you needed to do to stay alive. Let's call that a win."

He nodded. "Deal."

She glanced back at Jake, worried as she saw his body convulse with a shiver. "He's cold."

"Really? It's not cold in here."

"I'm worried he's getting a fever. An infection could already be setting in. Maybe we should go back to the village. Even if we can't get to a hospital, Jake's great-grandmother might be able to help him. She has a pharmacy of herbs in her backyard, and maybe she has some instruments I could use to get the bullet out."

"If that's what you want," TJ said. "But I do have to say that if Rodrigo's men are looking for us, that's where they'll go."

"You're right. We'll just keep him warm and quiet and wait until we think it's safe to leave or we're forced to go."

She stretched out on the bed next to Jake. She'd give him some of her body heat. Hopefully, that would help beat the chills.

TJ sat in the chair with the ottoman, and for a moment there was nothing but the sound of silence in the room. She was exhausted but too wired and too worried to sleep.

An hour later, she knew that her worst fears were coming true. Jake was racked with fever. She sat up, ready to take a risk and go back to the village, when she heard a car outside the cabin. The headlights flashed, then turned off.

"TJ," she said quietly, urgently, her heart beating a million miles a minute.

Her brother woke up with a jerk. "What—what's wrong?"

"There's a car outside."

He jumped to his feet to peer out the window.

"Can you see who it is? Please tell me it's not Rodrigo and his men." If they'd been discovered now, there was no way any of them was going to survive the night.

Seventeen

"I don't know who it—" TJ stopped. "Wait. It's a man and a woman."

She got off the bed and ran to the window. Sylvia and an older man were coming toward the cabin. She moved to the door and opened it. "Thank God you're here," she said with relief. "Jake is hurt."

Sylvia and her friend stepped inside. "I was worried about that. Paolo told me he'd given Jake the directions to this cabin. When I saw the fire on the mountain, I wanted to come here immediately, but Paolo persuaded me to wait, to make sure that no one would follow us."

"Jake was shot," Katherine said as Sylvia moved toward the bed. "In the left upper thigh. There's no exit wound. I put on a pressure bandage, but Jake has developed a fever. TJ and I weren't sure where the nearest hospital was, and we were debating whether or not it was safe enough to go to the village."

"You made the right decision to stay here," Sylvia said, putting her hand on Jake's forehead. "The nearest hospital is forty miles. It would take more than an hour to get there." She glanced back at Katherine. "You must take the bullet out. We will clean his wound. My bag is in the car." She motioned to Paolo, who left the cabin to retrieve her bag.

"I can't operate on Jake here," she protested. "I don't have the tools, and I have nothing to give him for the pain. She couldn't imagine doing surgery in these conditions."

"I have brought everything you will need," Sylvia said. "I'm not a doctor, and my hands are too shaky now, but I know how to treat a wound. I have plants that can attack the infection—after you take the bullet out. You can do this, Katherine. It's what you have trained to do."

"In a hospital, with lights and sterile equipment and an anesthesiologist and machines to watch his vitals." She shook her head, feeling more terrified than she'd ever felt when faced with a patient. "It's Jake, Sylvia. What if I make a mistake?"

"You won't," Sylvia said with confidence. "You're a good doctor, aren't you? I bet you were at the top of your class."

"She was," TJ interjected, drawing her gaze to his. "You know you can do this, Katherine. More importantly, you know you have to, because you're not going to let Jake die."

No, she wasn't going to let Jake die. And TJ's words reminded her of why she'd gotten into medicine so that she wouldn't feel helpless when someone was hurt, so she wouldn't have to sit and hold their hand while they were dying, the way she'd done with Hailey all those years ago.

Paolo came back with a large canvas duffel bag and set it on the bed. Sylvia gave her an expectant look. "I think I have everything you need."

"All right. Let's do this," she said, as she looked through Sylvia's bag. It would be a crude procedure, and if the bullet in Jake's leg had pierced an artery, removing it could put him at risk of bleeding out. But she couldn't think of the worst outcome. That wouldn't get her anywhere. She'd always been good at compartmentalizing and blocking out her emotions. She needed to do that now more than ever. Jake was her patient, and she wasn't going to lose him. She went into ruthless doctor mode. Fix the problem, save the patient. It was that simple.

When they were ready to begin, she put her hand on Jake's arm. He stirred but didn't open his eyes.

Sylvia came forward with an eyedropper. "A little of this under his tongue, and he will sleep pain-free while you take out the bullet."

"What is it?" she asked.

"The juice of the poppy."

Her chest tightened. It was some form of opium. She told herself that morphine was derived from the poppy, and opiates had been used for thousands of years, but she was still worried about Jake getting too large or too small of a dose. It could affect his breathing, his blood flow. A million bad scenarios ran through her mind in the space of a minute.

"You will trust me?" Sylvia asked.

She hesitated, then slowly nodded. "Yes, because I know Jake trusts you."

Sylvia smiled. "He does. He's my boy. Together, we will make him better."

After Sylvia slipped a few drops under Jake's tongue, Katherine prepared to begin. "I'll need you to hold his shoulders, TJ," she said. "In case he tries to move."

TJ placed his hands on Jake's shoulders. "I think he's out."

She really hoped so. Drawing in a deep breath, she used one of the small knives Sylvia had brought to cut around his bullet wound. Jake moaned and moved slightly, but TJ had his shoulders. As she dug around for the bullet, Sylvia wiped away the blood with a towel. Finally, she was able to use some tweezers to remove the bullet from Jake's leg. There was no massive rush of bleeding leading her to believe that the arteries in his leg were intact.

"Got it," she said.

"I will clean it," Sylvia said, using a different eyedropper to drop some liquefied medicinal herbs into the wound.

Katherine closed the incision, sewing it up with a needle and thread. Then she rewrapped his leg with some bandages

Sylvia had brought with her.

When it was done, she checked Jake's pulse. Finding a steady beat, she sank down on the end of the bed and blew out a breath of relief.

Sylvia gave her a reassuring smile. "You did well, Katherine."

"I hope so. We still need his fever to break."

"It will. I will stay here tonight with you. Paolo will come back in the morning, and then we can go to the hospital if we need to."

"Thank you, Sylvia. I think you saved Jake's life. I'd love to know what was in that eyedropper that you used to fight infection."

"I will tell you everything whenever you are ready to hear it. But you are tired."

"I am tired," she admitted.

"Do you know what's happening at the ranch—with the fire?" TJ asked.

Sylvia looked to Paolo to answer the question. The older man stepped forward. He'd kept his distance during the surgical procedure.

"I have heard that the ranch is gone, that several men are dead."

"Rodrigo?" Katherine asked hopefully.

Paolo said, "I don't know. The morning will bring answers."

"Is the fire still burning?" TJ asked.

"There were few volunteers willing to offer help," Paolo said. "The mountain is blazing with a fire that can be seen for fifty miles. Everyone in the village came out of their homes to watch. It was an incredible sight, beyond what I expected Jake to accomplish."

"Jake said he had some help from you, Sylvia. What did you do?" she asked.

Sylvia gave her a secret smile. "I just asked for help. And it came."

"Do you think anyone is looking for us?" TJ asked Paolo.

"I have not heard such a thing," Paolo replied. "But it is best you stay here for the night. There are many people on the roads now. It is difficult to know who is a friend and who is an enemy."

TJ nodded. "I understand." He glanced at Katherine. "The explosion combined with the lightning and the fires will probably take down thousands of acres. There's no way Rodrigo's operation survives, even if he does."

"I hope he doesn't," she said fiercely. She'd never wished anyone dead, but the death of that man with the evil smile and dreams of causing mass destruction would leave the world a better place.

"I will go," Paolo said, tipping his head. "I will return in the morning." He stopped and took a phone out of his pocket. "Shall I leave you this?"

"No," TJ said abruptly. "No phones with traceable signals."

"But what if we need something?" she protested.

"We can make it until morning. We can't risk someone using a phone to find us."

"It's Paolo's phone."

"Still..."

"All right," she said, as Paolo shrugged and put his phone back into his pocket. "We'll see you in the morning. Thank you for everything."

Paolo left the cabin, and Katherine turned back to the bed to check on Jake. His pulse was still reassuringly steady.

"You should rest, Katherine," Sylvia said. "Lay down next to Jake. He will feel your presence, and he will be comforted."

"You should lay down," she argued. "You must be exhausted. I can pull the other chair next to the bed."

"No, I will watch over Jake for you. I don't sleep much anymore. And when I do, the dreams exhaust me. Please," Sylvia added, tipping her head toward the bed.

Katherine felt a little awkward lying on the bed next to Jake, while his eighty-nine- year-old great-grandmother sat on a hard chair, but there was no arguing with Sylvia. TJ also offered up the armchair with the ottoman, but she refused, saying he would need his strength for the journey to come.

Katherine hoped she was just talking about TJ's journey home and not something more ominous, but she was too drained to worry about that now.

She put her hand on Jake's arm, happy that his skin was quickly becoming a more normal temperature, and closed her eyes.

She didn't know when she drifted asleep, but the early morning sun was lighting up the cabin when she awoke. Sylvia stood next to the bed, bathing Jake's head with a cloth. She gave Katherine a smile. "The fever is gone."

She sat up. "Thank God. I didn't mean to sleep all night. I was going to take turns watching Jake with you."

"The night passed quickly, and it is not often I get to take care of my great-grandson."

Katherine glanced over at the chair. TJ was slowly coming awake, fighting off the day with his usual grumpy groans as he shifted position to try to catch a few more minutes of sleep.

When she looked back at Jake, she saw his eyelids begin to flicker and then open. She'd never been so happy to see his amazing green eyes in her life.

"Beautiful Kat," he said with a dazed smile. Then he turned his head and saw his great-grandmother. "Mamich?" Confusion entered his eyes. "Where am I?"

"The cabin," Katherine said, drawing his attention back to her. "The safe house Paolo told you about. We came here last night. Do you remember?"

"I thought that was a dream. I got shot in the leg. You were trying to stop the bleeding."

"I had to do more. I had to take the bullet out. It was causing an infection."

"You did that here?"

She nodded. "With Sylvia's help."

"So am I going to make it, Doc?"

She smiled, knowing that he was feeling better if he could joke. "Yes, thanks to Sylvia's concoction of herbs. But we still should get you checked out at a hospital. Unfortunately, there's nothing around for about forty miles."

"I don't need to go to the hospital. I already have a doctor and a healer. What more could I need?"

"I'll let you know after I check your leg," she said. "You may need antibiotics."

As Katherine said the words, she felt like she was insulting Sylvia, but the woman just gave her a simple smile, and said, "You'll know what's best, Katherine."

"What happened at the ranch?" Jake asked.

"We don't know yet," Katherine told him. "Paolo is going to try to find out and tell us when he comes back this morning. He said the whole mountain looked like it was on fire. Rodrigo's hideout is definitely gone."

"What about Rodrigo?"

"Unknown."

TJ came over to the bed. "Good to see you awake, Jake. It got a little dicey there for a while."

"I'm tough to get rid of," Jake said.

TJ sniffed. "What's that smell? Am I so hungry that I'm imagining food?"

Katherine suddenly became aware of a delicious aroma as well.

"I made some soup," Sylvia said.

"You made soup in the middle of the night?" she asked in astonishment.

"No, I made it yesterday before I came here, and I heated it in the microwave this morning," Sylvia said with a laugh. "I'm not a witch. I can't make food appear magically."

"Just lightning," Jake said dryly. He scooted back in the bed so that he was sitting up against the pillows. He reached for the medallion around his neck. "This saved my life, Mamich. A bullet ricocheted off of it. If I hadn't been wearing it, I would have been shot in the chest."

Sylvia paled at his words, but she gave a tight nod. "I wanted to protect you from the lightning; I'm glad it also saved you from a bullet."

"Wait. I found another medallion outside the house," he said. "Where did it go? Do you have it, Katherine?"

She pulled it out of her pocket. "Yes. It's right here."

Sylvia let out a gasp as she saw the matching medallions. "No." She put up a hand and then took a step backward.

"What's wrong, Mamich?" Jake asked in alarm.

"That medallion. It was at the ranch?"

"I found it in the dirt." His brows drew together. "You said all the men in the family had one. Did this one belong to my grandfather?"

She shook her head. "No, his medallion was buried with him when he died." Sylvia drew in a shaky breath. "May I see it?"

Katherine put the medallion in her open palm.

She stared at the front for a long moment and then turned it over. "This is your father's medallion."

"That's impossible," Jake said. "He wore his medallion every time he flew. He had it on the day he died. He always told me the bird would keep him in the air."

"There is an engraving." Sylvia handed the medallion to Jake. "Your father's initials, WM."

Katherine moved closer so she could see the initials. Her heart stopped at the sight of those two little letters. Jake met her gaze. Shock, amazement, and anger ran through his eyes.

"I don't know what to think," he muttered.

She didn't, either.

"It was your father's," Sylvia said again.

"But how can that be?" Jake asked. "How could it get to the ranch?"

"He was there," Sylvia said. "That is the only answer.

You said you saw him holding it in his hand right before you found it. He was sending you a message. He made sure you found it. It's important to his story, to his journey."

"Did you know he went to that ranch?" Jake asked. "Was he here right before he died? When I visited you a year after his death, you said you hadn't seen him in several years. Was that true?"

"Yes, it was true," Sylvia said with sorrow in her eyes. "I had not seen him in three years. He did not come to the village, Jake. He was not here right before he died. But he must have been at that ranch."

"But…" Jake's voice trailed away as he traced his father's initials with his fingers. "I don't understand." He looked over at Katherine. "What do you think?"

"I have no idea," she said, shaken by this latest development. "Alicia said she thought there was more to your dad's accident than anyone knew. Maybe she was right."

"And it was Jerry who told her that. Jerry, my father's best friend," Jake said.

"Is it possible that your dad was involved in Jerry's scheme?" she asked tentatively, worried that Jake would immediately jump down her throat for suggesting such a thing.

"My dad died ten years ago. I don't even know if Jerry was doing whatever he was doing that long ago," Jake said. "My father was a good man and a patriot. I can't believe he would have been involved with anything illegal."

"Perhaps the ranch wasn't conducting that kind of business when your dad was there," she suggested.

"That's true. Rodrigo only came into power a few years ago." He looked at Sylvia. "When did Jose die?"

"It was before your father passed away," she said, a troubled expression on her face. "You must find the answers, Jake. So your father can find peace."

"I don't know how the hell I'm going to do that, especially now that the ranch is probably burned to the ground."

"You'll find a way," Sylvia said confidently. "Now, who wants soup?" She went over to the counter, poured some soup into a bowl and brought it over to the bed, along with a spoon. She handed it to Jake. "First things first."

He grudgingly accepted the soup. "Thank you. But this isn't over. There's something I'm missing here."

TJ helped Sylvia fill up three more bowls, and for several minutes there was nothing but silence in the small cabin. The delicious soup was warm and satisfying and Katherine felt much better after she ate. It had been a long stressful night, and who knew what the day would bring?

She rinsed out the bowls in the sink and had just finished doing that when she heard the sound of a vehicle coming up to the house.

TJ ran to the window. "It's Paolo," he said, then answered the door.

Paolo stepped into the room a moment later, a question in his eyes. "Is everyone all right?"

"Jake is much better," Sylvia told him.

"*Bueno*," Paolo said.

"Can you tell us what's been happening?" TJ asked. "Did Rodrigo and his men escape the fire? Is there any more information?"

"Rodrigo's body was found early this morning. El Diablo is dead," he said with a gleam of happiness in his eyes. "The village is rejoicing."

"Even though the money dries up?" Katherine asked.

"Blood money always ends in blood," Paolo said. "The town has seen too much blood the past few years."

"What about Rodrigo's army?" Jake asked.

"No one knows how many men were there, but they've discovered at least a half dozen bodies. Some may have escaped, but since they ran instead of trying to save the ranch, their allegiance to Rodrigo and the cartel is doubtful. I believe the danger to Jake and his friends is gone."

Katherine let out a sigh, feeling as if the last weight had slipped off her shoulders. She smiled at Jake and TJ. "It's over then. We can go home."

Neither man immediately agreed with her. "What? We can't go home?"

"Rodrigo was just one part of the problem," TJ said somberly. "He's dead, but who else is out there? If I go back to Texas, knowing as much as I know, will I be safe? Will Mom?"

And just like that, her worries came rushing back. "You need to talk to some high- level authorities. Alicia said she had a contact at the FBI. We'll start there."

"We can also ask Danielle for help," Jake put in. "She works for Senator Dillon. He'll be concerned about whatever is going on at MDT. They're a big company in his home state."

"A company that supports his campaigns," TJ said.

"Then he'll want to make sure they're clean," Katherine said.

"All right, I'm game," TJ said. "Obviously, I didn't do that well on my own, so I'll take some advice."

"I do think we should stay under the radar until we get out of Mexico," Jake said.

"How are we going to get out? We don't have passports or ID or money," she said, suddenly remembering that they'd lost everything.

"I'll talk to Rusty. He can fax copies of our passports to the airport in Tuxtla Gutiérrez. We'll hire a small plane. It will be easier, and when we get to the States, we'll get Alicia or Dani to help us with whatever we need," Jake said.

"My passport is probably still at the inn," TJ said. "Unless someone cleaned out my room."

"We'll check on the way to the airport," Katherine said. "And if not, I'm betting Mom still has a copy. We'll get one of her caregivers to look for it."

"That's settled then," Jake said, swinging his legs off the

side of the bed.

Katherine quickly moved to his side. "Don't get up for a second. Let me check your wound." She quickly unwrapped the bandage and was thrilled to see no sign of infection. "It looks good. I'm better than I thought."

Jake smiled. "You've always been better than you thought."

She smiled back. "Thanks." She re-bandaged his leg and then stood up.

"I have money for you," Sylvia said, pressing an envelope into Katherine's hand.

"We'll pay you back," Jake said.

"I'm not worried."

Paolo stepped forward. "You can take my truck to the airport. My cousin will drive me over there later to get it. I'll take Sylvia home."

"Thank you, Paolo—for everything," Jake said, shaking the older man's hand.

"You've freed our people from the devil. It is I who should thank you," Paolo said. "Sylvia? Shall we go?"

"A moment," she said. "I need to speak to my great-grandson before we leave."

Katherine stepped away from the bed. As Sylvia took Jake's hand, she decided to give them a little privacy. "We'll wait outside," she said, motioning for her brother to join her on the porch.

—➤➤◄◄—

"Jake," Sylvia said.

He squeezed his great-grandmother's hand as she gave him a loving and somewhat sad smile. "Thanks for saving my life, Mamich. I don't know how you called the lightning, but when I saw the jagged streaks of light raining down around me, I felt your power."

"The power of our ancestors. I have wondered these past

years what was left for me on this earth—why I was still here when so many others have gone before me. It was for this. I was waiting for you to come back."

He felt unsettled by her words. It sounded like she was ready to say good-bye. "We don't have all the answers yet, Mamich. We don't know how my father's medallion got to the ranch."

"You will find the truth, and then your father's soul will be free to move on."

He didn't know about freeing his father's spirit, but he would do everything in his power to find the truth.

"You didn't just rescue Katherine and her brother," Sylvia continued. "You stopped a lot of people from getting hurt."

He smiled at her. "I think *we* did that, Mamich. I wasn't a believer before, but I am now."

"You have the heart of a warrior." She leaned over and kissed his forehead. "One day you will hear of my passing. I do not want you to be sad. Remember that we had this adventure together. That we did something great."

He didn't want to hear her talk of death, but he could see she was determined to speak.

"Your father was a good man. If he was at the ranch, it was not because he was working with the cartel. It was because he, too, was trying to stop them. I believe that with all my heart."

"I know he was a good man. I have no doubts."

"I want to give you something else, Jake."

"You've already given me so much."

"It's not for you; it's for Danielle."

She pulled a heavy gold band off her finger. "This is the ring your great-grandfather gave me when we married. I want you to give it to Danielle." Sylvia smiled. "She won't like it. She'll think it's ugly, but tell her that if she needs strength, the ring will give it to her. She won't believe you, but it is true. She's the final piece in the puzzle."

He didn't think Dani would appreciate anything Sylvia was saying, but he took the ring and put it in his pocket. He'd make sure Dani took it, even if she just put it in her jewelry box. After his great-grandfather's medallion had saved him from a bullet, he didn't doubt that she knew best when it came to protecting her family.

"And tell Alicia that I leave her my house, my herbs, your father's letters, the story of our family. Tell her to come one day and collect whatever she needs."

He shook his head. "I will bring Alicia and Dani down here in the next few weeks. You can talk to them then. You can tell them what you're telling me."

"It would be good to see them," she said, but he could tell she was only saying what she thought he needed to hear. "But just in case—"

"No, Mamich. We're just getting reacquainted," he said. "Whoever is calling you from the other side—you tell them to wait. You have more to do here."

"My sweet Jake. Always know that wherever you are, I am watching over you. When the lightning strikes, it is only to show you what you need to see."

He nodded. She helped him to his feet, and they exchanged a long hug and then slowly made their way outside. Every step was painful, but for some reason the physical pain didn't feel as bad as the ache in heart as he watched Sylvia and Paolo get into their car.

"I was going to come and get you," Katherine said, putting her arm around him. "Everything all right?"

"Yes," he said, but his gaze followed Paolo's truck down the road. He had a feeling that he would never see his great-grandmother again. He would have been sad about her loss before this trip, but now he could feel the depth of the coming pain. He'd connected to her. They'd shared a powerful moment. He told himself he'd come back before too long and hope that she still had more time left on this earth. He turned back to Katherine. "Let's go home."

Eighteen

—➤➤◀◀←—

They made a brief stop at the inn on their way to the airport to retrieve TJ's passport. As Paolo had said, there seemed to be an air of celebration in the village with children playing, guitars strumming, and smiles on everyone's faces. Despite the festive atmosphere, Jake was happy when TJ got back in the truck, and they drove out of the village. He wanted to put as many miles as he could between themselves and any lingering members of Rodrigo's army.

"I almost forgot," Katherine said, handing him a cell phone. "Paolo gave me this. You should call Rusty."

He did so immediately and after making his conversation as brief and efficient as possible, he got Rusty to agree to find them a charter, pay for it and send copies of their passports to the airfield. While Katherine's name hadn't been on the charter to Mexico, Rusty had insisted on getting a copy of her passport before putting her on the plane. Now, Jake was happy that his boss had been so demanding.

After he hung up with Rusty, he called Alicia. There were so many things he had to tell his sister, he didn't know where to start, but he settled on the most pressing problem— making sure TJ would be safe once they got back to the States. He told Alicia that TJ had been kidnapped by a drug cartel who had probably been sold MDT-developed weapons by Jerry or someone else in the company. TJ had important information and was still in danger, so they needed to make sure he got help from the right people.

While Alicia had a million questions, she quickly realized that he couldn't answer most of them and told him she would call her contact at the FBI and see what they should do. He told her he would wait for her to call back and hung up.

"Alicia will make some calls," he told TJ and Katherine.

"You didn't tell her about your dad," Katherine commented.

"I wanted her to focus on TJ's situation. There will be time for all that later."

"Thanks for doing that," TJ said. "I probably should have called the FBI to start with, but MDT has a lot of friends in high places. I was too afraid to reach out on my own."

"You're not on your own anymore," Katherine said. "I'm not letting you out of my sight until I know you're going to be protected."

"I feel the same way about you," TJ said.

As the two exchanged a look, Jake wondered just what had gone on at the ranch before he'd gotten there. He had a feeling he was not going to like whatever it was. But he told himself that TJ and Katherine were fine; that was all that mattered.

Ten minutes later, Alicia called him back. "That was fast," he told her.

"I spoke to Special Agent Wolfe," Alicia said. "He's in DC. He thinks you guys should fly straight there rather than going back to Corpus Christi. He said a lot of governmental agencies will want to talk to you, and they can protect you."

"That makes sense," he replied.

"I spoke to Dani," Alicia continued. "She's going to talk to the senator as well. She said to come to her apartment when you land. I'm going to get on a plane, too, and meet you there."

"You don't have to do that."

"Are you kidding? I want to know everything, Jake."

Of course she did. "All right. I'll call Rusty and see if he can get us a flight to DC. I doubt we'll be there before tonight."

"Keep me posted and have a safe trip."

"Thanks." He ended the call and punched in Rusty's number. When Rusty answered, he said, "Looks like we need three seats on a plane to DC. Can you make that happen?" Rusty said he would do his best and to check in when they got to the airport.

Jake sighed and shifted positions as he handed Katherine the phone. He was a little cramped sharing the seat with Katherine—not that he'd ever complain about being too close to her, but his leg was starting to throb.

"Are you okay?" she asked.

"I'm good. Rusty is going to see what flights he can get us to DC."

"I'm sorry I ever doubted him, Jake."

"Don't worry about it."

"You should rest," she said, looking at him with a critical eye. "I think we've got a ways to go."

She was right. It took them almost two hours to get to the airport in Tuxtla Gutiérrez. They bypassed the main terminal for the smaller terminal on the other side of the airfield that serviced small private planes.

After calls between Rusty and the airport office, they were put on a plane shortly after eleven. It would be an eight-hour flight to DC. With the time change, they'd arrive around ten o'clock at night.

While they waited for their flight, they bought breakfast in the café with the money Sylvia had given them. Jake felt a lot better after downing an order of huevos rancheros and drinking two large glasses of orange juice.

"I'm glad you have an appetite," Katherine said.

"It never goes away," he said with a smile.

"I'm going to use the restroom," TJ said.

As TJ left the table, Jake saw Katherine's concerned gaze follow her brother across the room. "He's going to be okay," he assured her.

"I won't feel safe until we get in the air. I keep thinking someone is going to show up any second and try to stop us."

He couldn't deny that she had reason to be concerned. Rodrigo and his men might be dead, but whomever they were working with at MDT was alive and well.

Katherine turned her gaze back to him. "How are you feeling?"

"You have to stop asking me that. I'll tell you if there's a problem."

"I wish I could believe you would," she said pointedly. "But you're not a complainer."

"Finally, something you like about me," he teased.

"You know I like a lot of things about you. But I am worried the long flight is going to be too much for you."

"I'll make it."

"Those herbs your great-grandmother gave you are going to wear off, and you're going to hurt, Jake."

"I can take the pain. I'm so happy that we're alive, nothing else matters." He reached across the table and put his hand over hers. He had a dozen things he wanted to say to her, but before he could utter a word, TJ came back.

"Am I interrupting?" TJ asked. "Do you want me to wait outside?"

"No," Jake said, letting go of her hand. "It's time to go anyway, and I think the three of us should stay together."

"So you're worried, too," Katherine murmured as they headed toward the door.

"Like you, I'll feel better when we're off the ground."

The plane had eight passenger seats. Katherine took the window, while he sat on the aisle and TJ sat next to him on the opposite aisle. Also on board was an older couple in their sixties who said they were taking a second honeymoon. After some casual chatter, the couple turned their attention to their books and computers while TJ promptly fell asleep.

"Your brother is already out," Jake said as the plane took off.

"He's exhausted."

"You must be, too."

"I'm going to try to nap now that we're in the air." She tipped her head to the window, to the view unfolding before them. "Look at all that rain forest, Jake. I think we hiked through most of it."

"We did."

"I was beginning to wonder if we'd ever get out of it. I used to like being on the ground more than flying, but that's changed."

"It's a different perspective; that's for sure."

She glanced back at him. "Is it strange to be a passenger and not be in the pilot's seat?"

"Actually, I'm not too upset about it."

"Because you're in pain."

"It's not that bad."

"You have to tell me if you start feeling chilly, hot, or dizzy," she said, giving him a close look. "While Sylvia's herbal medicine seemed to take the infection right out of you, I don't know how long the effects will last."

"They'll last. She's good. So are you. Hailey would be proud."

A smile spread across Katherine's mouth. "She would have loved our adventure."

"I think she was with us."

"Me, too." Katherine paused. "When she died and I didn't, it made me feel like I had to do something important with my life, because she couldn't. That's part of what drove me, Jake."

"I know. And you did it, Kat. You're still doing it. Every day."

"So what did Sylvia say to you when you were alone in

the cabin?"

"She said good-bye. It felt...final."

"I guess at her age any visit from a relative probably feels like it could be the last," Katherine said carefully.

"It was more than that. It was as if she'd done what she was supposed to do. She kept saying this was why she'd lived so long—it was for our destinies to cross, for us to save the village from El Diablo."

"She does have a way with words," Katherine said.

"I know it's all crazy. If we tell anyone that we blew up the ranch with some matches and the help of a bad-assed lightning storm, no one will believe us."

"Or they'd say we just got lucky with the timing of the storm."

"And that's probably what it was."

"As a scientist, I'd have to agree with that, but despite words to the contrary, I think your great-grandmother is a little bit of a witch. She spooks me, anyway. Mostly in a good way, but I wouldn't want to get on her bad side."

He grinned. "Me, either. She told me how to save you, and Paolo helped me set everything else up. I just had this terrible fear when I got to the ranch that you might not actually be there."

"I wondered if you would find me, too, because I wasn't sure where I was. They kept me blindfolded until I was inside. Rodrigo was there; he had an evil smile. He told TJ that if he didn't fix the weapons system, they would hurt me. He gave him two hours. You got there just before the deadline."

His stomach turned over. "God, Katherine. I had no idea."

Her somber blue gaze met his. "You came in time. That's all that matters."

"You must have been terrified."

"I was," she admitted.

"I was, too," he said, looking into her eyes. "When I

realized they'd taken you from the yard, I felt a crushing blast of fear. I didn't know how I was going to save you." He took her hand. "I hate to think that you were so close—"

"Don't think about it," she said, cutting him off. "Because then I'll think about it, too, and I really don't want to."

He could see that despite her bravado, she was hanging on by a thread. "You should sleep, Kat. We'll talk it all out when we get to DC."

"We'll be able to keep TJ safe, right?"

He saw the lingering worry in her eyes. "We'll make sure of it."

"I wish I could have spoken to my mom."

Katherine had called her mother from the airport, but the caregiver had told Katherine that her mom was asleep, and Katherine hadn't wanted to leave a message.

"You'll talk to her when we get to DC."

"You're right."

He settled more comfortably into his seat. He wanted to keep talking to Katherine, but exhaustion was catching up to him. "I think I'm going to close my eyes."

"You should. I'll be here when you wake up."

He looked over at her. "You said that last night."

"And I was there in the morning," she reminded him.

"Will you always be there, Kat?" he asked sleepily, his brain shutting down even as he asked what was probably the most important question he could have asked. He just wished he could have stayed awake long enough to hear the answer.

———

Would she always be there?

How could she say yes?

On the other hand, how could she say no?

Leaving Jake before had been horrible, but at that time she'd been angry and hurt and desperate to get on with her life before she lost it.

Leaving Jake now…again…

That seemed impossible to contemplate. They'd bonded on their journey. They'd not only found each other again, they'd also found themselves. At least, she had.

She'd been hiding from so many things the past decade, but the biggest thing had been herself. She'd never wanted to look too closely at her thoughts or her actions, always afraid they would derail her. But trekking through Mexico had stripped all of her barriers away and changed her forever. She wasn't the same woman she was a week ago, and she was happy about that.

She'd been far too one-dimensional. That would change. She was going to be there for everyone; not just her patients, but her friends, her family, the people who really mattered— two of whom were in the plane with her.

As she watched Jake sleep, she felt a protective tenderness and an overwhelming love.

Would she always be there when Jake woke up?
How could she be anywhere else?

———⸎———

When Jake woke up, they were landing in DC. He couldn't believe he'd slept the entire flight. He looked over at Katherine, who was rubbing her sleepy eyes. "Did you catch a nap?"

"A long one," she said. "How about you?"

"I feel better now."

"I'm glad."

As she looked back at him, a hazy memory went around in his head. He felt like he should remember something, but he couldn't think what it was.

Katherine unbuckled her seat belt as the plane came to a stop. "We're back in the States."

"I've never been so happy to be home."

He looked over at TJ, who gave him a nod that finished

with a long yawn. "You ready for what's coming TJ?" he asked.

TJ shrugged. "It can't be any worse than what we've been through."

He couldn't help but agree.

After they got off the plane, Alicia met them at the gate and had apparently cleared their way into the country, because they were quickly on their way in a hired SUV to Danielle's Georgetown apartment.

"Special Agent Wolfe is going to meet us at Dani's place," Alicia said. "He wanted to pick you up at the airport, but I told him I had to see you first. I wanted to make sure you were all okay."

"And you want to get answers to your questions before the FBI whisks us away," Jake said dryly, knowing his baby sister very well.

"Maybe," Alicia conceded. "Can you blame me?"

"I guess not," Jake said. "Where's Michael?"

"He's in Miami. He had to work. He said to tell you he's glad you're okay." She gave Jake a speculative glance. "You look like shit, Jake. And what's with the ripped jeans and the bandage around your leg?"

"I got hurt, but I'm fine."

"He got shot," Katherine corrected.

Alicia's lips parted. "Are you serious?"

"Yep. Katherine dug a bullet out of my leg last night and stitched me up," Jake said.

"Are you going to be all right?"

"Fine."

"Katherine?" Alicia asked, obviously not taking his answer for truth.

"He will be fine; he's not quite there yet," Katherine said, sending him a pointed look.

"I can't believe it," Alicia said. "You should have told me that on the phone, Jake."

"I wanted to save that happy conversation for now," he

replied. "Ease up, Alicia. It's all good."

She made a face at him, and then turned to Katherine. "Thanks for taking care of him, even though I'm quite sure he's been a pain in the ass."

Katherine smiled. "He has definitely been that, but he also saved my life and TJ's, too, so I can't complain."

"See, not just a pain in the ass," he told his sister.

The car stopped in front of a brownstone, and they made their way up to Danielle's second-story apartment.

His sister greeted them at the door with a worried expression. She gave him a quick hug and then waved them inside.

"You remember Katherine?" Jake said.

"Of course I remember her," Dani said, giving Katherine a smile. "I have to say I am a little surprised you're together, though. Alicia has filled me in on some of what's been going on, but there are a lot of holes in the story."

"We'll try to fill them in," Jake said.

"This is my brother, TJ," Katherine said.

TJ gave Danielle a nod. "You probably don't remember me."

"I remember you were a lot shorter and skinnier," she said. "But good to see you again."

"Mind if I use your restroom?" TJ asked.

Danielle pointed down the hall.

As TJ left the room, Jake sat down on the couch. He felt tired, dirty, and hungry, and he would have loved to take a break before talking to the FBI, but on the other hand, the sooner they got TJ under federal protection, the better.

"We have water, juice, soda, and we ordered tons of Chinese food in case you're hungry," Alicia said.

"All of the above," he replied.

"And Dani and I went out and got you all some clothes," Alicia continued. "We had to guess at the men's sizes, but there's a bag for each of you. You said you lost everything."

"We did." He stretched his leg out on the coffee table.

"What happened to you?" Danielle asked as Alicia went into the kitchen to get the food and drinks.

"He got shot," Alicia yelled from the kitchen.

Dani raised an eyebrow as she looked at her brother. "I hope you shot back."

He grinned. "Spoken like a true Texas woman. Unfortunately, I didn't have a gun. But it turned out I didn't need one."

Alicia returned to the room and set cartons of Chinese food on the coffee table, along with forks and chopsticks. She made a quick trip back for drinks and then they settled in to eat when TJ came back from the bathroom.

"Okay," Alicia said. "Tell us what happened."

"It's a long story," Jake said, not sure where to begin.

"Jump to the part where Katherine and TJ were being held by a drug leader."

He looked at Katherine. "You want to explain? Some of what happened last night is fuzzy in my head."

"It was a ranch run by Rodrigo Calderon," Katherine said. "He was the leader of a drug cartel, but he was also amassing weapons."

"The most advanced weapons MDT makes," TJ put in. "I'm pretty sure he bought them from Jerry Caldwell."

Alicia nodded. "Finally, we know who Jerry was selling to."

"He had a couple smaller versions of our new railguns in the barn at the ranch, but they weren't working," TJ added. "They brought me in to fix the software that controls the weapon. I wasn't going to help them. And then Katherine showed up."

"They kidnapped me behind your great-grandmother's house," Katherine added. "And then they used me as leverage to get TJ to fix the system."

"Fortunately, none of that happened, because Jake created a diversionary fire," TJ continued. "It was massive."

"And I got some help from a fierce lightning storm," Jake

put in, seeing the gleam in Alicia's eyes. "That's right. *Lightning*. Mamich told me she was going to call the lightning down from the sky at the same time I lit the hillside on fire. And that's exactly what happened."

"The fire was so big," Katherine continued. "All the men went running. TJ and I broke out of the room we were in, and we saw Jake running toward us, but he got shot. The guard was going to take another shot, but the barn exploded. We ran to Jake and got him to safety."

"Thank God," Alicia murmured.

"Rodrigo and his men—at least some of them—are dead," Jake said. "But there's still a connection to MDT that needs to be figured out."

"I have a fairly good idea of at least one person who's involved," TJ said. "But I'm sure there's more, because she's not high enough in the company to have the kind of power to move those weapons. And I don't know what other weapons have been sold or to whom. Rodrigo hinted at a big plan to use those weapons. I don't think he was acting alone."

"That's why you need to get the Feds involved," Jake said. Hearing the story told again while he was conscious enough to make sense of it made him realize just how close they'd come to a really bad ending.

"They should be here soon," Alicia said.

"Before they come, I want to try my mother again," Katherine said. "Do you have a phone I can borrow?"

"Of course," Alicia said, handing over her cell phone.

"I'll call her with you," TJ said.

"You can use my bedroom if you want," Danielle offered.

"Thanks," Katherine said, as she and TJ went into the other room to make their call.

As Jake shifted his seat, something dug into his side, and he remembered the ring. He pulled it out of his pocket. "I have something for you, Danielle. This is from Mamich." He opened his palm to reveal the wedding ring. "She asked me to give it to you."

Danielle looked at the ring as if it might bite her and made no attempt to take it out of the palm of his hand. "Is that her wedding ring?"

He nodded. "Yes. She wanted you to have it. She said it would protect you, guide you, give you wisdom."

"How's it going to do that?" she asked doubtfully.

Jake sighed. "Just take it, Dani."

"I don't really want it. Maybe Alicia does."

"Sorry, Alicia, but she wanted Danielle to have it."

Both of his sisters looked unhappy with his reply.

"Look, Dani, Mamich said she knew you wouldn't want this, but I had to insist you take it. She said you don't have to wear it, but she wants you to keep it. One day she believes it will be important to you and that it will protect you."

"God, you sound just like her," Danielle said with a frown.

"I'm just telling you what she told me. So take the ring."

Dani reluctantly took the ring and then put it down on the coffee table.

"She didn't send me anything?" Alicia asked, a jealous note in her voice.

He smiled. "She told me to tell you that she is leaving you everything else—her house, her herb garden, Dad's letters and her house. You're in charge of guiding the next generation, making sure her story is told."

"You make it sound like she's dying," Alicia said.

He met her troubled gaze. "To be honest, she made it sound that way. I didn't want to hear any of it, but she forced me to listen."

"What did she leave you?" Dani asked curiously. "If I get the ring and Alicia gets everything else, what about you?"

He'd almost forgotten. His brain was definitely fuzzy and weaker than it normally was. He opened his shirt and pulled off the medallion he wore around his neck. "This belonged to our great-grandfather. She gave it to me before I went to rescue Katherine and TJ. She said it would protect me, and it did. One of the bullets ricocheted off of it, saving my heart."

"Seriously?" Dani asked in amazement.

"That looks like the medallion Dad used to wear," Alicia commented.

"It's an exact match." He reached back into his pocket and pulled out the second medallion. "This one was Dad's. It has his initials on it."

"I remember this." Alicia took it from Jake's hand. "He never took this off." She raised her gaze to Jake's, puzzlement in her dark eyes. "Wait a second. Dad had this on the night he crashed." She sucked in a breath. "Where did you find it?"

"At the ranch in the mountains where TJ and Katherine were being held."

"It was just sitting out on a table?" Alicia asked in bemusement.

"No, it was in the dirt on the outskirts of the property." He took a breath and held Alicia's gaze. "Only you would believe this, but when the lightning flashed, I saw the gold on the ground."

"You're both insane," Dani said, shaking her head. "I thought it was bad enough that Alicia chased storms. Now you're going to join her?"

"Trust me, I won't be chasing any more lightning," he said. "I've seen enough for a lifetime, but I can't deny what happened. On my way to Mexico, the lightning struck my instrument panel and took away my steering capabilities, which was why Katherine and I crashed in the jungle. In the middle of that storm, I saw Dad. He said 'Follow me' and I didn't know what choice I had since the plane was going down whether I liked it or not. I saw him again in the lightning flashes at the ranch. He was pointing toward the spot where I found the medallion."

Alicia leaned forward, enthralled by the story. "That's amazing. You actually saw Dad?"

"I thought it was my imagination."

"That's exactly what it was," Dani said. "Dad isn't a ghost lurking in the sky."

"Mamich believes there are many layers within the universe and that we travel from one to the other when we die," Alicia told Dani. "It's very possible that his spirit is strong enough to make contact with us."

Dani rolled her eyes. "Look, I think we need to stop investigating Dad's death."

"Are you kidding?" Alicia asked in shock. "We finally have a clue, Dani."

"What clue?"

"Dad's medallion was in Mexico. His plane didn't go down in the Gulf," Alicia said. "Right, Jake? He had to be at that ranch."

"I can't think of any other way his medallion got onto the property. I definitely don't think he crashed in the Gulf anymore."

"Maybe he lost the medallion or gave it to someone else," Dani suggested.

"He was wearing it that night," Alicia argued. "He always wore it when he flew. It was blessed."

"So what do you think happened, Jake?" Dani asked him.

"Yes, Jake, what do you think?" Alicia echoed.

He looked at both of his sisters and wished he had a good answer. "I think Dad was at the ranch, and it's possible he was killed there. I also think his death ties back to Jerry and what Jerry told you. Maybe Dad learned what Jerry was up to and tried to stop it."

"Was Jerry selling weapons and secrets ten years ago?" Dani challenged. "Do you know if his operation went that far back?"

He looked at Alicia. "Do you know?"

She shrugged. "I don't. It's certainly possible. But why wouldn't Dad have told anyone he was going to Mexico?"

"I'm not sure we'll ever know," he said.

"Well, I'm not ready to give up on finding out," Alicia

said. "I'll give Colin, my investigator, this information. Maybe it will lead him in a new direction. What about Mamich? Did you tell her that you think Dad was killed in Mexico?"

"She said she'd known for a long time that Dad's bones weren't where they were supposed to be."

Dani shuddered at his words. "That's a lovely thing to say."

"You know how she talks. Or maybe you don't," he said. "When did you last speak to her?"

"Years ago," Dani admitted. "That's why I don't understand why she sent me her wedding ring. We've never been close."

"She told me that you are the last piece of the puzzle."

"What does that mean?"

"I don't know. Maybe she just wants you to believe in her."

"Why would she care?"

"She cares about all of us. We're her family."

"Distant family."

"We're blood," he said. "In her world, blood matters."

"I want to go to Mexico," Alicia said. "I want to see Mamich and the ranch where Dad might have died."

"There may not be anything left to see. The buildings went down in the fire."

"But the land is still there. I feel like I need to walk in Dad's footsteps. We should all go together."

He could understand her desire, but they couldn't go yet. "Maybe in a while," he said. "It's too dangerous for any of us to be in Mexico right now."

"When this is over..." Alicia began.

"I'll go with you," he said. "And maybe Dani will come."

"I wouldn't count on it," Dani said.

He looked up as Katherine and TJ came back to the couch. "How is your mom?"

Katherine smiled. "She sounds better than she did the last

time I spoke to her. She said Rebecca stopped by and changed her medication. TJ and I called Rebecca to corroborate, and she told me that my mom was being overmedicated and that she actually could find no record of the doctor who wrote the prescription."

"What does that mean?" he asked in surprise.

"We think it means that Jasmine got someone to make Mom's condition worse," TJ replied heavily. "I gave her access to my life, and she took it."

"Why would she want to hurt your mother?" Alicia asked.

"Leverage," TJ said. "She might have thought she could use my mom's illness to make me desperate for money so I'd get involved in the operation. But when I shut her down on doing anything freelance, she went to plan B and got me to Mexico so Rodrigo's men could get to me." He paused. "I hope the Feds get here soon, because I want someone knocking on Jasmine's door as soon as possible, and preferably before she knows I'm alive and Calderon is dead."

The apartment buzzer went off. "Looks like you got your wish," Jake said as Danielle opened the door for two agents from the FBI.

Help had finally arrived.

Nineteen

The next three hours passed in a hazy blur for Katherine. Damon Wolfe, the lead agent, was an attractive man with dark hair and piercing blue eyes that were intelligent and impossible to read. His partner was an attractive brunette woman named Abby James. They both asked a lot of questions and rarely answered any that were directed at them.

She let TJ do most of the talking, although she and Jake made lengthy statements as well. Alicia also got involved, providing background from the case she'd been involved in. Katherine wished the agents had given more credence to Alicia's instincts. Maybe TJ's problems could have all been avoided if the FBI had not dropped the investigation into MDT quite so quickly. The fact that they had also led her to believe someone high up in the company was involved in a massive cover-up. She hoped now they would finally get caught.

Glancing over at Jake, she frowned. She didn't care for the pallor of his skin. He'd been rock solid through all the questioning, but she knew he was hurting. It was almost two o'clock in the morning, and there appeared to be no end in sight.

When Agent Wolfe glanced down at his notes and suggested that they go through each story one more time, she knew it was time to call a halt.

"No, that's enough for now," she said firmly.

Agent Wolfe gave her a sharp look. "We need to make sure we haven't missed anything."

"You can do that tomorrow. The three of us are exhausted. We need to find a hotel and call it a night. We can resume this conversation in the morning."

"Miss Barrett—" Agent James began.

"That's Dr. Barrett," she interrupted. "Look, we've answered all your questions, and while I am very aware of the importance of this conversation, we'll all think better with some sleep. I'm sure we'll be answering questions for many more days to come, but for tonight we're done." She got to her feet. "I'm going to call a cab to take us to a hotel."

"I made reservations for you," Dani said. "At the Hotel Marks down the street."

"We'll take you there," Agent Wolfe said. "And we'll have security outside your rooms tonight."

"Good." She turned to Alicia and Dani. "Thank you for everything, especially getting these guys to help us."

"It's about time the FBI listened to me," Alicia said. "I've been trying to get their attention for weeks."

Agent Wolfe gave Alicia a dry smile. "Believe me, you all have our full attention now."

Katherine gave Jake a hand, noting the lines of pain around his mouth and eyes as he stood up.

"Nicely done, Dr. Barrett," he murmured, swinging an arm around her shoulders. "I like when you go into doctor mode."

"I'll remind you of that sometime. I should have called a halt earlier. And I'm still wondering if I shouldn't be taking you to a hospital and not a hotel."

"I'd rather have my own personal physician watch over me. I'm just tired."

"You don't feel chilly or hot?"

He shook his head. "No fever, Doc."

"Okay, then."

"Don't forget the clothes," Alicia said, handing them each a bag. "We'll talk to you in the morning. Be safe tonight."

"I think it's the safest we've been in days," Katherine returned, following the agents out to their bulletproof black SUV.

Twenty minutes later, they had checked in to adjoining rooms at the hotel with two guards posted outside their doors.

TJ gave her a weary hug goodnight and then headed to bed. She left the door ajar between their rooms, needing to feel like she could hear him if anything went wrong.

Her brother could still be a target. The fact that the FBI felt the need to put guards outside the door backed up that idea. Until they brought Jasmine in for questioning, there were still a lot of unanswered questions.

But for now, she was going to let those questions go.

While Jake took a shower, she stripped off her clothes and put on one of the bathrobes hanging in the closet. She couldn't wait to get hot water on her head, but first she wanted to check Jake's wound and make sure there were no new signs of infection.

Walking over to the window, she glanced out at the lights of DC. What a different view she had tonight than she'd had any day the past week. She and Jake had been alone so much in such an isolated part of the world she'd almost forgotten what it was like to be in a city.

Jake came out of the bathroom with a towel around his hips.

Her exhausted body immediately perked up at the sight of him, but she told herself not to be ridiculous. The man needed sleep and nothing else.

He gave her a smile. "You could have joined me in the shower, babe."

"I want to look at your wound."

"Is that all you want to look at?" he teased.

She couldn't stop the blush that warmed her cheeks.

"How can you even have the strength to tease me?"

"I feel better now that I've had a shower. It woke me up."

"Well, you're not going to stay up. You need to sleep."

"I always sleep better after—"

"Don't say it," she interrupted. "As your doctor, I can't prescribe anything but a night of undisturbed rest."

His arms slid around her waist. "What about as the woman I really want to make love to?"

Her breath caught in her chest. "She would be way too worried about you over-exerting yourself. Seriously, Jake."

"Seriously," he echoed, leaning over to give her a kiss. "Man, I have been wanting to taste your mouth for a long time."

She couldn't help but kiss him back after a statement like that, but she forced herself to pull away. "Lie down on the bed. I want to check your wound."

He did as she ordered and stretched out on the soft mattress. "This feels a lot better than anything we've slept on this week."

As she sat down next to him, she had to agree. She pulled up the towel. "I see you took off the bandage." The wound was no longer red and inflamed. The stitches were holding well, and she actually thought he might not need to have them redone. "It looks good. I still have some bandages from Sylvia. Let me put one on."

He let her wrap his leg, then said, "Why don't you get into bed with me?"

"I'm going to take a shower first," she said, forcing herself to get up from the bed.

"Hurry back."

She told herself the last thing she should do was hurry back because there was a good chance Jake would talk her into activities that might be bad for him but really good for her.

She smiled to herself, thinking he wouldn't have a hard time persuading her to do anything he wanted. It had always been like that. It was one of the reasons she'd left him all those years ago. She couldn't trust herself to say no.

Getting into the shower, she rejoiced in the warm water spilling over her body. She spent a long time in the heated mist, shampooing her hair with lavender-smelling shampoo and luxuriating in the feeling of being clean again. When she got out of the shower, she blew her hair dry and then went back into the bedroom.

Despite Jake's words, he hadn't been able to wait for her. He was fast asleep—as he should be, she reminded herself.

She rummaged through the bag Alicia had given her, happy to find some PJs. She put them on, then got into bed and snuggled up next to Jake. For the first time in days she felt like she could really let go and sleep.

Jake rolled over onto the side of his good leg and wrapped his arm around her. "Beautiful Kat," he murmured sleepily. "Love you."

Her heart stopped at the words she hadn't heard in over a decade. She didn't know what to do. Should she say them back?

The little snore that came from his parted lips told her that she had at least until tomorrow to decide how she wanted to respond. Of course, there was a good chance that Jake hadn't even realized what he'd said.

"Love you, too," she whispered, then closed her eyes.

When Katherine woke up, she could hear Jake and TJ talking in the adjoining guestroom. She got up, dressed in new jeans and a sweater, then went to join them.

They were sitting at the table by the window, and the covered dishes in front of them smelled delicious.

"Perfect timing," Jake said, giving her a warm smile. "Breakfast is here. We saved you a little of everything."

TJ got up from his chair. "You can take my seat,

Katherine. I need to shave before we start another day of interrogation. I'm beginning to feel like we're the criminals."

"But we're not," she reminded him.

As TJ disappeared into the bathroom, she sat down across from Jake. "How are you feeling?"

"Good, but a little disappointed that I fell asleep on you," he said with a sexy smile.

"I was happy to see you were asleep. You needed to rest. You look better today. Your color is back."

"I'm on the mend. Can't let a gunshot wound stop me. I will tell you now that thing hurt like a son of a bitch."

She smiled. "I can't even imagine. You were incredibly brave."

"I didn't have a choice." He paused. "So, last night, I think I heard something."

Her pulse sped up. "Like a noise?"

"No, like some words, some very sweet words."

Before she could reply, a knock came at the door. "That must be Agent Wolfe or James," she said, jumping to her feet. "I'll get it." She was actually happy to have an interruption. Had Jake really heard her say she loved him? Well, he'd said it first. But still there were probably a lot of words that needed to be said before those particular ones.

She opened the door, and Agent Wolfe stepped into the room.

"Good morning," he said. "I trust it was an uneventful night."

"Very," she said.

"Is TJ here?" he asked.

"Right here," TJ said, as he came out of the bathroom.

"I have some news," the agent said, moving farther into the guest room.

Judging by his grim expression, Katherine didn't think it was good news. "What's happened?" she asked.

"Our agents in Corpus Christi were unable to locate Jasmine Portillo at her apartment last night."

"I knew she'd run," TJ said in disgust.

"Well, she didn't run far," Agent Wolfe continued. "There was a single-vehicle crash early this morning. Ms. Portillo was the sole occupant of the car. She did not survive."

Katherine let out a breath. "She's dead?"

"Yes," he confirmed.

"It wasn't an accident," TJ said, shaking his head. "Someone took her out."

"It appears that she may have taken herself out. There was a note in her car to you."

"Where is it?"

"It's currently being analyzed. I'll show it to you as soon as we get it back. I can tell you that she apologized for putting you in danger and hoped that one day you'd forgive her."

"Dammit," TJ said, running a hand through his hair. "She died and took all the information with her."

"It's too easy," Jake interjected. "Why would she kill herself now?"

"She must have realized that TJ was on to her," Katherine said.

"There will be a thorough investigation," Agent Wolfe said. "And we're not ruling out the possibility that this wasn't a suicide. We'll be going through every phone call, every text message, every email she sent. We'll interview her family, neighbors, friends, coworkers—anyone she might have had contact with in the past year. Hopefully, we'll find a trail to her partners in crime."

"Is MDT going to cooperate?" TJ asked. "Are they going to give you access?"

"Yes," Agent Wolfe replied. "I spoke to Reid Packer this morning. He's opened his own internal investigation and has assured us that he and his brother and all of the top executives will work with us—with complete transparency. They had no idea there were missing weapons, which makes the situation significantly more dangerous than just a technology leak." He paused. "Mr. Packer also asked me to pass on a message to you, Mr. Barrett. He said that you are welcome to return to your job and that every effort will be made to ensure your safety. In fact, he is offering you the office space next to his. However, I would recommend that you take a leave of absence until we dig a little deeper."

"I'm in no rush to go back," TJ said. "But I do need my salary."

"Mr. Packer said you'll be paid at your full salary for as much time as you need to take before coming back to work."

"That's a relief."

"I'll help, too," Katherine said. "I'm not going to let you carry the burden alone anymore, TJ."

"Thanks."

"What about Mexico?" Jake asked. "Do you know who survived the fire, whether all the weapons were destroyed?"

"There were seven bodies found at the ranch," Agent Wolfe replied. "Rodrigo Calderon has been positively identified. Some of the other identifications are pending. The US government is working with the Mexican government to investigate. It appears that the weapons you reportedly saw there were destroyed."

"Good," TJ said with a nod. "At least they can't use those weapons."

"We're going to ask MDT for a complete accounting of all products created by the company all over the world," Agent Wolfe continued. "If there has been any further siphoning of weapons, funds, or technology, we're going to find it." He paused, directing his gaze to Jake and Katherine. "We're satisfied with your statements—Dr. Barrett, Mr. Monroe. You're free to go back to your lives. If we have more questions, we'll be in touch. We would, however, like to continue talking to you, Mr. Barrett. We have a car waiting outside."

"Do you want me to go with you?" Katherine asked her brother.

"No, I'd like you to go home and check on Mom. Do you have time?"

"Of course. And when I get there, I'll make sure Mom is set up to get the best medical care." She paused, looking back at Agent Wolfe. "You will continue to look into Jasmine's relationship with my mother's caregivers? I know she's dead, but if those caregivers have knowingly poisoned my mother—"

"We're on it," Agent Wolfe replied. "And there's an agent at your mother's house right now, as well as a nurse who has been thoroughly checked out by our agency."

"Okay, good. Thank you."

"You're welcome. Mr. Barrett, I'll wait for you in the hall."

"I'll be right out," TJ said.

As the agent left, TJ gave Katherine a hug. "Thanks, sis. I owe you."

"I owe you, too, so let's call it even. Stay safe."

"You, too." TJ grabbed his bag of clothes and headed out the door.

"Looks like it's over," Jake said, holding open his arms.

She walked into his embrace and rested her head on his strong, broad chest. "Finally," she murmured.

"So, getting back to what you said last night..."

"Maybe we should talk about what you said instead..." She lifted her head to look into his sparkling green eyes.

"I didn't say anything," he denied.

"If you didn't, I didn't, either."

He laughed. "Kat, why can't you just tell me you love me to my face?"

"Why can't you?"

"Fine, you want me to go first?"

"You did last night."

"I don't remember that."

"It's true."

He pressed his lips against her mouth, then lifted his head

and said, "I love you, Katherine Barrett. I've loved you since I was sixteen years old."

"Not always..."

"Always," he corrected. "Even when I hated you."

"That doesn't make sense."

"Love isn't logical, Kat. Now, your turn."

She let out a little sigh as her feelings for this man threatened to overwhelm her. "I've loved you since I was sixteen years old, too, even when you hated me."

"You hated me, too."

She shook her head. "I wanted to, but I didn't. I was always afraid of you, not because you ever hurt me, but because what I felt for you was so powerful, so consuming. That's why I ran away."

He nodded. "I know. You were smart to run. I was dragging you down, Kat. I see that very clearly now; I didn't back then. I thought you abandoned me at the worst time of my life, but you were right when you said I was pushing you away. I was taking my grief and anger out on you. I *was* drowning, and if you'd stayed, I might have taken you down with me. But when you left, it was a wake-up call. It shook me out of that numb, crazy, restless state I was in." He let out a breath. "Can you forgive me?"

"Can you forgive me?" she asked, their gazes clinging together.

"I forgave you a long time ago."

"That's not the impression you gave me when I came to the airport."

"Well, I wasn't ready to admit it then." He brushed her hair away from her face. "My feelings for you have been just as overwhelming, Kat. You're such an amazing person. Look what you've accomplished. You're a doctor. You save lives. I'm sure as hell glad I didn't hold you back. I might not be here right now if I had."

"I'm proud of what I've accomplished, but the night that TJ called, the last night of my residency, I had this empty feeling inside. I had climbed this enormous mountain, but when I got to the top, it didn't feel as good as I'd expected. I had what I wanted, but I was alone. By choice," she added quickly. "I had friends, or at least people who wanted to be my friend, and I had family, but I'd distanced myself from everyone. The last few days have shown me that there is a huge world out there to see and that being a doctor is my job, but it doesn't have to be *who* I am or *all* that I am."

"I like the sound of that. Because you are many things, Katherine Barrett, many wonderful things."

"So are you, Jake."

"I just fly planes."

"Which is an important job. You get people where they need to go, and you have the opportunity to spend your life in the beautiful sky."

"You're becoming a fan of flying?"

"I am. I'm giving up on the idea of being able to control every aspect of my life, so flying is more fun now, and the view is a lot more interesting than the one on the ground. If I never see another tree..."

He laughed. "I know how you feel."

"Anyway, I think we both grew up pretty good."

"It took us long enough."

She grinned. "We're a little slow."

"Slow can be good."

She saw the passion flare in his eyes. "Really, Jake? You're still recovering. You could rip open your wound."

"You'll have to be gentle with me."

Smiling, she said, "I do love you, Jake."

"I love you, too. Let's go back to bed."

"And then what?"

"Then we'll go home and start planning our life together, because I know you'll want a plan, Katherine."

She shook her head in denial. "I'm ready to wing it."

"I doubt that, but I want you to know that if you don't want to live in Corpus Christi, I'm open to relocating. I've lived in Texas my whole life. I can live anywhere as long as you're there."

"I want to move back to Corpus Christi. I want to take care of my mom and TJ and be with you."

"See, I knew you had a plan."

"You know me too well." She kissed his lips and felt the familiar zing of pleasurable fire zip down her spine. "When you asked me on the plane if I'd always be there, I didn't get to answer you." She gazed into his eyes. "But the answer is yes. I'll always be there when you wake up. You never have to doubt that."

"And I'll always be there for you. You're the one, Kat. I intend to spend the rest of my life making you happy."

"I'm going to do the same for you."

"Why don't you start now?"

"With pleasure."

Epilogue

Eight weeks later…

As Danielle got out of the cab and approached her mother's house, she had mixed feelings about coming home. She was just getting her life started in DC, but it was Christmas Eve, and after the year they'd had, her mother had insisted that everyone come home for the holiday weekend. She'd still planned on begging off at the last minute, but a phone call the day before had destroyed that plan.

The front door flew open before she could reach for the knob, and Alicia enveloped her in a hug.

"You came," Alicia said happily. "I wasn't sure you would make it."

"You smell like pumpkin and onions at the same time," she said with a laugh. "And you have flour all over you." One of her mother's aprons enveloped Alicia's small frame, and it was covered in flour and some other unidentified substances.

"That's because Mom is sautéing onions for the stuffing, and I just made the pie. She actually let me do it. Although, she watched me like a hawk to make sure I didn't screw up."

"I'm sure it wasn't that bad."

"Are you sure?" Alicia asked with a raise of her eyebrow.

"Okay, it's Mom, so I get it, but it sounds like the two of

you have everything under control."

"Not entirely. Mom does not trust me to set the table. She said only you will know how to set out the pinecones, candy canes and candles that's she's collected for a centerpiece."

Danielle grinned back at her sister. "I am much better at that than you. So I don't blame her. Are you going to let me into the house?"

"In a minute. I wanted to tell you something first. Michael and I have set a wedding date."

"Really?" she asked. "When is it?"

"July fifteen."

"That's great. I'm really happy for you."

"I want you to be my maid of honor, Dani."

"Of course I'll be your maid of honor. There's no way I'm letting anyone else stand beside you. Plus, you'll need my help picking out the bridesmaids' dresses."

"And managing Mom's expectations," Alicia said.

"Have you told her you set the date?"

"I'm saving that for her Christmas present. Then maybe she'll stop sending me bridal magazines."

"Are you kidding? She'll send you more now. Are you going to do it in Miami? Or here?"

"We're going to do it here. I just couldn't kill Mom by having it anywhere else."

"Michael's family will have to travel, and your friends in Florida."

"We'll have a party there, too, but the ceremony will be here. I'm hoping Jake will walk me down the aisle."

"I'm sure he will. Is he here yet?"

"He and Katherine are on their way over, and they're bringing TJ and Katherine's mom, who is doing amazingly better since she got on the right medication. Her good days are much more frequent."

"That's great news." As Alicia rambled on about what else was going on in the family, Danielle felt a little disconnected. Her new life was busy, too, but it seemed very far removed from her old life, the one she'd led in this town. So many things had changed, and one change had hit her hard, harder than she'd imagined.

"Are you all right?" Alicia asked, her gaze narrowing. "You look a little—sad."

Before she could reply, Jake pulled up in front of the house, his car filled with people. She followed Alicia down to the sidewalk to greet everyone.

After hugs and hellos, she helped carry presents into the house.

Her mom and Michael met them in the living room, and there was another round of greetings. Then her mother and Debbie Barrett went into the kitchen, and TJ joined Michael in front of the family room TV to watch a football game. Jake was about to join the guys, but she asked him to wait.

As she looked into the expectant faces of Jake, Katherine, and Alicia, she wasn't sure what to say.

"What's wrong?" Alicia asked. "I knew something was up with you."

Jake frowned. "You do look tense, Dani. Whatever it is, just tell us."

"It's not that easy." She glanced toward the kitchen. "I should probably have Mom in here, too, but I thought it would be easier to tell you all first."

"Okay, you're scaring me," Alicia said.

"I got a call last night. I don't know why they called me and not either of you," she said. "But it was a man named Paolo. He was calling about Mamich."

Alicia put a hand to her mouth, her lips trembling. "Is she all right?"

Danielle shook her head. "No, she's not. She passed away yesterday."

"Oh, no," Katherine said, putting her arm around Jake.

Jake's jaw tightened, and he was clearly wrestling with his emotions. "Did he tell you what happened?"

"He said she went to sleep and didn't wake up. It was

peaceful. He said she wasn't even sick."

Jake nodded. "She told me when I was there that she didn't sleep anymore, but when sleep came again, it would be forever. She knew. She said goodbye."

"Not to me," Alicia protested.

"You got a letter from her last week," Jake reminded Alicia.

"But that wasn't good-bye." Alicia sank down on the couch, dabbing at her eyes. "Maybe it was goodbye, and I just didn't want to read it that way. I wanted to go see her. I wanted to take Michael down there, but now it's too late."

"You still have to go," Jake said. "Mamich wanted you to have everything, Alicia. She wanted you to go through her house and to have Dad's letters."

"I do want those."

"Paolo said that no one will touch the house until one of us comes down there," Dani said. "He told me that Mamich asked that you go, Alicia. She said all of us would be welcome, but she definitely wanted you to be the one to go through her things."

Alicia stared back at her. "Why did he call you?"

"I asked him that. He said that Mamich thought I could handle getting the news better than either of you. I guess she thought I didn't care as much." Even though she probably hadn't cared as much as her brother and sister, she had cared; she just hadn't felt the same connection with their great-grandmother as Jake and Alicia did. They were very different people.

"She knew you loved her," Alicia said, obviously reading her expression.

"I don't know how she could know that. I haven't spoken to her in years. Anyway, I'm sorry that I had to come here and tell you the bad news on Christmas Eve."

"Is that why you came?" Alicia asked, cocking her head to the right as she gave her a thoughtful look. "Because I got the feeling you were going to skip it at the last minute."

"I'm super busy at work, but once I got that call, I knew I had to come." She let out a breath, happy to have the bad news out of the way.

"Well, this sucks," Jake said.

"Big time," Alicia agreed.

"Should we tell Mom?" she asked.

"Let's wait until after Christmas," Jake said. "She's always been so weird about that side of the family. Let's give her the holiday and then break the bad news."

Danielle was fine with that plan. "So, changing the subject, if that's okay."

"It's okay," Jake said.

"How are you two doing?" she asked Jake and Katherine.

"We're great," Jake said, giving Katherine a loving smile. "Kat got a job at the hospital. Her mom is doing well."

"What about TJ? Is he back at MDT?"

"No, he has a new job in an entirely different industry," Katherine said. "In fact, he is moving to Dallas next week. Since his statements to the FBI have been covered by the news, he feels that he's safe from any reprisals. Whatever he knew, he has already told."

"I'm glad he's safe. I'm glad you're all safe."

"Do you know anything new?" Alicia asked. "I know Senator Dillon has talked to the press about the MDT investigation."

"I don't know anything more than you do. It seems that aside from the woman who committed suicide, everyone else has gone underground."

"Like rats scurrying back into their hiding places," Jake said.

"It's so frustrating," Alicia commented. "We get so far and then we hit a wall."

"Speaking of not over," Jake interrupted. "What's up with Colin? I haven't heard from you in a few weeks. I take it he hasn't discovered any groundbreaking news in regards to Dad's accident?"

Alicia sighed and shook her head. "No, but I haven't given up yet. I know there's more to come. This isn't over yet."

Danielle saw Jake give her a thoughtful look. "What?" she asked.

"It's just that Mamich said you'd be the last piece in the puzzle, Dani," he replied. "I always wondered what she meant by that."

A chill ran down her spine. "She was being dramatic. I want nothing to do with your puzzle. I have my own challenges to deal with."

"How is your job?" Alicia asked.

"It's hard, but it's good. I love the energy, the people, the power to make change. DC is where everything important happens, or at least what's important to me," she amended. "Now, I'm going to see if I can help Mom with the table."

"I'll help you," Alicia said.

"Finally, we're alone," Jake joked.

Katherine smiled up at him. "We've been alone a lot the last two months."

"Not enough for me. I know you wanted to bond with your mom and TJ again, but I have a proposition for you."

"Oh, really?"

He turned to face her, resting his hands on her waist as he gazed into her eyes. Her heart pounded against her chest. "Kat?"

"Yes?"

"I want to live with you."

She nodded, feeling a little let down. He'd been saying that for weeks. "I know. We're going to get a place. I told you that."

"I don't want to just share an apartment." He let go of her waist and dropped to one knee, reaching into his pocket as he did so.

"What are you doing?" she asked breathlessly.

"I think you know." He opened the velvet box to reveal a beautiful diamond ring.

"Oh, Jake." Her eyes blurred with tears.

"Don't start crying yet. I have to ask you a question."

"You better hurry."

He laughed. "I love you, Katherine Barrett, and I want you to marry me. What do you say?"

"I say yes." She looked into his eyes with so much love in her heart she felt like she could float up to the ceiling. "Yes," she repeated. "I'll marry you, and I'll love you for the rest of my life."

"And beyond," he said.

"And beyond," she echoed. "I didn't know you were going to do this now," she added, as he slipped the ring onto her finger.

"It's your Christmas present."

"Really? That's too bad."

"Why?"

"Because I just got you a shirt."

He laughed. "It better make me look hot."

"You look hot without a shirt," she said, leaning over to give him a kiss.

"What's this?" Alicia asked, as she and Dani walked back into the room. "Jake is on his knees."

"Oh, my God," Dani said. Then she turned and yelled, "Mom, get out here."

Soon everyone was crowding around, admiring her ring, giving her hugs and welcoming her to the family.

It was the happiest day of her life, made even happier when her mom put her arms around her and told her that she couldn't wait to see her get married to the man she'd loved since she was sixteen years old.

"I can't wait for that, either," she said.

"He asked my permission, you know," her mom added.

"You did?" she asked Jake, as he put his arm around her.

"Absolutely. She asked me what took me so long. I had to grow up first so I could be worthy of you. It took me a while."

"It took me a while to be worthy of you," she said. "But we made it."

"And we're always going to be there for each other."

"Always," she promised. As the party moved back into the kitchen, leaving them alone once again, she added, "I like my ring. It's perfect."

"I'm glad. I was going to ask for some sisterly advice, but decided to wing it on my own."

"You know what I like," she said, gazing into his eyes. "You know me better than I know myself."

"And you know me, beautiful Kat."

"We're going to be happy, Jake."

"So happy. Let's start right now," he said, as he lovingly touched his mouth to hers.

THE END

Don't miss the exciting conclusion of the

Lightning Strikes Trilogy

with Danielle's story in

SUMMER RAIN

Coming in August of 2016.

About The Author

 Barbara Freethy is a #1 New York Times Bestselling Author of 45 novels ranging from contemporary romance to romantic suspense and women's fiction. Traditionally published for many years, Barbara opened her own publishing company in 2011 and has since sold over 5 million books! Twenty of her titles have appeared on the New York Times and USA Today Bestseller Lists.

Known for her emotional and compelling stories of love, family, mystery and romance, Barbara enjoys writing about ordinary people caught up in extraordinary adventures. Barbara's books have won numerous awards. She is a six-time finalist for the RITA for best contemporary romance from Romance Writers of America and a two-time winner for DANIEL'S GIFT and THE WAY BACK HOME.

Barbara has lived all over the state of California and currently resides in Northern California where she draws much of her inspiration from the beautiful bay area.

For a complete listing of books, as well as excerpts and contests, and to connect with Barbara:

Visit Barbara's Website:
www.barbarafreethy.com

Join Barbara on Facebook:
www.facebook.com/barbarafreethybooks

Follow Barbara on Twitter:
www.twitter.com/barbarafreethy